The Weaver's Tapestry

The Weaver's Tapestry

Silk Road Series
Book 1

Anna C. Snyder

Nissi Press

Published by Nissi Press LLC Bend, Oregon

Library of Congress Control Number: 2025901636

ISBN: 979-8-9920270-1-3 (softcover)

ISBN: 979-8-9920270-2-0 (hardcover)

ISBN: 979-8-9920270-0-6 (ebook)

Cover Design by Hannah Linder Designs

Map Illustration by Gary L. Bartlett

To Adam, and to Isaiah, Caleb, and Naomi: the threads which make up the story of my life.

And

To the memory of my mom, Sandra Hutton.

Sweet to ride forth at evening from the wells
Where shadows pass gigantic on the sand,
And softly through the silence beat the bells
On the Golden Road to Samarkand.

We travel not for trafficking alone:
By hotter winds our fiery hearts are fanned:
For lust of knowing what should not be known
We take the Golden Road to Samarkand.

— James Elroy Flecker, Hassan (1913)

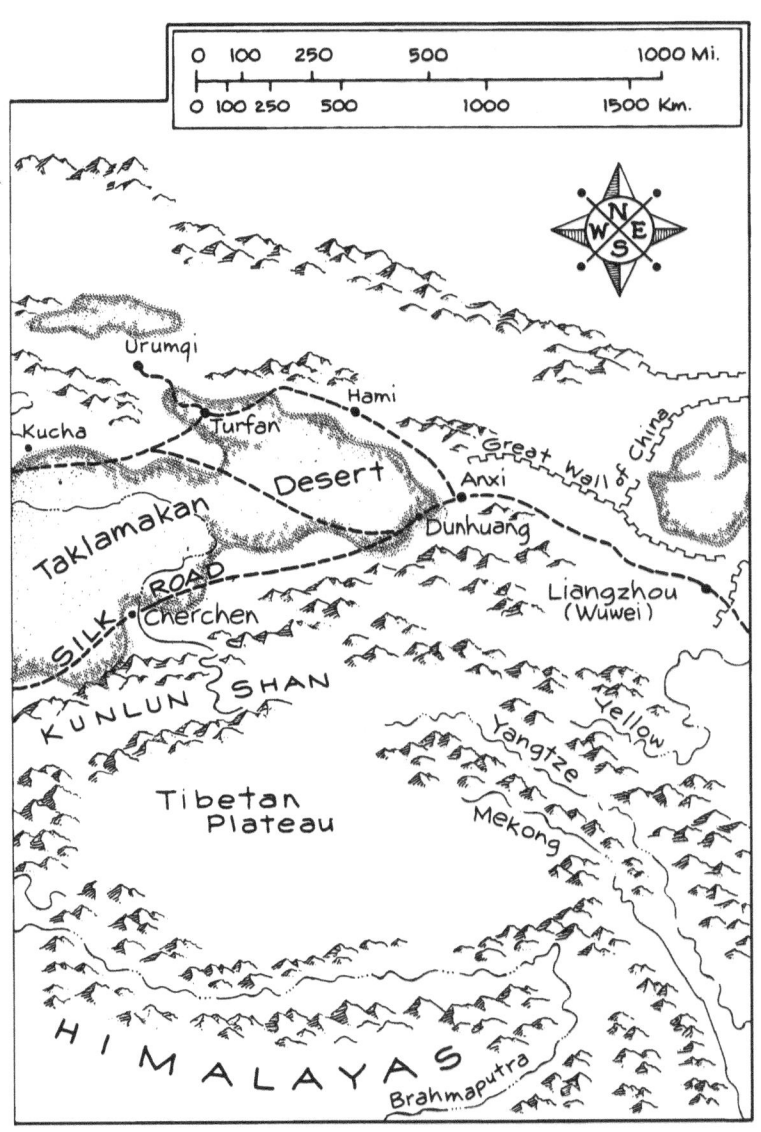

Chapter One

Samarkand
AD 634

S aina stood silently at the entrance of her mistress's sleeping
chamber, an ivory comb in one hand, wool bedclothes
draped over the other. "Are you ready, my lady?"

Bao Li looked up slowly from the scroll rolled out on her
small writing desk beneath the shuttered window. "Yes, enter,"
she said flatly, but her eyes did not meet Saina's. She returned her
gaze to the cinnabar characters painted on the scroll.

Saina set the bedclothes on the sleeping platform and then
carefully, so as not to disturb her mistress further, approached.
She studied the faint movement of Bao Li's lips, her drooping
shoulders, and the way her brows drew together.

When Saina had first come to live as a slave in Samarkand's
Grand Caravanserai, Bao Li insisted she learn to read. "All my
servants must learn this skill," she had said, placing a parchment
with the Sogdian script in front of Saina. "Understanding the
written word is your first measure of protection against those who

wish to deceive you." The skill had proven useful, and Saina was grateful. But as she looked over her mistress's shoulder, she saw that this letter was written in a language only Bao Li understood, the language of her homeland within the boundaries of China's Great Wall.

With the ivory comb in hand, Saina pulled out the gold *buyao* pinning Bao Li's hair in a tight bun. It fell to her shoulders in silvery, black waves. As she ran the comb through her mistress's hair, Saina noticed, as she often did lately, that it was not as thick as it once was, and the streaks of gray were more evident.

Evening had settled outside Bao Li's *khana*, the home she shared with her husband, Kang Dahan. But he had not been home in many months. As head *sartapao*, the chief caravanner, he spent most of his time trading goods along the Silk Road. Though Bao Li had never told her so, Saina noticed that in his absence Bao Li slept better, ate full meals, and smiled more often.

The crackle of fires and murmur of men's voices drifted in from the large courtyard outside Bao Li's room, breaking the weighty silence.

Bao Li dabbed her eyes with her silk kerchief and sighed. "My sister has written from Chang'an. Her eldest daughter gave birth to a son."

Saina's heart twisted at the familiar sorrow in Bao Li's countenance and the outpouring of heartache that would soon follow.

"Why does she torment me with such news?" Bao Li said bitterly. "She knows my husband grew weary of my barren womb long ago." Her mouth twisted. "My sister. My own blood. She mocked me when she learned that Kang Dahan took a young wife in order that an heir would finally be born to him."

Bao Li shoved the scroll aside and stood, rattling the porcelain tea jar on her desktop. "I wish to retire for the night."

Saina reached for the nightgown, but Bao Li stopped her. "Let me do it," she said, her voice weary.

Saina left Bao Li to dress herself and retrieved the warming stones she had brought from the kitchen earlier. "The clear skies have made for a cold night," she said, tucking them under the blankets at the foot of Bao Li's bed.

For the first time since Saina had walked in, Bao Li looked her in the eyes. "Thank you." She seemed to be searching for more words, but then her gaze shifted to the writing desk. "My tea jar needs to be replenished."

Saina carefully picked up the empty jar, a gift given to Bao Li and Kang Dahan by Emperor Taizong as a symbol of friendship extended to them from China's Tang Dynasty, and placed it in the crook of her arm.

It was a high honor to be entrusted with such a prized item, an honor Saina took great pride in. Though younger than most slaves in the caravanserai, she knew she was favored. "I will refill it and return in the morning with your tea," Saina said.

"There is no need. I have business in Samarkand at first light. With the rising cost of dyestuffs, the textile merchants are seeking new suppliers of indigo. They hope to send word to Kang Dahan before he reaches the city of Chach and an agreement is made."

"Will he receive it in time?" The moment Saina uttered the words she put her hand to her mouth. It was not her place to ask such questions.

Bao Li shrugged. "Uncertainty is the way of business on the Silk Road."

"Shall I wake you in the morning?" Saina said.

"No. Preparations have already been made for my early departure. But see that you help Vandakk with the morning meal. He is expecting you."

Saina nodded and turned to leave.

How strange that Bao Li saw fit to remind her of her duties. Saina had helped Vandakk every morning and evening since she was a child. And in that time, she had also seen to her mistress's needs without question or complaint. Indeed, she had come to anticipate them. But lately, a troubling question had begun to intrude in her thoughts. *Will anyone provide for my needs?*

Left unanswered, the question had worked its way into a sort of discontent. But this was a dangerous line of thinking, for what slave ever hoped for such things without falling headlong into despair.

"Saina," Bao Li called after her, holding out a small pouch of coins. "Ensure the *bahkshi* receives his payment before you return to the kitchen."

"Yes, my lady," Saina said, as she tucked the coins into the purse tied at her waist and walked away.

———

Saina cradled the empty porcelain jar against her chest and slipped between the heavy gilded doors. She studied the cool glow of the night sky extending beyond the high walls of Samarkand's Grand Caravanserai and shivered in her simple wool tunic. Her felt boots did little to ward off the chill seeping up from the stone ground.

"Bao Li has retired for the night," she said to Makh, the muscled guard standing outside her mistress's khana. "I am going to the storeroom to replenish her jar with more tea leaves. Can I bring you *chal*?"

Shadows cut sharp lines into his scarred face as Makh shook his head, denying Saina's offer of the fermented camel's milk, a popular drink among the guards on cold nights.

Saina expected his answer. He was a man with few expectations, an aged nomadic warrior who preferred the distraction of present difficulties to suffering the memories of war and the decimation of his clan.

Silent and watchful, Makh fixed his dark eyes on the great courtyard before them, where groups of merchants, traders, and sojourners reclined around warming fires. Having trekked across sun-choked deserts and cragged mountain peaks, they found protection here within the caravanserai's mud-brick walls.

Saina pulled the pouch of silver coins from her purse and wove through the courtyard, past outstretched bodies and sand-worn faces.

She approached the bahkshi, a gifted storyteller, who was hired by Bao Li to soothe the weary guests. With a silk caftan draping his thin shoulders, he sat cross-legged, plucking the strings of the *barbat*. Thin wisps of his gray beard grazed the pear-shaped base of the instrument set in his lap.

Kneeling beside him, Saina placed the pouch of coins, a generous payment from Bao Li, in the storyteller's reed basket.

The bahkshi nodded an acknowledgment of the payment, but his song did not slow. Captivated by the roll of his tongue, Saina listened as one of his many tales of the land poured from his lips.

A restless soul heeds the call
Gather the camels one and all
Come seek with me a distant land
Prepare the way to Samarkand

Beware the winds feared most by man
They drown the bells of the caravan
Dust thrown wide it blinds the eye
Apart from shelter they will die

The Merchants' Road of silken threads
Frayed the traveler edge to edge
Whose bones wrung dry lie bleached on sand
Found not their way to Samarkand

Saina's hands trembled around the jar. Was all that remained of her father a heap of disregarded bones, buried long ago in shifting sand?

Memories of the last time she saw him unspooled in her mind. She remembered the orange glow of the setting sun burning like fire on his face. She saw the pulse of his corded neck muscles and heard the bark of his voice silencing her cries. Panic thrummed in her chest like a thousand running horses. Her own father had sold her into a life of slavery and walked into the desert, pulling a donkey and three small sacks of grain in her place.

Cheers from the sojourners broke out, releasing Saina from the remembrance. She looked at the bahkshi, who held her in his gaze, his song and instrument quieted.

She shifted the jar in her hands and cleared her dry throat. Edging past the entranced merchants, she left them behind and continued across the courtyard.

Silk tapestries flanked the entrance of the arched hallway. Saina brushed past them as she walked into the long corridor. Inside, torchlight flickered, casting dark shadows on the walls. She walked the narrow hallway, grateful that the sounds from the courtyard and the stench of the stables were shut out. Here it was quiet, with only the shuffle of her feet and the murmur of distant voices deep within the belly of the caravanserai.

She knew these walls well, having walked past them countless times. The varied gaps and chips in the stone were as familiar to her as her own calloused hands.

But that same familiarity bred caution with the slightest change, a change Saina perceived even before it was illuminated by the dim torchlight. Ahead, the leather flap covering the entrance to the kitchen and storeroom had been pushed aside. She slowed her step, her brow creased. Had Vandakk left it open? It would be unlike him. The old cook was adamant about keeping the flap closed to protect the stored food.

"Vandakk?" She peered cautiously into the expansive storeroom, caution prickling her skin. But all was still. He was not there.

Pulling the flap closed behind her, Saina walked into the storeroom and examined the shelves lining the perimeter, stocked full of grains, spices, nuts, and herbs. The sweet scents of saffron and cardamom, used to season the evening meal of mutton and rice, still hung in the air.

Perhaps she forgot to close the flap earlier after she helped Vandakk prepare the meal. What would have caused her to be so careless? Nothing came to mind.

Baskets of vegetables in the center of the room were undisturbed. Not a single fly or gnat swarmed above them. Saina exhaled with relief, thankful she would not suffer Vandakk's disappointment for leaving the stored food unprotected.

After setting the porcelain tea jar on the table in the center of the storeroom, she approached the shelves and pulled out the red clay vessel.

Saina opened the lid and inhaled the dry scent of tea leaves. After all this time, she still could not tell the difference between the tea served daily to the merchants of the caravanserai and this tea, served only to Bao Li. Her mistress had once said that this tea was like a thread connecting her to the land of her youth and that each sip soothed a constant ache within her. A slave since childhood, Saina understood the longing for a home and family. If only she, too, had something to remember her old life by.

Saina pushed the thought away. It was no use dwelling on such matters. She had returned to the table and begun refilling the porcelain jar with tea leaves when she heard the shuffle of feet behind her. Expecting Vandakk, she turned and then gasped at the sight of young Upach quickly approaching.

"Where have you been?" Upach said, her voice filled with desperation.

"Upach," Saina said and reached her hand out to console the servant girl, who was a few years younger than Saina but stood half a head taller. She studied her untied hair, falling in thick, dark waves around her face. Her copper eyes were watery, pleading an unknown request.

"You know I tend to my mistress at this time of night," Saina continued. She looked past Upach and saw the flap covering the storeroom entrance had been pulled aside again.

Upach twisted the frayed end of the sash at her waist. "The unease between our mistresses, *both* of them wives of Kang

Dahan, means my presence is not welcome in Bao Li's khana, much less with the request that has forced me to seek you out."

Saina shook her head. "My chores are not finished for the day," she said, looking over her shoulder at the dishes from the evening meal piled in the kitchen. "I must help Vandakk..."

"Please, Saina," Upach begged. "Ning Po is in labor, and I...I cannot deliver this baby alone."

Cold dread rushed through Saina. "No, it cannot be. The baby is too early."

Upach reached for Saina's hand, but Saina stepped back, a silent warning that she should come no closer.

"Where is Umida?" Saina said, recalling the skilled herbalist and midwife Upach had befriended in the city. "This is her line of work. She will help you."

"Twice I have sent for her," Upach said, wiping tears from her eyes. "But she had already been called away to the home of another birthing mother."

"There are many other midwives in the city."

Upach shook her head. "Ning Po refused them all. Umida is the only midwife she trusts."

"I am not skilled in the task you require," Saina said. "How can you request this of me?" She regretted the harshness in her voice. Was it unfair of her to expect Upach, having barely reached the age of womanhood, to deliver this baby alone?

Saina and Upach had managed to carry on a cautious friendship despite the tension between the two mistresses they served, and Saina had taken care to help Upach understand the ways of servitude in the caravanserai when she had first come under Ning Po's charge. But this request—to help deliver Ning Po's baby and betray Bao Li's trust—Saina could not do. "I am sorry Upach, but I cannot—"

"Do not deny me this one plea, Saina. You and I both know Kang Dahan has longed for an heir. If he returns from his travels and learns something happened to this child, the consequences will be on my shoulders."

Saina's chest tightened at the sharp accusation in Upach's eyes, the eyes of a servant girl too young to comprehend why things are this way and why they must suffer because of it.

Saina's mind screamed, her stomach twisted in dread, but she nodded in agreement. What other choice did she have?

————

The dark corridors seemed to grow narrower as Saina hurried to keep up with Upach. The young servant girl stopped at the entrance to Ning Po's room. Saina stared at the wooden door separating her from the young woman inside. How strange it was to stand so close after working hard to keep her distance.

In the two years since Kang Dahan had brought Ning Po into the home he shared with Bao Li, her mistress had often reminded Saina of the humiliation she had carried since that day and the anger that still coursed through her veins.

Saina inhaled the stale air, thirsted for it, as though she had forgotten to breathe in the troubled span of time it took to rush from the storeroom to where she stood now.

Light spread out from beneath the door, landing on the tip of Upach's boot, but the girl did not seem to notice. She stood with her palm pressed against the door, looking at Saina.

Upach pushed open the door, flooding the hallway with light, but Saina remained at the threshold.

"Come in." Upach's demand hung in the air.

Saina stiffened, unable to look the young girl in the eyes. She considered telling Upach that she must return to the storeroom, to her chores, but Saina knew better. If she walked away now, she would not return.

Ning Po's low groans broke the silence.

With her gaze fixed on the ground, Saina walked into the room as guilt at the betrayal of her own barren mistress snaked through her heart.

Candlelight flickered on the walls, casting a golden glow over

9

the fine silk rug with its intricate design of delicate vines and lotus buds spread across the floor. Standing at the edge of the rug, Saina hesitated. She glanced at Upach and then to the wooden sleeping platform in the far corner of the room. The thick down mattress and silk bedding had been rolled up and pushed aside, replaced with a wool birthing mat. On the low table beside the mat, a wick of incense burned, sending up a thin swirl of smoke.

Ning Po sat propped against several large pillows, the skin of her swollen belly stretched thin, and her forehead beaded with sweat. She clutched the edges of the birthing mat and stared at Upach, as though to draw strength from her presence.

Pulling her chin to her chest, Ning Po groaned as her body bore down. Upach knelt beside her, taking her mistress's hand in her own, her wide eyes pleading silently with Saina.

When the birthing pain receded, Ning Po leaned her head back. Damp hair clung to her forehead.

Saina pressed her lips together and stepped forward. Ning Po's gaze fell upon her, and her eyes flashed in anger. "Why are you here? Get out!"

Saina's body shook, but she did not move. "Upach," she said, her flat voice echoing in the room. "In the closet down the hall, you will find a stack of small basins. Fill one with water from the cistern in the courtyard, and bring it here."

Ning Po jerked her head toward Upach and grabbed hold of her wrist. "Do not leave me alone with Bao Li's servant."

"Upach, do what is required, or I will leave. Are you prepared to deliver this baby alone?"

Upach closed her eyes and turned away from Ning Po, as though harnessing courage to defy her mistress's orders. When she opened her eyes, she gathered the hem of her tunic and stood up.

"If anyone should ask what you are doing, say only that your mistress requires water for washing. Nothing more," Saina said.

Upach nodded and rushed out of the room. The door slammed closed behind her.

Saina shifted her weight.

"I did not ask for you," Ning Po's sharp voice cut through the tension. Her eyes narrowed as she stared at Saina. "Upach is a stupid girl for bringing you here."

"She was desperate. Your refusal of all other midwives left her no choice," Saina said, not regretting the sharpness in her voice.

"She could have brought any slave except you," Ning Po screamed, but as quickly as her anger flooded the room, it dissipated. A low groan slowly built as another contraction contorted her face with pain. She clutched the edge of the birthing mat.

The air in the room was thick, brined in the sweat of a woman giving birth. It was followed shortly by a putrid tang, faint at first but growing stronger.

Saina looked toward the door. She was not wanted here; she could leave now and return to her chores without giving it another thought. Ning Po had brought this upon herself. But just before the decision was finalized in her mind, Upach pushed through the door.

"I brought some clean cloths too," Upach said. She approached with quick steps, pulled by the weight of the water basin in her arms. Setting it on the ground beside Ning Po, she dipped a cloth into the water and wiped Ning Po's forehead.

Saina dropped her shoulders and looked away. In the presence of Upach's loyalty to her mistress, she had little to offer.

The birthing pains receded. In their wake Upach stroked Ning Po's hair. "Soon you will hold your baby in your arms and your suffering will be like a distant memory, carried on the wind far away from you."

Saina could not deny the tenderness with which Upach spoke to her mistress. If she allowed her thoughts to slip away, she could even come to understand the depths of her loyalty. But Upach had not been a servant in the caravanserai long enough to know that Ning Po's very presence was like a slow poison seeping into these walls.

Upach leaned close to Ning Po and whispered, "With this

child, your bitter portion will end. You will find favor in Kang Dahan's eyes and finally be regarded with honor as the only wife who could bear his child."

Saina's jaw tightened. As long as she served her own barren mistress, Bao Li, and Upach served Ning Po, their friendship would be divided by differing loyalties. Despite the terrible risk she took in helping deliver this baby, nothing would change that.

"The baby is coming," Ning Po's ragged breath startled Saina.

Pulling her thoughts back to the task, Saina crouched between Ning Po's legs and readied the blanket in her lap.

Upach leaned close as Ning Po bore down once more, her cries piercing the air.

The baby slipped into Saina's shaking hands.

In a moment of stunned silence, Saina stared wide-eyed at the tiny baby in her arms. Laughter escaped her lips, and she did not concern herself with who might have heard it. Awakened to the beauty of birth, the sacred work of a woman's body, her arms trembled.

"A girl," Saina said.

Ning Po exhaled and laid her head back as tears fell from the corners of her eyes. Her chest heaved, and a smile of contented relief spread across her face.

"You did it," Upach said, her chin quivering. "You found your hidden gem."

Saina pulled the baby close, drying her skin with a soft blanket. She noted her downy black hair, the tiny dimple above her full lips, and her delicate skin, perfectly formed. She leaned closer. How bluish pale and translucent she seemed, like silk spun from its cocoon before the colors of the earth had a chance to penetrate her.

An eerie stillness emanated from the baby. Saina's stomach clenched in dread. She pressed her ear close to the baby's chest, to hear her breath and feel it rise against her cheek, but all she heard was silence.

"Give me my baby," Ning Po stretched out her hands toward Saina.

The baby's body was cold against Saina's skin.

"Will you not give her to me?" Ning Po said, the smile that softened her face earlier had faded. Her eyes narrowed. "What is it? What have you done?"

Ash from the incense wick on the table beside the birthing mat fell into the dish below, sending a small curl of smoke, a final breath, into the room. Like a brief vapor, it disappeared.

Saina opened her mouth to answer, but the silence grew deafening.

Chapter Two

At dawn the next day, Saina woke from a shallow sleep. She groaned and rolled over, wearied from her mind's unending replay of the night's events. So tiresome were her thoughts, she could bear them no longer.

She sat up, shivering against the crisp morning air, and blackness surrounding her.

Her cramped room, a storeroom for grain before Bao Li had ordered it to be cleared out and given to Saina, was barely wide enough for her sleeping mat and small earthen vessel set in the corner near her head. Few would be impressed by the modest room with its bare walls and narrow wooden door, but Saina was grateful for a space of her own.

Tucked away at the far end of the caravanserai's second floor, the entrance to her room was dwarfed by the grandeur of the arched doorways preceding it. Most passed by unaware of its existence. It was a luxury not afforded the other servants, but last night she had yearned for the warmth found among the sleeping bodies in the servants' quarters and the comfort their presence would have brought.

Saina shook her head at the foolish thought. Nothing would ease the torment of the recurring memory of the lifeless baby growing cold in her arms or Ning Po's false accusations still ringing in her ears.

"You killed my baby," Ning Po had wailed. Tears had poured down her face, landing on the delicate baby clutched at her breast.

"No, do not speak such evil," Saina said, panic rising in her chest.

"Get out!" Ning Po screamed, her dark eyes flashing in anger.

"Please, Ning Po," Saina said, reaching out her hand. "I would do no such thing."

But Saina's protest only kindled Ning Po's rage. "Murderer," she screamed, writhing on the birthing mat like a feral animal. She tore off her blankets and knocked over the ashen incense wick.

Saina stepped back. She looked to Upach to calm her mistress and offer words in Saina's defense, but the young servant girl lay slumped in the corner, weeping bitterly.

"Kang Dahan will know," Ning Po screamed again. "You killed his long-desired heir. You did it out of loyalty to his barren wife. I will tell him myself."

Such false, poisonous words were too much to bear. Without looking back, Saina had fled the room.

Pushing aside the memory of last night, Saina stood up and, with shaking hands, braided her thick hair. She tied off the ends with a thin strip of leather, then dressed herself in her felt trousers and wool tunic, which were piled at the end of her bed mat. She had left them where they fell last night, just before collapsing onto her mat, sobbing.

She unlocked the heavy iron latch that Bao Li had insisted be installed on her door and that Saina faithfully locked every night. She stepped onto the balcony overlooking the courtyard below, finding solace in the slivers of pale morning light etched across the sky. She tied the leather belt around her waist and peered over the railing at Vandakk, who shuffled into the courtyard carrying disks of camel dung and whistling a tune. His gray hair curled out from beneath his embroidered *doppa*, the familiar black skullcap adorning his head.

She watched him stoke the fires beneath the cauldrons, drawing strength from the comfort of his kind and humble presence.

His reputation as the finest cook in Samarkand had spread far and wide, but his passion and his work were borne from a deep grief.

Vandakk had once told Saina he had never thought of life beyond shepherding. His young wife had worked beside him among other Uighur shepherds, harvesting wild herbs and berries high in the Tian Shan mountains. She was creative with the flavorful offerings given by the land, using them to season their meals. He had learned well from her.

"Our lives were cleaved together as one," Vandakk had said, his green eyes shimmering behind the tears that often gathered whenever he spoke of her. "And I was in want of nothing more."

But his love was not enough to sustain his wife during the cruel illness that ravaged her body. Their life together was cut short. And though her voice was silenced long ago, her legacy lived on in his desire to nourish the bodies of weary travelers, as she did for him in the early days of their love and as he did for her in the waning days of her life.

Saina pushed away from the balcony and descended the steep stairs, taking care not to wake any merchants. On clear nights such as this, many chose to sleep in the open-air courtyard, not the private rooms bordering its perimeter.

She walked up beside Vandakk, offering her arm for support as he pushed to stand.

He straightened. "My dear Saina, what would I do without your careful eye always watching over me?"

"You must take care," Saina said. "Who will feed all these hungry merchants if you injure yourself?"

Vandakk patted her shoulder and chuckled.

Saina continued, "I am certain I could not carry such a heavy burden."

"Why do you doubt yourself?" Vandakk said. "I have properly

trained your hand in the few years Bao Li has granted me." He paused and leaned closer. "It is not only I, but Bao Li, who has great confidence in you."

Saina's chest tightened. Until last night, he would have been correct in his telling, but now it pained her greatly to hear of Bao Li's undeserved trust in her. She was no longer worthy of it. But with the wound still raw, she could not speak of these things just yet. She forced a smile. "Perhaps what you say is true, but my concern still remains that you push yourself too hard. It would please me to begin lighting the morning fires so you may rest longer."

"It is a small matter," Vandakk said, brushing away her concerns. He peered into the iron cauldron beside him. "The cold mornings stiffen my knees, but I am as strong as a wild yak." The cauldron captured the lilt of his voice, returning it as a tinny echo into the still air.

"And as stubborn as a donkey," Saina quipped.

He threw his head back and laughed, his green eyes flashing with delight. "But a donkey gets the job done. Already I have set fire beneath the tandoor oven and am fetching water for tea." He picked up the water bucket beside the cauldron and straightened. "There are just a few simple dishes left to prepare for the morning meal. See to it that they are finished."

He started to walk away, then turned back. "Saina, if you have time, fill the lamps with fresh oil. We will need them to burn long for the evening arrival of several large caravans."

———

Saina walked into the storeroom and inhaled the yeasty scent of rising dough. Bowls of tart *suzma* and drizzled honey were placed alongside serving trays piled with dried apples and peaches. In the kitchen, just beyond the storeroom, a kettle of hot water boiled. Vandakk had been hard at work.

In the far corner, three wide shelves had been stacked from

floor to ceiling with rounds of dough rising above warming bricks. Saina glanced over them.

It had been more than a few years since Vandakk first entrusted her with the task of preparing the bread for baking. Just nine years old at the time, she still had the hands of a small child and was nearly paralyzed by the great responsibility.

"I trust you will know when the dough is ready to be cooked," he had said. But his trust was unfounded. The dough had barely risen when Saina pulled it from the shelves. The resulting bread was small and dense, and the merchants were loud with their displeasure.

Red from shame, Saina hid behind the shelves in the storeroom until Vandakk came in search of her. "Do not hang your head," he said, kneeling down before her. He lifted her chin with the crook of his finger. "To gain mastery over anything, we must first taste the bitterness of humility."

The memory wearied Saina. Humility was her constant companion, a bitter tang upon her tongue. But Vandakk was correct. It was, perhaps, the greatest teacher. She glanced over the delicate dough rounds. Though mastery seemed to be far from her, she had learned to give the dough proper time to rest. The rounds would be ready to bake when the tandoor's fire burned down to coals.

She dropped quail eggs into the kettle of boiling water and, when they were finished, ladled them into prepared baskets. She looked around the room. With the morning meal nearly ready, she left to fill the oil lamps, which were stored in the closet at the far end of the dim corridor.

Standing in the narrow closet, Saina finished pouring the oil into the last lamp base then set the heavy jar of oil on the floor and straightened. Her arms ached, but the chore, having taken longer than she expected, was finally finished. She left the storage closet and was walking down the corridor when ahead, the door to Ning Po's room was flung open. Upach stood in the doorway holding a candle, its small flame flickering.

Saina quickly stepped into the shadows of the empty room beside her. Had Upach seen her? With shallow breath, she pressed her back against the cool wall and waited.

"Do you have the burial shroud?" Ning Po said, her voice empty, as if stripped bare by grief.

"Yes," came Upach's reply, her voice as toneless as Ning Po's. "I found some perfumed oils and spices in the storeroom. We will pick some flowers along the way and use them as a fragrant balm for her burial."

Saina heard the sharp intake of breath as Ning Po's quiet sobs slowly built into prolonged groans.

"My lady," Upach said. "I have prepared the donkey and filled the cart with provisions for our time away. Please drink the tea I have set out for you. It will build back your blood and give you some strength to face what must come."

Ning Po's weeping slowly faded. A thick silence extended into the hallway.

"It is sweet. What is this drink?" Ning Po said. "And how do you know of such things?"

"It is called 'eight treasures tea,'" Upach said. "Umida taught me how to prepare it for when you gave birth."

Saina's dared not move for fear of drawing their attention.

"You are shaking with exhaustion," Upach said. "Your body is weak and your blood flows heavily. Please, let me hold her while you rest for a moment."

"Do you seek to take her from me too?" Ning Po said, her voice strained.

"No, my lady, I—"

"Then speak no more of it. My time with her is fleeting," Ning Po said. "I will hold her until the very last moment, for the weakness in my body pales in comparison to the ache in my heart."

"Forgive me," Upach said. "It was a thoughtless request, spoken only out of concern." There was a long pause before Upach spoke again. "If it truly is your wish to bury her in the place of the ancient trees, the distance is too great for you to walk. But you can take your rest in the cart. I have packed many thick blankets and pillows for your comfort."

"My daughter deserves nothing less than to rest beneath their covering, to lie in the loam of the earth that sustains them," Ning Po said.

"Then we must leave now, while the caravanserai is quiet, and the merchants are still asleep."

A murmur of voices carried from deep within the corridors.

"We must go, my lady," Upach said. "The servants are rising."

Saina waited until the sound of their footsteps had faded in the hall, then stepped out from the shadows of the room and glanced down the hallway. She could hide no longer. By now, the coals beneath the tandoor oven would be hot enough and Vandakk would be expecting her.

Chapter Three

Two days had passed since Ning Po and Upach left to bury the baby, but Saina had little time to consider their absence, for her work had not ceased. Even Bao Li had been too busy visiting with dignitaries in Samarkand and dealing with matters of business these past days to call upon her.

The caravanserai bustled with the ebb and flow of sojourners and merchants seeking a place of respite for themselves and their beasts of burden. All servants were on hand, working long before the sun peeked over the Pamir mountains and well into the night, when the last of the merchants bedded down.

In the courtyard, Saina stirred the simple morning meal of rice porridge, adding honey, milk, and dried fruit as it thickened. With little time to purchase more supplies, the fresh food and many of their stored grains had nearly disappeared.

From across the courtyard, Vandakk approached, wrapping his threadbare coat around his shoulders. "I have received word that another large caravan is arriving tonight," he said, a sense of urgency in his voice. "I need you to purchase supplies from the bazaar and return as soon as possible." He dropped a pouch of coins in her hands.

"Will you not accompany me?" Saina said.

"There is no time," he said, straightening his doppa. "I have ordered various meats from the butcher in Samarkand and must leave immediately to pick them up."

Frowning, Saina followed him. "How will we take in another large caravan when we are filled to capacity already? Many of our guests do not plan to leave until tomorrow."

Vandakk turned around, censoring her with a firm gaze. "Do not concern yourself with such questions. Bao Li has demanded that we receive them. We will find room, as we always do." He paused a moment, then continued. "Take that ill-tempered donkey with you. You are the only person with the confidence and ability to deal with her."

Saina looked toward the stables as Vandakk walked away. The irritable donkey was well known in the caravanserai. All other servants refused to deal with her, but as a young girl, she had watched her father use a gentle hand when working with such animals. Employing the consistent practice and patience she saw exercised by her father, Saina taught the donkey to respect and respond to her authority.

———

Having set servants to the task of making final preparations for the morning meal, Saina hitched the donkey to the cart and walked through the gates of the caravanserai, shielding her eyes against the blaze of the morning sun. Far in the distance, a haze had settled above the sprawling city of Samarkand and the grand bazaar set outside its walls.

Saina stood at the diverging path. To the left was the Silk Road, which wound along the Zarafshan River. It was wide and well-kept and led to the northern entrance of the city. But as its name suggested, the road was congested with the foot traffic of man and beast, and today, Saina could not be slowed by lumbering caravans and keen-eyed merchants.

Gripping the donkey's lead rope, Saina turned right, taking the southern route. She preferred its solitude anyway.

It was not a road as much as a strip of worn-down earth. Rutted and rocky, the path meandered along the canal and peach orchards that reached far beyond the western edge of Samarkand. Birdsong filled the air.

Ahead was the grove of mighty *karagach* trees growing at the edge of the oasis. Sometimes Saina cooled herself under the outstretched limbs that offered shelter for birds and animals, as well. But as she approached, admiring the beauty of the trees, she gave thought to the sudden, thick silence around her and the stillness within the grove. How dark and foreboding it seemed, as though something unseen was watching her.

The skin on her neck prickled. What did the silent birds sense was hiding in the grove that her own eyes could not see?

She did not want to remain long enough to learn the answer to her own question.

With quickened steps, she rushed past the place, and the donkey obediently kept pace at her side. The unease lifted only when she crested the final hill and viewed the entirety of Samarkand, the city of ancient shadows, and the bazaar set just outside of its walls.

Saina fixed her gaze down the walkway knotted with people. Colorful awnings extended down both sides, shading merchants who hawked their goods to anyone passing by. Men and women bumped shoulders, bartering over almonds, sour cherries, dried apricots, and figs. Vendors filled small pouches with spices, threading the air with the scent. Men wove through the press of people, carrying bulging sacks of rice, wheat, and barley on their strong backs.

A woman passed by carrying a small baby, and its soft cry pierced Saina's heart with remembrance of Ning Po and the shattered hope she had placed in the life of her daughter.

Saina slowed. How was it possible to ache for someone who

had acted so cruelly or to be consumed by loneliness while standing in the midst of a crowd?

"Move!" A man's angry voice called out from behind her.

Startled, Saina pressed herself against the donkey as two men brushed past her, carrying giant reed baskets filled with dill fronds and mint. But the younger of the two slowed enough to glance back, offering a weak smile before he continued on.

Light shifted as thin clouds passed overhead. The scent of baked bread drew her toward the bread maker's stall. She found Zimat bent over his tandoor, pulling out blistered rounds with a thick wooden paddle.

"Saina," he greeted her as he stood and wiped his brow with a cloth. "I have just finished Vandakk's order." He dipped his fingers into a bowl of herbs and sprinkled them over the loaves. "And I have set one aside just for you." Zimat smiled proudly, extending one out to her.

Saina tore off a warm strip and put it in her mouth, savoring the earthy seasoning. "Vandakk will regret not coming to the bazaar today. He insists your bread is superior to any other baker in the city."

"I do not believe it," Zimat said, throwing his head back, his belly shaking with laughter. "How can a student surpass his teacher?"

"If there is one to do it, it would be you," Saina said, dropping three coins into Zimat's hand.

He took the coins, a wide grin spreading across his face. "I am honored to be called upon in his time of need, but I dare not compare myself with a master such as he." He moved two large baskets of hot bread out from behind the tandoor and placed them in Saina's cart.

By the time Saina had worked her way through the bazaar, morning had given way to midday. She took off her overcoat and tossed it into the cart, which now sagged under the weight of large sacks of rice and grains, as well as pungent spices, fresh fruit, and vegetables.

The small round of bread Zimat had given her earlier had not sustained her throughout the day, and a pang of hunger burned a pit in her belly. She could ignore it no longer.

Drawn by the tantalizing smells, Saina stopped at the food stall of a Tajik woman, who seemed close to Saina's age, turning kebabs on a long grill. A small child, with a head full of dark curls and a face wet with tears, clung to the woman's legs. The kebabs hissed as their juices dripped into the coals, sending smoke billowing into the awning above. Saina purchased two and smiled at the child, who responded by burying his face in his mother's homespun tunic.

When she stepped back, the mother pulled the boy into her arms. He giggled contentedly, his laughter following Saina as she turned down another walkway, empty of all but a few lingering patrons.

If things were different, she would have been married by now with a child on her hip. *But my body will never take the full shape of a mother*, she thought. *My heart will never know such love.* This thought had occurred to her for the first time several moon cycles ago. She could find no words to describe the growing ache its revelation brought.

At least her work provided ample distraction. She shrugged. Perhaps in time she would be grateful for it. She led the sturdy donkey and cart past the perfumer's stall. Inside, the perfumer and his daughter were arranging glass jars and silver vials filled with scented oils. Farther down, a jeweler forged strands of gold into fine necklaces and bracelets.

Ahead, the walkway was blocked by two emaciated men struggling to carry a long roll of white felt on their shoulders. Their master, a tentmaker, stood nearby, abusing them with careless words. "Useless slaves," he said, his embroidered kaftan barely covering his round belly. "If you get even a speck of dust on this felt, you will suffer my heavy hand," he hollered.

The servants gritted their teeth, their bodies soaked in sweat. Saina did not doubt the truth in the master's cruel threats, but she could not bear to see them mistreated any longer. For this she felt a pang of guilt. Bao Li had treated all her slaves fairly. Things could have been different.

Waiting for the men to clear the walkway, she peered inside the large tent at her side and saw gold-threaded textiles and richly hued silks displayed throughout. Drawn by the resplendent colors, Saina slipped under the inviting shade of the awning.

Bolts of fabric, embroidered cloths, and woven sashes, all skillfully crafted, were carefully displayed.

Then, as if he had suddenly appeared, she saw the silhouette of a man sitting on a small stool at the base of a wooden loom. His shoulders drooped like wax beneath a silk lampas robe, his head bowed low as he moved the shuttle back and forth, weaving threads between the warp. His hands, though gnarled and bent, moved with the ease of a master weaver as the rhythmic clack of his shuttle reached Saina's ears.

He seemed unaware of her presence. But as he leaned forward, running his fingers over the taut threads, Saina noticed the garment hanging behind him. Her heart skipped a beat. Could it be? She stepped closer to study the garment with its familiar embroidery—set within a floral roundel were two horsemen facing each other, each gripping a spear. Yes. A chill spread through her body. This garment once belonged to her father.

She remembered the first time she had looked upon it as a young girl. Saina had been standing outside the stables of the heavenly horses when her father approached her after his long day's work of training the highly prized warhorses. With a proud smile, he held the garment out before her. "Have you ever seen such fine craftmanship?" he asked. "Touch it, Saina," he said, taking her hand in his. "Do you feel how tight the weave is, how soft it is in your hands?"

Saina nodded slowly. "Where did you get it?" She ran her fingers down the embroidered edge, noticed the discrepancy between the garment's fine threads and the dirt caked beneath her fingernails. She pulled her hand away.

"Look at the horsemen," her father said, draping it over his shoulders and turning his back to her so she could see the woven pattern. "They are warriors, just like the Sassanian who offered this as payment for training his horse." Saina could not remember ever seeing him look so happy. At the same time, it seemed to her that he held a deeper contentment, a reason beyond any the garment could provide.

He wrapped her in his arms and set her upon his horse. "Come, it is time we return to your mother, for she is heavy with child and expecting us home."

The memory twisted a knot inside Saina. What great weight had been lifted from her father's shoulders that day? She shook her head at the foolish thought. She would never know the answer to that question.

A loud clatter startled Saina. The donkey jerked its head up, yanking her arm.

The tentmaker's angry voice filled the walkway. "What have you done?" He ran toward the collapsed awning and roll of felt lying in the dirt beneath it. Curious onlookers stepped out from their stalls as he threw off his cap and ran his hands over his bald head.

The donkey lifted her head and brayed in fright. Saina had barely wrapped her hands around the lead rope when the donkey began to kick. The cart jerked and shuddered, threatening to overturn. Saina gripped the lead rope tighter, pulling the donkey's head down, and shielded her vision. With steady movements she stroked the tight muscles along her neck. She clicked her tongue, just as her father had shown her, and the beast began to settle.

"You have a way with animals," a raspy voice said.

Saina turned around to see the weaver smiling at her, his face creased with age. "I have never seen a donkey settle so quickly. Certainly not with a hand as gentle as yours."

She was drawn to the kindness emanating from his smile. "I learned by watching my father," Saina said. She heard the strength in her own voice as she remembered the kindness her father showed her in his daily life, not what he did in his darkest moment.

Saina looked again at the tapestry hanging behind the weaver, and he followed her gaze. When he turned back to face her, he tilted his head. "What is your name, girl?"

"Saina."

The weaver's eyes widened as he leaned forward on his wooden stool. "You are from Samarkand?"

"Yes," she responded slowly. There was no fear in her regard, only careful admiration. "But I live in the caravanserai outside the city. My claim to Samarkand is only through the toil of a servant now."

"Servants are the backbone of any great man." He squinted as he pushed to stand and shuffled to the entrance of his stall. "Please, come closer," he motioned to her. "I no longer see with the clear eyes of a young man."

"I cannot remain long," Saina said, stepping closer. She took in the weaver's cerulean eyes, so blue it was as though the sky was borne within them. "I came to the bazaar only to complete important errands."

The weaver bowed his head slightly. "So did I, my child. So did I."

She paused, uncertain what to make of his comment, which seemed to hold a secret knowledge. What was it about this man that both intrigued and unsettled her? She pointed to the garment behind him. "How did you come to have that in your possession?"

The weaver closed his eyes, a thin smile spread across his face. "Ah, you recognize it?"

The statement sent a tremor through Saina's hands. She nodded as she struggled to loosen her tongue. "Do you know about the man it belonged to?"

The weaver's eyes remained fixed on Saina's as he slowly exhaled, filling the air with his deep, raspy breath. Though no words were uttered, she sensed her question had fulfilled an expectancy on his part.

How foolish she felt standing before him in the silence, hoping to find a thread connecting her to her father. Perhaps the weaver never intended to give a response.

"I wove that garment," he finally said.

Saina put her hand to her chest to ease the sudden stab of pain. Why, after all these years, was she still clinging to the foolish hope of seeing her father again? She looked away, hoping the weaver would not see the tears stinging her eyes or the disappointment on her face. "Forgive me for taking your time. I see you are a busy man. It is just that I saw this garment and I...I have seen one like it, and I thought —"

"I assure you that this is the only garment of its kind. There is no other," the weaver said.

"But my father...he..." Saina shook her head. "It was a foolish thought." She backed out of the tent, but turning to leave, stumbled into someone standing behind her.

She felt a firm grip on her arm, holding her steady until she found her footing. When she looked up and regarded a young man with clove-colored eyes and dark hair standing before her, her heartbeat quickened.

"Are you steady?" he said, adjusting the wool sack hanging off his shoulder.

"Forgive me, I was not paying attention," she said, her face burning hot with embarrassment.

The young man's eyes softened. A shy smile pushed up one side of his mouth, but Saina sensed a great confidence and strength in him.

He cleared his throat, and Saina dropped her head, fixing her gaze on the ground. Had she stared too long?

"Narisaf, my boy," said the weaver. The delight filling his voice set Saina at ease. She looked up.

"Grandfather," Narisaf said. He slowly took his eyes off Saina and entered the tent.

"I wondered what became of you," the weaver said. "I was concerned that you lost your way in this unfamiliar city."

Narisaf pulled the sack off his shoulder and set it on the ground. He pulled the weaver into his arms and kissed him on both cheeks. "Your directions were clear. It is my mind that wandered," he said with a deep laugh.

Letting go of the weaver, he turned to Saina and held her in his gaze. "The beauty of Samarkand has captivated me," he said. "It is filled with all manner of sights to distract the eye, from lush gardens and *chaikhanas* flowing with tea to skilled workmen adept in their trades." He leaned down and untied the sack. "Yet I managed to break free from the distraction and purchase what you requested," he said, as he pulled out several large spools of colorful thread along with two bolts of silk. "And a little extra," he reached inside and took a clay jar out from the cloth it was wrapped in.

Narisaf opened the lid, and the weaver leaned in. "Roasted duck?" he said, clapping his hands together. "Where did you find such a delicacy?" He took the jar and inhaled the scent. A proud smile spread across his face.

"The rumors we heard are true. The flavors of the world can be found within Samarkand." He unwrapped bread from another cloth.

The loneliness that had been Saina's constant companion seemed to compound. She mustered courage to remain standing alone as the deep bond between the two men unfolded before her.

"Saina," the weaver said. "Meet my grandson, Narisaf." He gripped Narisaf's muscular shoulder. "He is better to me than one hundred sons ever could be."

"Saina," Narisaf said thoughtfully, as though her name had fulfilled a longing.

She liked the way her name rolled off his tongue.

"We arrived only yesterday, and I did not anticipate having a guest," Narisaf bowed his head. He set a round of bread on top of a second clay jar and held it out. "Please, take my portion."

Saina cleared her throat against the tickle of sudden dryness. She raised her hand to protest his offering, but her tongue, as dried out as the dust on which she stood, clung to the roof of her mouth.

"Our travels were long and arduous," the weaver said, breaking the silence. "Fatigue has settled in my bones, but it seems to have stolen Narisaf's mind, for I have never seen him offer his own food to anyone."

"Grandfather," Narisaf said as a hint of pink spread across his face, but the weaver laughed.

"I am honored by your offering, but I have already eaten and must take my leave," Saina said, though it pained her greatly to say so. She pointed toward the cart loaded with supplies. "These goods are expected at the caravanserai. I cannot be late." She would not say more. The weaver knew her low position, knew the price all servants pay when their work is not sufficient. If Narisaf had not noticed already, he would have seen it in her plain tunic and undressed hair soon enough.

Ashamed of her unworthiness and overwhelmed by the sudden urge to flee, Saina desired to put space between these two men and the swirl of unexpected emotions they caused within her. She bowed her head and quickly left the shade of the tent.

"Saina," the weaver said, stopping her.

She inhaled a deep breath and turned to face him.

He pressed his lips together as though to choose his next words carefully. His refusal to look Saina in the eyes tightened threads of dread around her heart. Finally, he cleared his throat.

"When painful moments in our lives are not dealt with, when we cannot be honest with the reasons we were hurt so deeply, then these things will carve a hollow remembrance. They will leave us empty. Bitter. But to accept the truth of your past is to find healing in the well of your soul."

Saina could not take her eyes off of him. Why was he saying this to her? "I do not understand," she finally said.

The weaver looked at the warhorse garment, then back at Saina. "When you are ready for the answers, I will be here."

Chapter Four

I t was midmorning when the final caravan departed. Saina watched the last two camels lumber through the gates, the colorful tassels on their saddlebags swaying beneath the goods cinched on their strong backs.

She had set to clearing trays and remaining morsels of the morning meal when the increasing volume of men's voices drew her attention.

Several traders gathered in the shade of the sycamore tree, watching Peroz and Basir toss stones into the narrow opening of a reed basket. The two merchants, whose trade routes brought them through Samarkand often, were frequent patrons of the caravanserai.

Peroz jostled a stone in his hands as he squinted into the bright sun, studying the basket set fifteen paces away. He turned toward his old friend. "With this final toss, my victory will be secured, Basir. You would be wise to purchase that pitcher of *kvass* right now. I will need the fermented drink to quench my thirst."

"Be careful, Peroz." Basir smiled. "Soon you will eat your words."

"A bet is a bet," Peroz said. With a fling of his wrist, he tossed the stone. It glided past the basket and hit the ground five paces beyond it.

Laughter filled the courtyard.

His striped kaftan rippled as Peroz spun on his heel and threw up his hands. "The basket moved! I saw it." He extended his arm toward the traders beneath the tree. "Tell me you saw it too."

Basir, with his long nose and drooping eyelids, threw his arm around his friend's shoulders. "You have no aim, Peroz," he said, his face red from laughter. "It is to your good fortune that you are skilled in forging metal. For if your family relied on you to provide for them with a bow and arrow, I am certain they would starve."

Peroz shook his head, his smile fading. "I have a skill, Basir, but I cannot say the same for you." He pointed to the threadbare mat beneath the sycamore tree. "You claim to be a weaver, but it looks like you did little more than pull wool from a thornbush."

Basir's eyes widened and his mouth dropped open as deep laughter rang out once again from the men resting nearby in the shade of the tree.

Saina laughed, too, delighted by their friendly banter. She set out a pitcher of the fermented *kvass* then returned to her chore of clearing the morning dishes.

"Perhaps you can take lessons from the grandest weaver of all," Peroz said, retrieving his stone. "I heard a rumor that the weaver of Merv has come to Samarkand."

The weaver? Saina stilled. Was he speaking of the same man she saw in the bazaar yesterday?

Basir perked up. "He is here...in Samarkand?" He walked into the shade of the tree. "Why would a man of his age make the dangerous trek from Merv? That section of the Silk Road would take him straight through the red sands of the Kyzylkum Desert. It is terrible enough on young men in their prime."

"His grandson is with him," another man said as he sat up from where he reclined beneath the tree. "Narisaf has a warrior's heart, just like his own father. I trust the weaver will be well cared for. Why concern yourself with such matters?"

Basir shook his head. "I do not understand why he has chosen to come here now. How many years has it been since the death of his son? And in all that time he has refused to leave Merv."

"Who can say?" Peroz said. "His work is highly sought after. Perhaps he came at the request of a dignitary. A man with his mastery would be in high demand." He leaned forward. "But I was told that the last time the weaver stepped foot in Samarkand, it was to seek a wife for his son. Could it be he is doing the same for Narisaf now?"

The tray slipped from Saina's hands and rang out as it hit the ground, but she remained standing, unable to move. Was it true? Had the weaver come this far just to find a wife for his grandson? The thought gnawed a tender spot within her.

"Saina," Peroz hollered from the shade of the tree. "Tell Vandakk to drizzle some honey on the trays. They will stick to your hands better."

Heat crept into her face as she knelt, then quickly gathered the tray and spilled crumbs. Any food left on the ground would invite not only vermin but a stern warning from Vandakk. Rising, she pulled the tray close and rushed out of the courtyard.

"Ignore him," Basir called out behind her. "He is sore from losing to me once again."

Upon entering the cool hallway, Saina slowed and gathered her thoughts. If what Peroz said was true, why would the weaver make such a dangerous trek to find a wife for Narisaf? Surely there were many suitable women in Merv.

Saina shook her head and strode quickly toward the storeroom. And why would she care anyway?

She yanked the leather flap open and walked inside.

"Saina?" Vandakk said, looking at her from the table where he was measuring flour in a bowl. "You startled me. Is something the matter?"

Saina could not think beyond the strange rush of emotions. "Nothing, I...I dropped the tray, and..." her voice trailed off. She did not know what to say.

Vandakk nodded. "The days have been terribly long, and we are all weary," he said. "I was going to tend the garden when I finished preparing the dough for dumplings. Perhaps the chore would suit you better?"

Comforted by his invitation, Saina smiled. "It would please me greatly." She set the trays on the table in the kitchen before returning to him. Working in the soil and harvesting its produce had always brought her solace.

"Vandakk," Saina said, thoughtfully. "Have you heard mention of the weaver?"

Vandakk slowed and tilted his head as he added a little salt to the flour. "Which weaver do you speak of? The streets of Samarkand are full of them."

Saina shook her head. "I know of the many fine weavers in the city. I am speaking of the weaver who comes from Merv."

"Ah, the Grand Weaver?" Vandakk said, awe building in his voice.

Saina nodded.

"Of course, I have heard of him. He is well known along the entirety of the Silk Road. Why do you ask?"

"He has come to Samarkand. Peroz and Basir were speaking of him in the courtyard just now."

Vandakk raised his brows and laughed. "Those two? Who can know what is true and what is fable coming from their mouths."

Saina stepped forward. "What they say is true. I met the weaver in the bazaar yesterday."

Vandakk shot her a sideways glance as he cracked eggs into his bowl. "You are certain of this?"

"Yes," Saina said. "Basir spoke of the weaver's grandson, Narisaf. He is the same man I met in the weaver's stall."

Vandakk seemed to consider this news for a moment before he spoke. "Does he plan to stay for some time?"

Saina shrugged. "He came only to complete an errand," she said. She thought of the many striking women in the city who would be happy to become Narisaf's wife. "But I do not know how long it will take."

"He has traveled quite a distance for an errand," Vandakk said. "There must be more to it." He dumped the stirred contents of his bowl onto the wooden board and began kneading the dough. "We can speak more on this later. For now, we have more pressing matters to consider, the garden being first among them."

Saina nodded. "I will go now," she said, grateful for the reprieve.

Torchlight danced on the dark walls as she walked down the corridor and approached Ning Po's room. Still no light seeped beneath the door, the murmur of their voices remained unheard.

She continued on past rooms reserved for hired entertainers and storage closets holding extra bedding, ewers, and oil lamps. Few had reason or desire to come this far into the inner corridors, with the narrow walls and dancing shadows.

The first time Saina had walked here as a young girl, Bao Li and Vandakk had been at her side, casting knowing glances at one another. She had not yet lived within the caravanserai for a full cycle of seasons, and the sorrow of her abandonment seemed to fill her so completely that no relief was felt.

"Open the door," Bao Li had said, pointing to an ornately carved door tucked at the very end of the corridor.

Saina looked from Bao Li's smile to the door. She studied its thick metal hinges and iron lock. A sliver of light shone through a crack and came to rest on her dirty tunic, the spot where her heart beat its constant rhythm. "What is it?" Saina had asked, wondering at the source of brilliant light coming from the other side.

Vandakk pressed his hand against Saina's back, gently urging her forward.

Saina inhaled a deep breath, then gripped the large handle and pulled open the heavy door. Shielding her eyes against the glare of golden sunlight flooding the hallway, she stepped onto the stone path extending before her. The sight stilled her breath.

Dried and brittle plants lined the path winding through the overgrown space. Shrubs drooped beside an empty pond. There were remnants of a small orchard with trees whose gnarled branches hung low and wild, and twisted vines wrapped around faded, broken trellises.

One did not need a grand imagination to know this unkempt garden was beautiful in its time.

Saina looked up at Bao Li. Despite the respect the older woman commanded and the hard lines on her face, Saina had come to regard her as deeply kind and caring. "I do not understand. What are you showing me?"

"A gift...for you," Bao Li said. "We wanted to revive this old garden and knew you would be the perfect helper to do so. It will be a lot of work, of course, and will require Vandakk's help to tend it." She looked at Vandakk standing proudly beside her. "A task he has agreed to."

Saina straightened.

"But there is one condition, Saina," Bao Li's eyes narrowed. "You must give me your word that you will not step foot in this garden until your daily chores have been completed."

"Yes, my lady," Saina said. She understood the warning, even as her chest swelled with pride at the task set before her.

Despite keeping her promise to Bao Li all these years, Saina had found ample time to work in the garden, to give it life once again. She walked the stone path lined with fragrant sweet briar rose and the spring colors of budding tulips and irises.

The warmth of the sun spread over her as she glanced at the peach, apple, and almond trees that had matured and grown thick enough to cast their cool shade. Pale-colored larks flitted through the low hanging branches of shrubs and orchard trees, swooping over the water lilies that had spread across the pond.

Saina bent down, pulling weeds that threatened to choke out the tender shoots from the seeds she and Vandakk had planted earlier in the season. In every way, she had learned to tend the garden by imitating him.

She snapped off a twig of tarragon and held it to her nose. Its sweet scent wafted into the air as she studied its severed end. Her toil in the garden had been a soothing balm against the painful severing caused by her father's abandonment.

The memory of that terrible day often came to her in the quiet of the night. But now she sensed its darkness spreading over her like a shadow even as she stood in the light of the garden. She gripped the tarragon tighter in her hand, and her heart began to race as the memory of her father's tear-stained face returned to her.

"Pack your things," her father had said when he walked into their home. His cheeks were streaked with dirt from burying her dead mother and the newborn baby who had never lived.

"Where are we going?" she said, stuffing the only other tunic she owned into her small satchel.

"Away," he said, then turned around and walked out the door.

With a final glance at the baby clothes and leather rattle her mother had sewn in anticipation of the baby's arrival, she ran after him. She struggled to keep up as her father walked away. But he was all she had left in this world, and she would learn to keep his pace or risk losing him too.

He did not speak, did not look at her until they arrived outside the towering walls of the caravanserai where they were met by a dark-haired woman who greeted them with rigid posture and her mouth in a straight line. "I received your message," she said, as her guard stood silently behind her, an imposing, fearsome-looking man.

"My bones ache with grief, Bao Li. My life has been torn from me," Saina's father had said to the woman dressed in fine silk. The last rays of sunlight draped her black hair like a golden veil. She looked at Saina with sorrowful eyes.

Saina looked away and adjusted the strap of her satchel higher up on her shoulder, then tugged on her father's hand. "Please, let us go." She wanted to leave this place, to never come back.

"I beg of you, take my daughter from me," he said, then

pressed his hand firmly into Saina's back, forcing her toward Bao Li.

Confused, Saina turned to face her father, but he had looked away, his gaze fixed in the direction of the setting sun, a distant mark in the vast desert.

"If I agree, Turghar," Bao Li said, grimacing, "what would you require in return?"

A muscle twitched in her father's jaw. "All I request is a donkey and some grain," he said. He bit his lip, stopping the quiver in his chin. "I will leave her life to unfold as it will, but promise me she will be cared for. To think otherwise is too great a burden."

"Makh," Bao Li said, motioning to the guard standing behind her. He leaned forward and she whispered to him. She watched him walk away before turning back to face them. "Very well. Your daughter will be a servant in the caravanserai and will receive compensation as such. I offer nothing more," Bao Li said, shaking her head.

Saina stepped closer to her father and put her small hand on his clenched fist, but he pulled away.

Confused, Saina watched Bao Li reach into her sash and pull out a scroll. "I am sorry to learn about the death of your wife and unborn child," Bao Li said, looking away. "I do not despise you for your reasons in leaving. I request that you do not despise me for treating this as a matter of business." Her face was pinched as though speaking such words pained her. "This contract states you have relinquished your daughter to me. In exchange for food and shelter, she is indebted to a life of servitude in my caravanserai." She held out the scroll.

He took the scroll and marked it with the symbol of the heavenly horse. As a trainer of warhorses, he had taken the symbol as his signature. He crushed the scroll in his hands before giving it back to her.

The guard returned with the donkey and Bao Li put her hands on Saina's shoulder. "She is no longer your concern."

The muscles of her father's neck tightened to cords. He grabbed the donkey's lead rope and turned away.

Saina's eyes widened as she looked from her father to Bao Li. "Father!" she screamed. Her chest filled with panic.

Bao Li grabbed her arm, but Saina pulled away.

"I am going with him," Saina said, stumbling.

"Makh, hold her," Bao Li yelled.

The guard grabbed Saina, wrapping her in his arms as they fell to the ground. "No," Saina cried. "My father is leaving. I must go with him." Her feet slid in the dust as she pressed her body against Makh's, but she was no match for his strength.

She writhed in his arms until she crumpled in exhaustion. Her cries were swallowed up by the desert's expanse as she watched her father walk away, pulling a stubborn ass and three sacks of grain in her place.

The caw of a bird echoed through the garden, releasing Saina from the terrible memory. Searching, she found the bird perched on the wall, straws of alfalfa sticking out from its black beak.

It is the season of toil for all creatures, Saina thought, feeling drained of strength. Who was she to expect lesser toil than even the birds of the air?

With great effort she churned compost and spread it around the plants. The garden had been her respite from the abiding ache left by her father, but it had taken Saina many seasons to understand that this had been Bao Li's intention the day she offered her the opportunity to build new life from a barren place.

How is it that I have repaid Bao Li's kindness with betrayal? Her shoulders slumped.

Now that the caravanserai was finally quiet, Saina expected Bao Li would call upon her soon. When that happened, she vowed to confess the truth about the stillbirth. She could not bear to keep it from her any longer.

The door creaked open, and Vandakk appeared, carrying a small basket.

"You have accomplished much in a short time," he said,

looking around. He set the basket on the stone path. "There is not a single patch of loam left for me to tend." He pulled a knife from its sheath hanging at his waist and cut a handful of herbs.

"This is my favorite place to be," Saina said. "It is not work when I am here."

"From the very beginning, I understood that about you," he said. "But do not get too comfortable out here in the sun." He held up the cut trimmings, then tossed them into the basket. "With the addition of these herbs, Bao Li's midday meal will be complete, and she has requested that you bring it to her."

He said this without ceremony and left before Saina could offer her response. But it was just as well. The moment he uttered Bao Li's wishes, dread rolled like a millstone through her body. The certainty she had felt moments earlier was ground to dust.

Chapter Five

S aina walked into the courtyard carrying Bao Li's meal of steamed dumplings, a kettle of tea, and her porcelain jar. She inhaled a slow breath, trying to still her trembling hands.

Faded tapestries, hanging from the second-floor balcony, snapped in the breeze. The flowing banners welcomed the early arrival of a large caravan as camels and their livestock handlers poured through the gates. The beasts grumbled and kicked up dust as they circled the courtyard and came to a stop, but this did not seem to bother Basir, who sat in the shade of the sycamore tree, an array of colorful wool spread around him. He looked up as Saina walked past him.

"You work from the dawn of day until well past dusk," Basir said. "Do you ever find rest?"

Saina paused, grateful for the distraction. "What is rest, Basir, that I should seek it? My work is to serve my mistress. But my reward is the knowledge gleaned from merchants and traders who bring news and stories from the outside world."

He clicked his tongue. "You are a servant among servants. It is clear to all why Bao Li esteems you, even though you do not see it.

I hope that one day you are granted reprieve from your years of loyal service."

Saina smiled, if only to indulge him for a moment. But she knew better. How many slaves were freed because they were highly favored? She had not known a single one.

The camels settled, and the handlers immersed themselves in the work of unloading goods from their sturdy backs. Saina left Basir and continued through the courtyard. The sweet scent of spices drifted in the air as servants rushed to store crates of cinnamon bark and mace, nutmeg and sandalwood. Others hauled dyed textiles, furs, and glass beads into rooms that had been prepared for their arrival.

But at the far end, where unburdened animals were led toward the stables to be refreshed with troughs of fresh water and alfalfa hay, a shadowed figured of a woman caught Saina's eye.

Draped in a black shawl, the woman's head and shoulders were slumped, her hands pulled toward her chest. She walked as though every step required great effort, unaware of the servants struggling to keep their animals from trampling her underfoot.

Who was this woman who took no caution of those around her? Saina had barely thought the question when Upach appeared behind the woman, carrying an armload of blankets.

The woman snapped her head up and swept the courtyard with a glance. Her dark eyes settled on Saina. *Ning Po?* Saina drew back.

It seemed to her that the boisterous sounds of the caravanserai fell silent. Saina could not move, could not look away, shocked as she was by Ning Po's sunken presence.

"My lady, you are hungry," Upach said, her voice breaking the hold between them. "Let us return these blankets to your room and request a meal be prepared." She placed her hand on Ning Po's shoulder, urging her forward.

The despair in Ning Po's eyes softened Saina's heart, but a prickle of caution rolled up her spine. Saina kept her eyes fixed upon them, refusing to turn away, until they were swallowed up in the crowd.

By the time she walked up the stairs leading to Bao Li's khana, her throat ached. The small cup of water she had swallowed in the storeroom had not slaked her thirst.

Built as the core of the caravanserai, yet meant to stand alone, the khana brought a sense of awe to those who looked upon its grandeur. Its hewn-stone walls were softened by ornately carved shutters and fine silk curtains draped from the overhanging portico. But standing in front of the massive, gilded doors, she observed the dragons carved into the wood. Their fierce eyes and bared teeth seemed to hold a measure of warning.

Saina shifted the tray in her hands, taking care not to topple the delicate tea jar. How would she tell Bao Li all that had happened since she last stepped foot inside these doors?

She had dreaded this moment, but standing here in contemplation only made it worse. Saina opened the heavy door and walked inside. It closed behind her, shutting out the bark of the merchant's voices and stench of their camels.

Down the narrow hallway she entered the large, vaulted room where Bao Li received her guests. Parchments lay unrolled on the wooden desk at the far end, but her mistress was not there.

Saina removed her felt boots and walked across the silk rug spanning the entire length of the room. Intricately woven, it had taken a team of weavers several years to complete.

But as striking as the rug was, it was the giant mural on the opposite wall that caught Saina's attention. With the scent of fresh egg paint still lingering in the air, its vibrant colors and lush landscape awed her.

Saina had seen the artists entering the khana the past few days but only from a distance. Bao Li had not granted access to any servants, including Saina, until the painters were finished. She set the tray of tea and dumplings on the desk and walked toward the mural.

A lush forest extended across the background, with tree-covered mountains jutting up into the cerulean sky where birds soared with outstretched wings. In the foreground, at the base of pink flowering trees, a young version of Kang Dahan stood beneath a white wedding canopy. His black hair was tied neatly behind his gold, pointed Sogdian hat. Beside him, Bao Li leaned her head on his arm, her pale shoulders exposed beneath a wide silk scarf.

Saina looked away. She had never seen such intimacy shared between them.

"Do you like it?" Bao Li said.

Startled, Saina spun around and saw Bao Li standing just steps from her. "It is beautiful," she said. Bao Li wore her favorite silk coat, which was richly embroidered along the hem. In one arm, she cradled two leather scrolls, and a single willow stick used for writing.

"I have heard of verdant green mountains but have never seen them with my own eyes. Is it true that such a place exists?"

Bao Li nodded. "This is the city of Chang'an, the land of my youth," Bao Li said, her chin held high. "It is a beautiful, fertile land, with washing rains and abundant foliage. It cannot be rivaled by this desert city of Samarkand, where one chokes on the sand carried in by storms."

Saina fixed her gaze on the ground. She had come to expect Bao Li's disdain for Samarkand, but having never stepped foot outside this place, she had considered only its beauty. Nothing less.

"Before Kang Dahan left on his recent journey, he hired an artist to paint a mural of our wedding day," Bao Li said. "It was his gift to me in hopes that we would never forget the importance of that day." She huffed. "I hated the idea, but I could not speak against the wishes of my husband.

"My marriage to Kang Dahan was not a union made from love but the result of a business contract between him and my father. Kang Dahan agreed to transport my father's porcelain to distant lands on the Silk Road, earning him untold wealth. But

Kang Dahan's offer was self-serving. He was no fool. In return for such generosity, my father would be required to give me in marriage to him.

"I refused at first. I even told my father that I loved another man, but he closed his ears to me." Bao Li's eyes pooled. "I argued with my father, pleaded with him not to do this, but a swift blow from his hand split my lip and silenced my will."

The sadness in Bao Li's eyes pained Saina, but what could she say in the wake of Bao Li's admission? To stand silently beside her, sharing in their mutual sufferings of loss, seemed to be enough.

Bao Li sighed. "It mattered not to Kang Dahan that I was miserable. He would not concern himself with my grief, for he had received his reward." She looked once again at the mural. "Do you see how I smile? That was how Kang Dahan remembered it. For him, the truth was not as important as the lie he wished to convey.

"The truth is that I was not smiling on that day," Bao Li continued, "or the many moon cycles afterward. Those months we spent trekking across the Taklamakan Desert and Tian Shan mountains were bitter for me. But I had a choice to make. Rather than let my hatred for him grow, I set my mind to useful things. I became adept in my husband's business, assuring dyers of their cloth and merchants of their spices, all brought on the backs of his camels. I filled the caravanserai's coffers to overflowing and built a team of servants and cooks envied by all. In the end he repaid me by taking a second wife, claiming it was only to help ease my duties." Bao Li's voice was like fire, but it was the anger in her eyes that lit the flame. "Does he think I am stupid?"

Saina could not speak as she watched Bao Li slide her hand across the mural, her finger coming to rest on a peasant boy standing in front of a grove of trees holding a basket of fish.

"This young man was painted upon my request," Bao Li said slowly, as though every word tasted of sweet honey. "While my husband sought comfort in the arms of a younger woman and an heir in her womb, I sought only to gaze upon the distant memory of the *only* man I have ever loved."

Saina inhaled, felt pressure swelling in her chest. She dared not move; she could barely breathe. What was this admission? Had Bao Li truly loved another?

Bao Li had carried this secret for years and Saina was deeply honored that she trusted her with it. She resolved to tuck Bao Li's admission of love in her heart and guard it carefully.

Saina stepped forward. "I am sorry for your grief, my lady," Saina's voice was thick with emotion. "How terrible it must have been to lose that which you loved more than any other, what you thought would always belong to you."

Bao Li snapped her head up, as if surprised she had spoken her thoughts aloud. She looked once more at the painting of the peasant boy, then stepped away from the mural and knelt at the desk. Unrolling the scroll in her hand, she readied her writing tool and set to recording the daily finances and contracts for the caravanserai.

Saina arranged Bao Li's meal and prepared her tea. Stepping back, she stood silently, watching over the older woman's shoulder. She tried to summon the courage to speak, to tell her Ning Po had already given birth and that Kang Dahan's heir had not survived. But fear overwhelmed her. What would happen when Bao Li learned of her betrayal? Would she send her away like her own father had done?

Bao Li ran her finger along the porcelain jar, then reached out and picked a dumpling from the tray. She turned toward Saina and stopped. "I should not have shared such private matters. You are correct that we share a similar fate, but it was careless of me. I see that it weighs heavily upon you."

Saina stepped forward. "I am not weighed down by your admission. But there is something I must tell you..." She saw the sadness in Bao Li's eyes and shook her head. Now was not the time.

"What was his name?" Saina blurted. She regretted asking the question as soon as she spoke it, but she had to say something. Anything.

Bao Li tilted her head, her mouth open, but she did not speak.

"The boy you loved, the one holding the basket of fish. What was his name?"

Bao Li closed her eyes, a smile creased her aged face. "Chen Tien," she finally said, her voice light, as though it brought great relief to speak of him. "I have not spoken his name out loud in many years." She put her finger to her heart. "I have only held it here.

"Our love was forbidden, so we kept it a secret. But given enough time, all secrets are exposed to the light," Bao Li said, shaking her head. "We had even planned to run away, but by then it was too late, my father had already betrothed me to Kang Dahan." Her voice was suddenly older than her years. "I have often wondered if my closed womb was the result of all my sorrow." She hung her head, and her shoulders shook with sobs.

Saina knelt before Bao Li and took her mistress's hand in hers. "I can see in your eyes how you love Chen Tien still—"

From down the hallway, Saina heard the doors of the khana swing open. She looked over her shoulder at the sound of rushing, heavy footsteps.

Ning Po appeared at the entrance to the room, her teeth bared like the carved dragons on the gilded doors. She did not wait to be granted entrance but ran straight toward them.

Saina's stomach clenched. "No, Ning Po," she said, rising to meet her. She stared into the fury of Ning Po's countenance and held out her hand to stop her from coming any closer, but Ning Po shoved past her and lunged forward.

Bao Li's eyes were wide with shock, and she stumbled back as Ning Po fell upon her.

"You did this," Ning Po's voice quaked with rage. She clawed at Bao Li. "You cursed my child, the seed of my husband."

Saina grabbed Ning Po's arm and tried to pull her back. "Stop! Bao Li knows nothing of this!"

"You cannot contain your jealousy," Ning Po screamed. She raised her clenched fists.

Saina threw herself in front of Bao Li as Ning Po swung her arms in a torrent of anger. The ache of knuckle on bone spread above her eye. Pain pulsed down her face, tearing into her jaw, but Saina remained over Bao Li, protecting her from the terrible blows.

Only when the sound of a man's voice was over them did Ning Po finally stop.

Saina's body shook as she pulled her hands away from her head and looked up from where she cowered. Makh stood above them, his arms wrapped around Ning Po's waist, yanking her back.

"I will speak to Kang Dahan upon his return," Ning Po cried. "You will pay harshly for conspiring to murder his child." She tore at Makh's arms, trying to escape his grip as he pulled her out of the room. Her eyes, like tiny, black stones, fixed on Saina, then Bao Li. "I will get my revenge on you and your worthless slave," she hissed. Her words snaked around the corner and out the gilded doors as Makh dragged her away.

With a throbbing head, Saina helped Bao Li stand, steadying her. Bao Li's nostrils flared. Her ragged breath was the only sound in the settling silence.

She held Saina in her long gaze. Streaks of silver glistened like frost down the loose strands of hair that had been pulled from her tight bun.

"I have given Kang Dahan many seasons of my life, but he disregarded me, heaping bitterness upon my sorrow by taking Ning Po as his second wife," Bao Li said, her voice rising as she pointed to the ground beside her desk. "And now this destruction?"

Saina turned as saw the porcelain tea jar shattered on the floor and stiffened, her body suddenly cold.

"How dare she accuse me of such lies and not fear the consequences," Bao Li said, her anger swelling, as though it were a dreadful, living thing. "And why was I not informed that she already gave birth?"

Saina stepped back and swallowed down the knot forming in her throat.

Bao Li's eyes narrowed. "Stand before me, Saina, and answer my question."

Saina's legs trembled beneath her.

"Why would Ning Po accuse me of murdering her child?"

Saina could not raise her head. Tears burned her eyes, blurring the woven rug into a pool of shapeless color.

"Answer me!" Bao Li's voice split the silence.

"I was asked to help deliver Ning Po's baby," Saina said, the words spilling from her mouth. "The midwife had been called away, and Ning Po refused all others. She said she did not trust them. Her servant, Upach, was too young to tend to the task alone. There was no one else." She stopped, then continued quietly. "Ning Po's baby came too early. There was no life in her, but Ning Po refused to see it. She accused me of snuffing out the life of her daughter."

"And you did not see fit to tell me this news?"

Saina nodded. Nothing would excuse what she had done.

"My husband took another wife because of my barren womb." Bao Li laughed bitterly. "How fitting that even his second wife cannot succeed in bearing his children."

"I beg your forgiveness. It was not my intent to keep it from you. But you were busy with the painters and...and dignitaries." Saina searched Bao Li's eyes, hoping to ease her up from the depths of her anger. But she saw only her reflection in Bao Li's blank stare.

"I knew Kang Dahan held no loyalty when I married him, but never once did I consider that *you* would treat me in the same manner in order to protect this...this harlot."

"It was only for Upach's sake that I helped. Please, I beg of you, it was not to dishonor you—"

"Saina," Bao Li said, her voice breaking. "I do not place blame on you for helping the young servant, Upach." Tears pooled. "But you did not trust me enough to tell me the truth, and that hurts me more than anything."

"My lady?"

"Leave me," Bao Li said, wiping a tear from her cheek. She turned her back to Saina and walked away.

Saina stared after her, wanting to cry out her defense, but she bit down on her tongue, tasted the tinge of blood. She swallowed it along with her explanation. Nothing she could say now would fix what she had done.

Chapter Six

Ning Po had succeeded.

The sun descended three times in the western sky, each night setting the horizon ablaze in its fiery glow, but still, Bao Li did not call upon Saina. How similar those untamed skies were to Saina's time of waiting, when despair burned in her and her hope was charred black.

"I have prepared your favorite meal," Vandakk said. He slid a bowl of *laghman* noodles onto the table in front of her. Saina turned away, wiping her eyes.

Midmorning the next day, he approached again, setting a bowl of plain rice before her. "Please, Saina, you must eat." She put it to her mouth but could not force herself to swallow it. Pushing away the bowl of pale grain, she bore her hunger silently.

The stale air of the storeroom worsened the turbulence in Saina's heart, but she could not bring herself to emerge from the dark walls that offered her protection from the curious stares of other servants. Vandakk had allowed her to remain in the storeroom, preparing the daily meals while the swelling in her face subsided, but she could not expect him to shoulder the weight of her responsibilities much longer.

After Vandakk left to clean the cauldrons, Saina paced in

front of the shelves, taking note of the remaining supplies. Only a few sacks each of rice and wheat remained. Both would be consumed by tomorrow. The pressing need to feed sojourners would require a trip to the bazaar, but she was certain that Vandakk would not expect her to go with him, not in the state she was in.

She put her fingertips to her brow, felt the tender bruise and dull throb pulsing down her face. Some servants looked at her with pity in their eyes, but others would not even raise their heads as they walked past. Saina did not know which was worse. Had gossip about her lost favor spread even beyond the walls of the caravanserai? It was a painful thought. She could only hope Bao Li would see beyond her offense and forgive her.

She pulled three strips of salt fish from a basket on the top shelf and set them on the plate along with a handful of sour cherries, a boiled egg, and two honey cakes. If Bao Li called upon her, she was prepared to present her with the sweet offering.

Vandakk's voice echoed in the hallway, growing louder as he approached. Saina picked up the plate of food and faced the entrance as he walked inside. She stared at the young stable girl who followed closely behind him with her hands clasped tightly at her waist and her eyes downcast.

The girl was small for her age, but Saina had seen her working in the stables and marveled at her strength as she heaved bales of alfalfa hay twice her size into empty troughs. Even the stableboys who worked alongside her shook their heads in disbelief. But the stable girl looked more delicate standing before her now, with her hair tied up in an ochre scarf and clothed in a clean tunic.

What was her purpose for being here? Saina searched Vandakk's eyes for answers, but he did not meet her gaze. She pulled the dish closer to her body.

Vandakk stepped forward. "Is that Bao Li's meal?" he asked, hesitation in his voice.

Saina swallowed. "Yes." She looked from Vandakk to the stable girl. "Has Bao Li called upon me?"

Vandakk turned to the stable girl. "Fetch the small kettle of hot tea in the kitchen," he said, pointing toward the back of the room. "Bao Li will require it with her meal." When she walked away, he looked at Saina, his face pained. "Do not lose heart," he whispered. "You must allow time to soften the sharp edges of Bao Li's anger. It will not burn against you for long, but it is the only way."

The news brought a stab of pain to Saina's heart. She set the dish on the table and steadied herself.

"I am sorry, Saina," Vandakk said, dropping his head. "For now, Bao Li has requested that the stable girl tend to her needs." He placed his hand on Saina's shoulder, squeezing her gently before walking out of the storeroom.

Tears burned Saina's eyes. The task of tending to Bao Li had been ripped from her hands. Ashamed of how far she had fallen, she pressed herself against the wall and wept.

———

On the following afternoon a shift occurred. Its stirring was miniscule at first but having spent several long days in the dimly lit storeroom, Saina sensed it in the marrow of her bones.

She finished putting away the supplies Vandakk had purchased from the bazaar and set to preparing the evening meal.

She pulled a large sack of ripe dates from the top shelf and piled them into the oversized, bronze bowl. On top, she drizzled honey from the comb and crumbled goat cheese. Before setting it aside, she took a bite of the fruit, savoring its sweetness.

Earlier in the day, Vandakk had given word that the long-expected architects who were traveling from the west had arrived, along with their apprentices and teams of servants. Musicians from Samarkand trickled in, hired to entertain them during the evening feast.

It was common for all who lived and worked within the cara-vanserai to be filled with anticipation on such evenings. Saina heard it in the lilt of the servants' voices that carried through the corridors as they swept the floors outside the storeroom and was surprised at its effects on her too. Her steps seemed lighter, her thoughts clearer. It did not serve her well to remain in solitude and continue to thresh her disloyalty.

She picked up the bowl of dates, surprised at its weightiness, and walked out of the storeroom. How weak she had become these past few days.

The cumbersome bowl grew heavier as she entered the courtyard. Her arms ached, and the harsh glare of the desert sun throbbed in her temples. She squinted, seeking out a narrow path between the merchants unloading their goods from their animals.

Beyond the tangle of supplies strewn throughout the courtyard, Saina saw Vandakk arranging platters of dried apricots and sweet honeycomb beside a mounding basket of steaming flatbread. His gray hair stood on end. Their eyes met, and Vandakk smiled, beckoning her with a wave of his hand.

She shifted the bowl and wove through the maze of goods, past bolts of woolen cloth and delicate wooden cages filled with birds whose striking wings resembled colorful topaz and Persian turquoise.

Beside the cages sat a woman with a gold hoop pierced through her nose. She tilted her head and peered at Saina as she passed by, her agile hands working quickly, knotting the loose fibers of an unfinished basket in her lap.

Saina looked away from the woman's intense gaze just as a dark-haired camel rose up from the ground before her. Red and gold tassels hanging from its saddlebags bounced and swayed. Saina shuffled to the side, trying to avoid being trampled beneath the beast, but the momentum of the heavy bowl proved too much for her fatigued arms. It burst through her hands and fell to the ground, crushing a bird cage beneath it.

Stunned, Saina could only watch as two birds flew away from the splintered cage and came to rest on the opposite wall of the caravanserai. On the ground, a single bird remained, fluttering and dazed at her feet. Merchants turned and stared at the commotion, but Saina could not move. Humiliation rooted her legs firmly to the ground.

A gray-haired man rushed toward her, his back bent with age, flailing his arms like the startled birds confined in the remaining wooden cages. Scooping the bird into his gnarled hands, he dropped it into another cage. He slammed the doors shut, then turned to Saina.

"What have you done?" he spat, pointing a shaking finger in her face. "You must pay for this."

"Forgive me, the bowl slipped..." Saina said. He shook his head angrily, then suddenly grew still, his gaze fixed on the ground.

Saina looked to where the long beak and splayed wings of a motionless bird protruded beneath the splintered mess.

Whimpering, the old man knelt down. He pulled the colorful wing, sliding the bird out from the rubble.

Saina's stomach knotted. Her life, like a poorly crafted tapestry, had come undone. The familiar heaviness that had plagued her these past days, returned. If only she had remained in the storeroom, she would not have caused more trouble. How long must she bear the heavy hand of guilt that pressed upon her?

Vandakk approached her, but his presence brought no consolation. He did not stop to speak with Saina. Instead, he put himself between her and the angry merchant. With his hand held out, he tried to calm him.

"These birds are very expensive and in high demand," the old man said, shaking the dead bird in Vandakk's face. "You must hold this servant accountable for the trouble she has caused."

Saina sought to drown out his voice. She picked up the bowl and turned it over, breaking loose a small turquoise feather. Its downy tips were mangled and burdened with fine dust. She picked it up and turned it over in her hands. How beautiful it was despite being torn away from the living creature it had belonged to.

She tucked the feather into her felt boot and stood up as Vandakk dropped a handful of coins into the old man's hands.

Bao Li had entrusted Vandakk with money for situations such as this, with the expectation that he give an accounting for money paid out. Saina was struck with dread. What would Bao Li think to learn Saina was the cause of more trouble?

The old man dropped the coins into his small leather satchel hanging at his waist. He turned his back and walked away, tossing his prized bird on the pile of shattered cage and dirt-caked dates.

"Look up there," Vandakk said, placing his hand on Saina's shoulder. With his other arm, he pointed at the two turquoise feathered birds perched high on the caravanserai wall overlooking the courtyard below. "They were never meant to live in cages," he said, his voice resolute. "Man tries to subdue that which is wild, but all creatures long to be free."

There was truth in what he said, but Saina could not crawl out from beneath her despair. "Still, what the old man said is true. I have caused more trouble than I am worth."

Vandakk clicked his tongue. "When vulnerable, we all believe lies spoken over us, but you must not allow one man's anger to consume you. Consider the birds. Are they disappointed in you?" he asked.

Saina looked up at the birds as they flew from the wall, catching the air with outstretched wings. They swooped and circled overhead, and their chirps echoed over the courtyard, drawing the attention of several merchants who craned their necks at the sound. In a few strokes of their vibrant wings, they flew over the wall and out of sight.

"Sometimes death must occur for others to be free," Vandakk said, patting Saina's shoulder.

Saina looked down as he walked away, noticing the caged birds, silent and still at her feet, and feared she would always be like them.

———

Evening spread its long shadow over the desert oasis and the caravanserai responded in kind, with warming fires and torchlight casting a warm glow throughout. Saina had just finished lighting the last oil lamps when the musicians took their place in the courtyard, warming up their fingers on the three strings of the *tanbur* and filling the night air with soft melodies as they blew into slender *ney*.

All at once the music came together; the tempo increased. Weary merchants were drawn from their rooms, gathering as the scent of mutton pilaf cooking in the cauldrons wafted throughout the courtyard.

The architects and their apprentices circled together, tended by their private servants. They would be on their way to Chach at dawn's first light, and Saina suspected this was why they showed little interest in mingling with the other travelers. It was just as well. With the caravanserai full and all but one room occupied, there was little time to tend to the tiresome needs of such dignitaries.

Saina offered the guests pitchers of wine brought in earlier from the local vineyards. The fermented drink was highly prized among travelers coming from the west, who for three days had slaked their thirst on tepid water carried from the Karez well. But the architects dismissed her with a wave of the hand.

"Pour your wine into my cup," said a copper-haired man sitting among a group of merchants as he raised his cup into the air. His face held the deep creases of aged leather. The Silk Road had taken its toll on him. "I am not too proud to drink from your vineyard."

"With a face like yours, you cannot afford to be proud," said a gaunt man sitting next to him. Several others grunted in agreement.

As soon as Saina filled his cup, he put it to his mouth and gulped it down. Dragging the back of his hand across his mouth, he narrowed his eyes. "Do not be foolish, even your wife prefers my face over yours," he said, drawing barks of laughter from the others. He looked around the courtyard, a smile spread wide across his mouth.

"Your face looks like a pile of camel dung. No woman would be drawn to it," the gaunt merchant replied. He pinched pilaf between a strip of torn bread and put it to his mouth. Looking out across the courtyard, his eyes widened. He pointed toward the gates. "But there is a man who would steal the eyes of all our women."

Saina looked across the courtyard to see a man with dark hair and leather-cuffed wrists speaking with Makh. The din of the merchants' voices faded as she studied the metallic-colored horse that accompanied him. Saina could not look away from its muscled body and confident stance.

Such warhorses were rarely seen outside the battlefield, but Saina had grown accustomed to the beasts when, as a young girl, she had watched her father train them. The presence of this one comforted her.

Makh motioned to the stableboy who took hold of the reins and led the horse away. Speaking to the horseman once more, Makh turned and pointed toward Saina.

It was then that Saina recognized him from the weaver's stall. "Narisaf?" she said under her breath, the surprise in her voice spilling into the night.

"You know this man?" the copper-haired merchant asked.

Saina did not respond. She gripped the handle of the pitcher tighter as Narisaf walked toward her, his gait smooth, his eyes set on hers. A long knife with a carved bone handle was fastened to his belt.

She became aware of the questioning stares coming from the architects and merchants. From the corner of her eye, she saw them pressing their foreheads together, whispering.

She stepped away from the fire, feeling the cool air seep into her skin as she closed the distance between them, putting the distraction of the merchants' curiosity at her back. What reason did Narisaf have in coming to the caravanserai? And why would he risk the trip after the sun had set?

Narisaf must have sensed her curiosity.

"I have been sent on an errand by my grandfather," he said. Flames from the warming fire behind Saina danced in his clove-colored eyes. "The guard said you could take me to the merchant who sells gold embroidery. My grandfather has awaited his arrival for several days."

Saina struggled to gather words, to make sense of what Narisaf had asked of her. She shook her head, releasing the thoughts that seemed to tangle in his presence.

"Renchou is who you seek," Saina finally said, pulling her gaze from Narisaf and searching for the merchant. "He arrived earlier in the day with teams of camels and goods under heavy guard."

"We have awaited news of his coming," Narisaf said. "My grandfather hoped to see him in person, but he is still recovering from our journey from Merv. It would have been too much to bring him here tonight."

"It is just as well," Saina said. "I was told they are leaving at first light." She led him to where Renchou sat outside his room, sharing a meal with his servants and handlers.

Dressed like a dignitary, Renchou wore clothes made from fine threads in rich hues, with thick hems embroidered in cords of gold and silver. But it was his kindness toward all people that distinguished him. He had always welcomed the servants in the caravanserai and engaged them in conversation. His servants were equally mannered, and their presence always set Saina at ease.

He set his food on the mat laid out beneath him and stood. The men surrounding him did the same.

"I could not help but notice your horse," Renchou said, his deep voice carrying the familiar rasp Saina had come to know. He cleared his throat, straightening his overcoat. "Your arrival on that beast was as swift as the wind and as black as night. It is no wonder that heavenly horses are feared on the battlefield. Tell me, how does one come by such an animal?"

"She belonged to my father," Narisaf said, "but even in her advanced age she has proven herself to be more intelligent and trustworthy than most of the tradesmen we met on our journey to Samarkand."

Renchou threw his head back and laughed. "Any man who has spent a day on the Silk Road has learned to put more trust in his animals than the stranger traveling beside him. It is rare to find a man who seeks not his own gain."

"We avoided them well enough, preferring to travel in our own company, but we would have welcomed the company of your caravan had we been given the opportunity."

Renchou placed his hand on his chest and looked into Narisaf's eyes. "You are a man of discernment. Your keen eye, coupled with the skills of your horse, would prove useful to me. If you wish, it is not too late to join me and my men on the Silk Road. The job is a difficult one, of course, but it promises immeasurable rewards."

"Your offer is a generous one," Narisaf said to Renchou. "But I came to Samarkand with my grandfather. It was at his urging that we left our homeland in Merv and traveled here. My duty and honor are to remain by him."

Saina waited at their side listening to their conversation. It was one of only a few benefits of being a slave— present but invisible.

"You are a good man," Renchou said. "I admire your loyalty to your grandfather, even with the great risk you took in coming this far."

"He is all I have left of my family, and I trust his wisdom," said Narisaf. "But tonight, I have come on more pressing matters."

"Of course," Renchou said, nodding. "And I have been expecting you. I have already set aside the threads your grandfather requested, but I understand if you would like to see all that I offer."

He spoke briefly to his servant who pulled a torch from the

wall and slipped into the room behind them, then continued. "I had planned to remain in Samarkand for several days, for no other reason than to meet your grandfather in person. But our travels were delayed when thieves robbed two caravans only a day's journey ahead of us."

"Did you come upon trouble as well?" Narisaf said.

"We narrowly escaped them. Even with my trained guards, it can be difficult to defend against their numbers," Renchou said, waving his hand as though dismissing any concern. "Such is the price we must pay to make our living on the Silk Road. Weak-minded men do not survive its demands."

The servant opened the door and whispered into Renchou's ear. Renchou nodded. "Narisaf, the room has been prepared. Please, come inside and have your pick of choice threads."

Saina backed away, but Renchou stopped her. "Saina, my good servant, prepare a meal for the weaver's grandson, for tonight he will feast among us."

Chapter Seven

The giant sycamore tree in the courtyard was rumored to have set root in the ground long before Kang Dahan's ancestors built the caravanserai around it. Drawn to its grandeur and hardiness at the edge of the oasis, they took great care to lay the foundation in hopes that their well-intentioned plans would bear much fruit when built on the same loam that sustained the tree.

If Kang Dahan's ancestors felt concern about the caravanserai's success, it was for naught. Merchants never ceased to come, and the sycamore tree continued to flourish, extending its mighty branches over the courtyard. Its generous canopy offered protection from the heat of the day and delighted tired eyes at night, when light from the warming fires danced through its tangled leaves, casting shadows on anyone sitting nearby.

Saina walked past the tree, intent on preparing food for Narisaf and Renchou, but the pale-faced merchant locked eyes with her and thrust his cup into the air. "Have you a drop of wine left in that pitcher?" he said, leaning against its trunk. Firelight illuminated his copper hair and glassy eyes.

She shook her head. "It is empty, but I will fetch another servant to fill your cup."

He lowered his hand and turned to the men nearby. "This girl is too good for us now that the horseman has arrived," he grumbled.

Gripping the handle of the pitcher tighter, Saina left them. There was no time to give ear to his displeasure. She found Sapan, the stableman who shared the nightly chore of tending to merchants, standing near Vandakk. He was a young man of few words, with a shaved head and kind, dark eyes. He nodded when she told him of the thirsty merchant sitting beneath the sycamore tree.

When he walked away, Vandakk leaned over the iron cauldron, churning the pilaf with a thick, wooden paddle. "With all this food, even the servants of the caravanserai are guaranteed to feast tonight. I hope your appetite has returned."

The scent of herbed pilaf and baked bread wafted from the trays in front of Saina. Her mouth watered, and hunger pangs twisted her belly. "I could eat everything set before me, but for now, I have been sent to prepare a meal for Renchou's guest."

"Ah, yes," Vandakk said, raising his eyebrows. "The young man's arrival seemed to turn the head of every merchant in the courtyard. Who is he?"

Saina spooned pilaf into a bowl, placing several dolma and a round of flatbread on top of the rice. "He is Narisaf, grandson of the weaver of Merv," Saina said, surprised at how easily his name flowed from her lips. Indeed, the very mention of his name sent a thrum through her chest.

A smile of understanding flashed across Vandakk's face.

Saina blushed. Had she given herself away? Vandakk would not have looked at her the way he did otherwise.

Vandakk shifted his gaze to the courtyard and stared long, as was his custom whenever he was deep in thought. "Does he intend to stay in the caravanserai tonight?" he said.

Saina shook her head. "I cannot speak of his intentions. Only that he came to purchase threads from Renchou."

Her answer seemed to satisfy Vandakk. He looked over the

tray of food in Saina's hand, then picked up a plate and filled it with dates, crumbled cheese, and honey. "Take me to Narisaf. Together we will present him with this fine meal."

But with each step, Vandakk's pace seemed to slow, hastening Saina's urgency to return to Narisaf.

When a group of men stopped Vandakk to offer their praise of his food, Saina continued walking, her attention fixed on the golden light pouring from the open door and Renchou's gravelly voice coming from the inside.

His servant stood outside the door and smiled. "Renchou is expecting you," he said to Saina, extending his hand toward the room.

Inside, large wooden chests and trunks were open, a vast display of beautifully dyed threads set out. Narisaf leaned over a crate filled with threads of indigo and purple. Several brightly colored skeins of silk were already tucked in the crook of his arm.

"It is my strong desire that you take up my offer to remain here for the night," Renchou said. "Even with the short distance to Samarkand, many unseen dangers lurk in the dark. And with goods such as those in your hand, thieves would do well to come by them."

"There was a time when I would have ignored such warnings," Narisaf said. "But I left those days of foolishness behind in my youth, for plenty are the men who seek to spill blood for these." He held up the skein of golden strands twisted into indigo thread.

"And you, Saina, what do you think?" Renchou said, looking at her from across the room.

Narisaf looked up, and Saina saw the way his eyes brightened.

Saina tried to calm her racing pulse and the way her thoughts seemed to scatter. She had served many dignitaries in her years in the caravanserai, each having brought with them the finest goods produced in the lands they traveled from. But she had never seen anything as alluring as what she looked upon now. How strange it was to regard the richly hued threads, resplendent in every way, yet be more affected by the man holding them.

"They are unlike anything my eyes have beheld," Saina said. She looked down, fearful to say more and risk her true admiration being found out.

Narisaf turned back to Renchou. "It has been settled then," he said. "I will take this indigo thread as well."

"You have made a worthy choice," Renchou said. "For that hue is highly sought after and even more difficult to come by."

Renchou motioned to the dish in Saina's hand. "Come, Narisaf, let us eat before the meal grows cold."

Outside, Narisaf took his place beside Renchou and his men, and Saina set the bowl of pilaf and bread on the ground in front of him. When she stood, Vandakk approached.

"Vandakk," Renchou said. "I see the caravanserai is full tonight. Do you have any rooms left for Narisaf, or must he make his bed among me and my men?"

"We have one room left, but I regret that it is near the kitchen," Vandakk said, turning to Narisaf. "If it pleases you, I will send Saina to prepare it for you now."

Narisaf glanced at Saina and raised his brow. "It would please me greatly, but only if it is not too much trouble."

At Narisaf's acceptance, a strange new energy pulsed within Saina. The room Vandakk spoke of was being used to store extra flour. It would need to be cleared out and swept clean, but she was eager to set her hands to the late evening chore.

"Trouble?" Vandakk said. "We are here to serve the needs of any man who stays within these walls. It is what we do."

With a nod from Vandakk, Saina bowed her head and took her leave. As she walked across the courtyard, she beamed. She could not contain it. What Vandakk said was true. Preparing a room for Narisaf was no trouble at all.

The architects had retired to their rooms and the musicians were putting away their instruments by the time Saina returned.

Across the courtyard, Narisaf and Renchou were deep in conversation, their voices drowned out by the scattered groups of merchants nursing what remained of their fermented drink.

Saina wound through the courtyard, clearing dishes and setting them on trays, then stopped for a moment near the sycamore tree. Light from the warming fires danced in its canopy. It was in the golden glow that she looked over her shoulder and saw Narisaf watching her.

Saina swallowed, felt a tightening in her chest, but she could not look away. His skin was smooth, not yet creased with age and toil, and there was a hint of boyishness still lurking at the corners of his mouth. He was perfect. His presence stole any reasonable thought in her mind.

"Why are you staring at him?" the copper-haired merchant slurred as he propped himself up on his elbow. "Do you think a man of his standing would have an eye for a slave girl like you?" His voice dripped with mockery.

Saina stared at his reddening face, his glazed eyes. She stepped back, but he grabbed the hem of her tunic. "I asked you a question. Dare you insult me with your silence?"

She pulled away. "I do not answer to you."

"You are worthless," he spat. But as soon as he spoke, his eyes widened.

Narisaf appeared at Saina's side.

The copper-haired merchant sat up, but he seemed to comprehend little in his drunkenness. "Have you come to protect this slave?"

A few men sitting nearby urged the merchant to calm down.

"Be silent," he barked at the men.

Narisaf crouched down and leaned close. "I have come to warn you that if you touch her again, you will pay a heavy price," he said, his voice low and threatening.

"I am head of a caravan of fifteen men and seventy camels,

strong in numbers and might." He extended his arm, pointing to the men sitting near him who were shifting with unease. "We trekked across the Kyzylkum Desert with less trouble and insult than we have had in one afternoon here. This slave has given you all her attention. She would not even pour our wine."

Shame twisted a knot in Saina's throat. She tried to swallow it down.

A muscle tensed in Narisaf's jaw. "You and your caravan of mighty men trekked across the Kyzylkum Desert?"

The merchant narrowed his eyes. "I did not stutter."

Narisaf looked at Saina, a smile playing at the corner of his lips, before turning back to the merchant. "And yet you are incapable of trekking across the courtyard to pour your own wine?" Silence hung between them, but Narisaf did not shift his gaze. "It seems to me that you would be wise to reconsider your trade, my friend."

The merchant opened his mouth but had no recourse, sobered as he was by Narisaf's chastisement.

"We warned you to keep silent," another merchant said. "You have made fools of us all."

When Narisaf stood his arm grazed Saina's, spreading a shock of sensation through her body and releasing the tension that bound her moments ago.

Most of the merchants had retired to their rooms and Saina had finished gathering the dishes in the courtyard when Narisaf approached her carrying his leather satchel of newly purchased threads. "You have not stopped working all evening, which is why I am hesitant to disturb you, but"—he pointed to the rooms encircling the courtyard—"I do not know where I am sleeping tonight."

Saina smiled. "You seemed to be enjoying your time visiting with Renchou, so I did not want to interrupt. Come, I will take you to your room."

They entered the hallway, and Saina turned to Narisaf. "Thank you for...helping me."

"Is that behavior tolerated here?" Narisaf said.

"No." Saina was thoughtful for a moment. "Kang Dahan has earned great respect along the Silk Road. Few would dare enter his caravanserai and disrespect his property or servants. But on those rare occurrences when their behavior gets out of control, the guards throw them out."

"He is still here, though."

"I think it is because everyone enjoyed watching you put the merchant in his place," Saina laughed. "I have a feeling he will be gone before the sun rises so as not to show his face."

"You were not bothered by him?" Narisaf said.

"Of course, I was," Saina said. "I do not understand why people like that drunkard desire to remind me that I am a slave, as though I do not know this. I wake every morning aware of my low position."

"He is a fool," Narisaf said. "A man driven by drink is no less enslaved. In the end, his master exacts a harsher toll."

Saina put her hand on the door of his room and looked up at him. Who was this man who would defend her, a worthless servant girl?

She opened the door and stepped aside as he walked in.

She had taken care to clear it out and prepare the space with heavy, wool blankets folded at the base of the thickest sleeping mat she could find. She had placed a ewer of water on the low table in the corner, along with a small plate of pistachios and sour cherries. Looking at them now, she wondered if such preparations would be too simple for him. He lived among the colorful threads and vibrant tapestries of a master weaver. Would the meager furnishings of the room seem dull?

There was no hint of displeasure or flash of dismay in his countenance. He seemed pleased as he set his satchel on the floor and glanced around the room. His shoulders relaxed. A deep sigh escaped his lips.

He turned to Saina, his eyes shining. "Your preparations have ensured my comfort tonight."

Saina bowed her head and inhaled a slow breath.

"Vandakk serves a meal at first light every morning. Many merchants are eager to start their journey before the heat of the day and leave before it has been prepared. It is our hope that you will remain long enough to enjoy the meal."

Narisaf sat on the mat and pulled off his sandals. "I would be foolish to miss it."

———

Beneath the stars that shone like flecks of gold in the clear night sky, Saina gripped her bowl of pilaf and rushed through the empty courtyard. She shivered, her breath curling into the air, like the plumes of smoke from the warming fires that had burned out long ago.

She climbed the stairs with ease, surprised at the strength flowing through her body, as though a fire, lit anew, burned deep within her.

Stepping into her room, she closed the door and set the bowl on the ground beside her sleeping mat. Taking off her shoes, she saw the feather tumble out. She watched it fall silently to the ground.

For a moment she sat, pondering the broken cage, the freed birds, and the tiresome merchant. But each seemed distant memories, events that happened long ago, not earlier in the day. It was Narisaf's presence that pressed urgency upon her now. Who was he, and why was she drawn to him? These questions set root within her.

Her pilaf had grown cold by the time she put it to her mouth, but as she savored the meal and swallowed it, she felt satisfied, its richness a delight.

Chapter Eight

A donkey brayed, signaling the first hints of dawn, but the sky had not yet welcomed its light.

Saina stepped onto the balcony and looked out over the courtyard, where Vandakk was tending small fires that burned beneath the cooking cauldrons. Growing flames licked the iron bases, sending steam swirling into the morning air.

She glanced toward the hallway leading to the kitchen. From the moment she had awakened, her thoughts had been on Narisaf. The anticipation of seeing him again made her restless. She pushed away from the balcony and rushed down the stairs, feeling the coming day thick with promise.

Vandakk smiled as she approached. "You are up early," he said, a weariness in his voice.

"I woke to the scent of baking bread and thought I had overslept." Saina looked at the baskets filled with freshly baked, hardcrust bread. "Were you up all night?"

He nodded.

"Why did you not ask for my help?"

"I learned late last night that the architects expected provisions for their early morning departure. You needed rest, so I enlisted the help of a night servant." He pointed to another basket filled with flattened, misshapen bread and shook his head. "But it only doubled my work."

Saina tried to hide her smile, but it was no use. She stepped closer to him and sighed. "And you wonder why rumors that you do not sleep have spread among the servants."

Vandakk's eyes widened, as though surprised such things were spoken about him. He chuckled. "I have begun to believe it myself. But I must keep going. If I stop moving at my age, I will not start again."

"I am certain to find you sleeping by the warming stones in the kitchen later," Saina said. She would be sure to set a thick mat out for him to lie on.

"You know me too well," Vandakk said. "But do not tell that to the servants and risk me being found out." He laughed again.

Saina's thoughts drifted to Narisaf sleeping near the kitchen. Unable to restrain herself, she peered toward the hallway once again. It was foolish to believe he would be awake this early, but maybe...

Vandakk cleared his throat, and Saina snapped her head back.

He motioned toward the architects emerging from their rooms like silent shadows. Several teams of camels, urged forward by livestock handlers, emerged from the stables, their loud bleats breaking the stillness of the morning. If that did not wake the rest of the merchants, the chime of the bells draping their necks would.

When the last camel entered the courtyard, Bao Li's new servant girl stepped out from behind it, holding a ewer and wash-basin. Saina's heart twisted as she watched the girl approach Bao Li's khana.

Rooted in place, Saina felt the glimmer of hope drain through her feet, consumed by the hard stone on which she stood. Why would the servant girl enter Bao Li's khana at such an early hour? Not even Saina was granted entrance until the full light of day. *Bao Li will be sure to reprimand the girl for such a careless action.*

"Saina," Vandakk said, his hand on her shoulder.

She sucked in her breath and felt tears burning her eyes. "It is too early, and Bao Li will not be pleased." She started toward the girl. "Someone must tell her."

Vandakk placed his hand on her arm, stopping her.

"It does you no good to dwell upon it. For now, set your mind to your chores. Eggs need to be boiled and dried fruit set out for the morning meal, and I have prepared suzma, which must be seasoned as well."

Saina glanced toward the girl as she walked into the khana, the gilded doors closing behind her. The sight stung, but she looked back at Vandakk. He was correct. It would not serve her well to wish things were different. If she hoped to earn Bao Li's favor once again, she would have to prove herself.

———

Saina plunged the ladle into the pot of boiling water. She spooned out the eggs and left them to cool, then arranged several platters of dried peaches, apricots, and dates. By the time she had sprinkled flour over the rounds of dough and worked them into flat disks, the voices of waking merchants echoed in the corridor.

By now, Bao Li would have had her tea. *Does the new servant girl prepare it better than I did? When the servant girl walks through the khana, does Bao Li have to remind her to tread quietly like she used to tell me when I was younger?*

She shook her head to rid herself of the gnawing questions. She must give it time. Until then, she would set her mind to her work.

Reaching into the reed basket, she pulled out a head of garlic. If she rushed, she could finish preparing the suzma in time to help Vandakk cook bread in the open air...and see Narisaf.

As she set the large bowl of tart yogurt on the table, Vandakk entered the room.

"I meant to bring this earlier," he said, placing a handful of dill fronds beside the yogurt. "Add it to the bowl. Simple flavors are best this morning."

He closed his eyes for a moment, and Saina watched him sway slightly.

"Vandakk, are you well?" Saina said.

He rubbed his eyes. "Yes, just tired." He looked around the room then sighed heavily. "But there is no time for rest. When the morning meal is finished, I need to take stock of our supplies and go to the bazaar."

Saina studied his drooped shoulders, his heavy steps. He always put duty above his own needs, but this time, she sensed it would be too much. "Stay here; I will go in your place," she said, even as her heart fell in her chest.

He shook his head, denying her offer, but Saina put her hand on his arm. "Vandakk, you often remind me that draining my own cistern dry only leaves me unable to supply the needs of others. Will you not heed your own advice?"

Vandakk gave a sheepish smile. "You are good to me, Saina," he said, picking up the platter of dried fruit and boiled eggs.

"You have given several years of your own time and passions to train me up in the ways of the caravanserai," Saina said. "My duty is to you."

"I will have Sapan prepare the donkey and cart for your journey," Vandakk said.

Saina watched him leave, her chest growing tighter. Though she felt glad to help ease Vandakk's burden, there was no chance she would see Narisaf now.

———

With the leather lead rope in her hands, Saina set out on the southern road, winding along the canal and vast peach orchards. The cart's wheels set a rhythm as they jarred and creaked over scars of thick roots and deep ruts, picking up a thin layer of dirt from the morning dew.

Having memorized every curve in the path and rocky outcropping along its border, she let her mind turn to thoughts of Narisaf. How foolish she had been in her yearning to see him this morning, even at the high cost of putting off her duties. After all, as a slave, she had no right to act upon the feelings that were awakened within her. Besides, she was certain Narisaf had already returned to the city without a thought of her.

By the time she reached the grove of karagach trees, her disappointment had eased.

The sun pressed down upon her and sweat beaded on her forehead. She stopped to cool herself in the shade of the overhanging branches and pulled off her overcoat, placing it in the cart. When she turned around, she caught a glimpse of something at the base of the tallest tree. She peered closer. Slivers of light burst through the canopy overhead, illuminating a tiny mound of freshly dug earth, its perimeter lined with a row of smooth stones.

"A grave?" she said aloud. Birds flitted in the overhanging trees.

Glancing over her shoulder, Saina walked into the shade, taking care not to disturb the loam on which she stood. She knelt down, felt the cold ground against her knees. A small wreath made of dried flowers had been set on top of the mound. And the scent of perfumed oils—the same oils Upach packed for the baby's burial—still lingered in the air.

Ning Po's baby.

A shiver coursed through Saina's body at the realization. Ashes, remnants of vigil fires, flitted in the light breeze and gathered at the base of the stones. How appropriate they seemed near the shadowy grave, colorless in a world drained of color.

If only Upach had never asked for Saina's help or Ning Po's baby had survived, then things would be different. She would be the one bringing Bao Li her morning tea. Not the stable girl.

She thought of her own mother and unborn baby, the dirt from their grave streaked across her father's face. An ache settled in her throat. Indeed, how different her life would have been had her own mother lived.

Saina rubbed her forehead and groaned. What use was it to dwell upon these things? She could not change the past. But she could find favor in Bao Li's eyes once again. That was the only hope for her future.

At the sound of distant horse's hooves, Saina stood. She quickly brushed away the ashes that had gathered on her tunic and listened as it drew nearer. Who could it be? Few people knew about this road. Even fewer chose to make their way to Samarkand along it.

She pushed through the tangle of low-hanging branches and rushed out to look down the path. The rhythmic pounding coming from the direction of the caravanserai grew louder. Had Ning Po sent someone to keep guard over the grave? What would happen if Ning Po received word that Saina was seen here?

Reaching for the lead rope, Saina positioned the donkey between her and the approaching horseman. She gripped the rope tightly and straightened as the horseman, his dark hair and muscled figure, came into view.

Narisaf? The thrum in her chest quickened despite her earlier convictions.

Narisaf's eyes opened wide, and he pulled back on the reins. His horse threw back its head and came to a sudden stop. "Saina..." Narisaf said. A slow smile spread across his face as he shifted on his horse, the dust billowing around them.

It was a moment before words made their way to Saina's mouth. "I did not expect to see you," she said. "This road is only frequented by orchard workers. It is rare for other travelers to come this way."

"Vandakk directed me here. He said it would be safer with the expensive threads in my possession." Narisaf dismounted his horse.

Saina swallowed. She had never been alone in the company of a man like Narisaf.

He peered into her cart and raised his eyebrows. "This is a large cart for such a small basket."

At his teasing, Saina's body relaxed. She smiled. "I assure you it will be full on my return from the bazaar," she said. "This basket holds the bread rejected by the architects. They said it was not formed well enough for their liking, so it will be given to the children of the laborers living outside the city instead."

The answer seemed to satisfy him.

"I thought you left the caravanserai earlier," Saina said.

Narisaf shook his head. "Vandakk wanted to prepare a meal for my grandfather, so I delayed my return." He slowed. "If you have time, you could come with me. My grandfather would be pleased to see you again."

His invitation brought a swell of pride to Saina's heart. She wanted to stand closer to him, to walk at his side on this dusty path, but she held the reins of the donkey, keeping it between them. "I would be honored to go with you but must take care to finish purchasing supplies and return to Vandakk by the afternoon." She said this more as a warning to herself, certain that if she was not careful, Narisaf's presence would cause her to lose all sense of time.

Saina thought she saw a flicker of delight in Narisaf's eyes before he quickly hid it away. "My grandfather still speaks fondly of the time he and my father came to Samarkand. Though it has been many years, he says he can still taste the roasted duck with pomegranate sauce and the giant melons dripping with sweetness. But since our arrival, the memory of my father seems to have grown stronger. Now whenever my grandfather recalls him, his eyes become glistening pools, and his voice grows heavy with emotion."

"Is that why he has come, to remember your father?" Saina said. She was aware of the silence around them, as though to listen to Narisaf speak was to drown out the rest of the world.

"I do not know," Narisaf said, shaking his head. "At first, I saw only foolishness in his plan to come here and even made my thoughts known to him. The Kyzylkum Desert is treacherous and unforgiving. But he was resolute in his purpose and I...well...what could I say? It is my duty to respect my grandfather, and he has proved himself trustworthy. Besides, I learned long ago that he cannot be swayed when compelled by that which he believes God had called him to do."

They approached the children of the fieldworkers who had gathered outside their erected tents. With screams and squeals, the children circled Saina and Narisaf, receiving the bread with wide grins. When the last of the bread was handed out, they left the children to enjoy their treat and continued on.

The bazaar was within sight, and Saina could hear the unbroken hum of bartering voices. Plumes of smoke from cooking fires swirled into the air, spreading above the varied stalls and colorful awnings.

Saina turned to Narisaf. "Whatever the reason your grandfather has come to Samarkand, I hope he finds what he seeks."

"I sometimes think upon it as a grand tapestry," Narisaf said. "His plans live in his mind. He does not share them with me. But they are like threads stretched across the warp. Only when one has built upon another do I begin to see a pattern emerge. In this same way, he will accomplish what he has set out to achieve. There is no other way with him."

He fell silent as they merged with the men and women pushing carts and carrying baskets through the main entrance. The crowd spread out, the sound of bartering filled the walkway, but Narisaf remained by Saina's side, drawing long stares and whispered comments about the young man and his warhorse.

Chapter Nine

The rhythmic clack of the weaver's shuttle spilled out from his stall. Its rise and fall extended a welcoming cadence as Saina tied her donkey next to Narisaf's horse and followed him into the shade.

Bent over his loom, the weaver sat immersed in the work before him and seemed to have no knowledge of their presence. When he stopped to adjust a single stretch of thread across the warp, Narisaf approached him.

"Grandfather, you will be pleased with my purchase from Renchou," he said, bending down and kissing him on the cheek. He held out the skein of indigo thread twisted with fine, gold strands.

The weaver turned it over in his hands and smiled. "In all my years, I have never seen such fine filament. Tell me, how did he come by it?"

Narisaf shrugged. "Renchou did not give away his secrets. But he expressed his desire to offer it to you first. How could I deny it?"

"You made a wise choice," the weaver said.

"Not just me. Saina too. She encouraged me to purchase it."

The weaver's eyes fell on Saina. "Is it true? Are you the reason I hold this thread?"

Saina shot a glance at Narisaf and shook her head. "I only commented on its beauty. It is not my place to recommend such a purchase." She had barely uttered her defense when Narisaf winked at her. Her face grew hot. He was teasing her.

The weaver chuckled quietly as he shuffled to the corner of his tent and set a kettle of water over a small cook fire. "Pay no mind to my grandson. He is just like his father. Would you believe he used to be the shyest boy in our village, afraid to open his mouth around any girl who came near?"

This time it was Narisaf's turn for embarrassment. "Grandfather," he said, then he laughed, the deep resonant sound filling the stall.

Saina had been invited into their banter and was glad for it. She smiled as she studied Narisaf. He stood a head taller than the weaver, his strong back erect, not worn and melting like his grandfather's. There was a glint in his youthful eyes, hinting at his ability to pull small joys out of a life of toil. She desired to learn his secret and know from where he drew his contentment.

"Tea," the weaver said, turning to Saina.

She shook her head. "I was sent to purchase supplies and must return to the caravanserai soon. I only came on Narisaf's request to present a welcome offering from our cook, Vandakk."

Narisaf pulled a small basket from his satchel and gave it to the weaver. He peered inside, then looked up, his cerulean eyes bright. "Dolma?"

Saina nodded. "Vandakk filled the first vine leaves of the season with seasoned mutton and rice," she said.

"It will be more flavorful than the plain rice you were eating," Narisaf said, pointing to the bowl next to the loom.

"I ate alone," the weaver said, almost in a whisper. "Why prepare a rich meal if there is no one to share it with?"

Narisaf chuckled. "I would have returned last night, but

Renchou convinced me it was not safe to leave the caravanserai after dark with these threads."

The weaver looked doubtful.

"Besides," Narisaf shrugged. "How could I turn down the feast that was offered?"

"I know your reasons for staying," the weaver said, nudging his grandson.

Narisaf shook his head slightly as he leaned against the wood beam in the center of the stall, his face turning a light shade of red.

The weaver held up the basket of dolma, then closed his eyes and tilted his chin up. "Thank You, Father, for providing this unexpected meal."

Saina looked away. It was not the prayer that troubled her. She had grown accustomed to the countless religions and hand-fashioned gods that were shared along the Silk Road, but she had no faith in them. They all seemed empty. What was she to make of gods who demanded worship but gave nothing in return?

The weaver tilted his head. "I see you are troubled with a question for which you have no answer."

Saina shrugged. It was all the confirmation she could offer. She would not betray her sore journey of accepting the life her father sold her into—if indeed, she had ever really accepted it. But to hope that any sort of god would provide what her heart truly longed for was to open herself up to countless heartaches. She had felt every terrible sting of that hollow expectation and had learned to protect herself.

"It is not a trite thing to say that a man's plight is to suffer unanswerable questions," the weaver said. "Narisaf was a boy when his father was killed in battle. When we received the terrible news, he clung to me, refusing to leave my side. For a full moon cycle, he asked why his father would be taken from him." His eyes shimmered. "As his grandfather, the torment of having no answer for his question was unbearable."

Saina's heart twisted for the sorrow Narisaf experienced as a boy. She knew it well.

"I understand now that such heartache will never be satisfied by a single answer," the weaver continued. "So, we must be open to the opportunities that might ease our pain—even if just for a moment. This happened the day my son's warhorse was returned to us. It was the first time I saw Narisaf smile in many months. Our healing began the day we saw the horse for the gift that she was."

The weaver stepped away from Narisaf, and Saina's eyes fell upon the warhorse garment behind him.

Her throat began to burn. She recalled her father's pride that evening when he draped it over his shoulders and sat behind her as they rode their horse home to her mother. Even as the setting sun cooled the air and cast long shadows before them, blanketing the rolling hills in darkness, Saina was not fearful. Her father had always kept her safe. As a child, she had not known any different. But now she did.

The weaver looked at her, his eyes softening. "It is rare to have something returned that once belonged to the fathers we lost."

How had he known to answer this way? Silence stretched between them as Saina mustered the boldness to speak of her long-held sorrow. "My father's leaving was not honorable. Looking upon this garment now brings back memories I wish to never recall. When I think about him using it to comfort himself on the coldest desert nights, I wonder if he has ever truly felt warm since the day his heart turned cold against me."

From the corner of her eye, Saina saw Narisaf straighten. She regretted having expressed the hurt that had plagued her since her youth. But if the weaver was bothered by her outburst, he did not show it.

"You may not have known what threads of grief were woven into your father's young life," the weaver said gently. "Or how one last rending of what he held dear would cause him to come unspooled. But these difficult things are never the end. You can choose to become bitter and let it stop you from living. Or you can gather the disparate threads of his leaving and use them to weave a new story." He returned to the kettle, which began to boil.

Saina pondered his words, spoken as though he held some secret knowledge of her father. But how could that be? She began to back away. Even if the weaver wanted to tell her the truth, she could not bear it. She did not have the inner strength Narisaf had. Not yet.

The weaver poured water into a single mug and looked at Saina from across the tent. "You know this bazaar well. Would it trouble you to bring Narisaf along on your errands and show him the best stalls to purchase supplies?"

Saina straightened and glanced at Narisaf, who was studying her carefully, his arms crossed in front of his chest.

"Our needs are simple," the weaver continued. "He will not require much of your time."

"I would be glad to," Saina said, the words flowing from her mouth without hesitation. "It is helpful to know where the best goods are sold and which merchants use dishonest scales."

Narisaf's face relaxed as though relieved that their time together had not yet come to an end. She knew hers reflected the same pleasure.

———

They walked through the colorful stalls of the spice merchants and grain sellers, the air around them smelling sweetly of frankincense and turmeric. Narisaf loaded large sacks of rice and fine flour into the cart while Saina purchased hot peppers, sugarcane, cucumbers, and rounds of goat cheese.

She led him to a corner stall where thick braids of dried melon hung from ropes strung across the awning and along the back wall. "The giant melons your grandfather spoke about are not yet ripe in their season, but even dried, they hold the same sweetness."

Narisaf purchased a bundle from the fruit seller, then pulled out two strands and gave one to Saina.

It was the first bite of food Saina had eaten all day, and the small morsel stirred her hunger. "Come, I will take you to one of my favorite food stalls so you can tell your grandfather that I kept my word," Saina said. "The cook is the finest noodle maker in Samarkand and a friend of Vandakk's."

A small crowd had gathered to watch Barchukh stretch and twist large mounds of dough into long, thin strands. He worked at the steady pace of a man who had grown old in years but, with his three sons at his side, still found purpose in his toil.

The black doppa adorning his head was similar to the one Vandakk wore, indicating their shared heritage. So alike were he and Vandakk in manner and appearance that had they told Saina they were brothers, she would have believed them.

Barchukh dropped the noodles into the cauldron of boiling lamb stew. When he looked up, his eyes met Saina's, and his smile widened within the thin, gray wisps of his beard.

"You are busy today," Saina said.

"Yes," Barchukh said. "The people have come to eat our noodles once more, for in two days' time my family and I will make the trek back to our homeland."

"You are leaving?" Saina said, her heart growing heavy. She looked at his sons talking among themselves; their smiles and kind nature were so much like their father's. Could this be the last time she would ever see them?

He nodded slowly. "Samarkand has been good to us, but my wife is ill with longing for home, and my sons want to raise their children in the land of our forefathers. It is time we returned to Kashgar."

His eyes softened. "Do not lose heart. Though separated by a great distance, we can still cast our eyes on the same mountains and think upon our shared memories." He traced his finger across the sky. "The only difference is that in Samarkand, the sun rises over the Pamirs and sets in the Kyzylkum Desert. But in Kashgar, the sun rises over the Taklamakan desert and sets in the Pamirs."

Saina hid her disappointment behind her smile. She could

look at the mountains and think of countless memories of Barchukh from her earliest years when she would come to the bazaar as a child with her parents and eat his noodle stew.

"Does Vandakk know you are leaving?" Saina said.

Barchukh's shoulders dropped, he shook his head. "He knows that our yearning for home has grown in our hearts. Perhaps he even sensed its imminent approach but said nothing about it. Nevertheless, the decision came suddenly. The mountain passes have opened, and the weather has settled. We must leave now for the best chance of a safe trek."

"This news will sadden him. Your friendship has kept the ties to his people alive. He will want to search you out before you leave," Saina said.

"I will expect him," Barchukh said. He ladled noodles and soup into two bowls and offered them to Saina and Narisaf. "Please, take this meal as my parting gift to you and the weavers grandson."

"You have met?" Saina said, surprised.

"No, no," Barchukh said, his green eyes shining. He turned to Narisaf. "I heard rumors that your grandfather had come. When I saw you walk past me earlier with that warhorse, I knew they were true."

Narisaf laughed. "I have been told it is uncommon to see heavenly horses near the city."

"Most have not seen them up close," Barchukh said, bowing his head. "But Saina knows those warhorses well. Her father trained them."

Saina's stomach tensed as Narisaf turned to her, his brows drawn close. "That was long ago," she said, trying to push down the memory of a life she could no longer claim.

"Life has a curious way of calling us back to where we belong," Barchukh said. "No matter our age." He smiled once more before returning to his work.

Saina leaned against the cart, eating *laghman* noodles in

silence next to Narisaf. His presence was strong and sturdy beside her, but she sensed a question looming between them.

He leaned toward her. "I did not know your father trained warhorses. I thought that—"

She spun around and faced him. "You thought I was born a slave?"

"No," he said, his eyes widening. "I thought...I hoped you would be impressed by my rare horse." He looked at her, a smile playing on his lips.

Saina drew back and searched his face. "Are you teasing me again?"

He shook his head and laughed. "I am only surprised to learn of your father's work and your knowledge of the heavenly horses. Why did you not speak of it?"

Saina pondered the question as she looked at the people crowding the narrow street pushing handcarts and carrying baskets filled with provisions. Finally, she turned back to Narisaf. "That life is as distant from me as the faded memories of my youth. I cannot form a clear picture of them anymore. Besides, I have lived longer as a slave in Kang Dahan's caravanserai than I did in my own father's home."

Narisaf did not blink, did not shift in place as she told him this, and Saina did not know what to make of it. Had she shared too much? Would he withdraw his friendship upon learning the truth? She sighed heavily and shook her head. "Forgive me, I should not have burdened you with this telling..."

"Do you think me weak that I cannot handle this news or shallow that I would look down upon you for it?" Narisaf said.

She shook her head, her resolve faltering. "It is because you are not these things that I hesitate to tell you."

"Why did your father leave?" he said, his voice tender.

Saina stared into the bowl with its remaining noodles. She did not know how to answer the question at first. Could she muster the courage to speak, to form it into proper words?

Inhaling a deep breath, she looked up at Narisaf. "My father was good to me when I was young," she said, surprised that after all this time, she still regarded him with undue loyalty. "Our life was simple. Happy. My mother swelled with the baby growing inside her.

"I remember it was the birthing season for the horses. It was a busy time for my father. He was away when my mother went into labor." Saina paused, trying to swallow down the stab of pain in her throat. "My mother said it was too early. I tried to help her. I filled a washbasin and wiped her forehead, but it was no use. Her blood came, but the baby never did." She shook her head, feeling tears pool in her eyes.

Narisaf did not move, did not speak.

"I sat alone in the darkness until my father returned. By then her body had long grown cold, and a sticky pool of blood dried around her. He looked at my mother, and I saw the life drain from his eyes. Then he looked at me and said..." Her heart twisted at the words her father spoke next, words that bound her heart and kept her prisoner to their poison. "He said...'What have you done, Saina?'"

Narisaf shook his head and exhaled sharply.

"The next day he sold me to Bao Li in return for a donkey and three sacks of grain. And I have carried the guilt of my mother's death ever since."

"It was not your fault." His words hung in the air.

"But I bear the consequences as though it was," Saina said. It was the first time she had ever spoken about it. The words changed nothing, but she felt as though a weight had been lifted.

Narisaf did not respond, and Saina did not expect him to. His presence was enough.

Her heartbeat seemed to quicken. Who was this man that did not cower from the truth? She wanted to stay at his side, to learn the reason for his strength, but the day was growing warmer, and Vandakk expected her soon.

Silence swelled between them.

"I must return to the caravanserai." Saina pointed toward the cart. "Vandakk is waiting on some of these goods in order to prepare tonight's meal."

A shadow of disappointment crossed Narisaf's face. He stepped closer, running his hand along the cart. "When will you come back?"

She shrugged. "I do not know. We purchase supplies from the bazaar once or twice per week, but Vandakk does not always request my help. And it is not common for me to come alone unless he has been called away by another matter."

Narisaf motioned toward her. "I will walk with you to the edge of the bazaar."

With her belly full and the cart sagging under the weight of purchased goods, Saina walked slowly, not wanting to rush what little time remained with Narisaf. She was surprised when he continued with her well past the bazaar, until the caravan traffic from the city merged with the Silk Road.

"My childhood home is there," Saina said, pointing toward the hills across the Zarafshan River where grazing animals and mud-brick homes dotted the flowing grasslands.

"Have you been back to see it?" Narisaf said.

Saina shook her head. "I hope Bao Li will grant me the freedom to visit one day, but I have not worked up the courage to ask her yet. There is a rumor that the house still lies empty. Perhaps no one wanted the curse of that land after we left."

Narisaf fixed his gaze in the distance, his thoughts seemed as far away as the rolling hills. He stepped toward Saina, his hand brushing hers. "Or perhaps it is waiting for the right time to be restored," he said.

At his touch, Saina's thoughts scattered. She walked onto the road and fell in step behind a caravan of lumbering camels, laden with goods. Often, when she walked along the section of the road, her mind would be filled with the endless chores that would be waiting upon her return. But now she was consumed with pleasant thoughts about Narisaf and wondered how she would find the time to see him again soon.

Chapter Ten

The next day, Saina entered through Samarkand's city gates. She gripped the donkey's lead rope as she pressed through the crowd.

She had not stopped thinking about Narisaf since yesterday when she left him standing at the edge of the Silk Road. And now, she was so close to the bazaar...and him. If only she could see him again. But not today. Vandakk was adamant that she complete her errand to purchase honey in the city and return to the caravanserai, while he bid Barchukh and his family farewell.

She walked behind a small family of sojourners. A black-haired yak accompanied them, but they carried all they seemed to own in thin bags slung over their shoulders. The young girl let go of her mother's hand and with wide eyes turned in a circle. A small gasp escaped her lips.

Saina smiled at the girl. It had been years since she saw the city through the eyes of a small child. The moment gave her pause. How beautiful its lush gardens were, like emeralds shining beneath an azure canopy. The storefronts bustled with craftsmen who forged metal or carved wood from thick trees felled in the outlying forests. Lamb kebabs hissed on long grills. The scent of charred meat and seasoned pilaf made her salivate.

Like the girl, Saina longed to lose herself in childish delight, but duty pushed her forward. The heat of the day pressed heavily upon her, and the desert air felt unusually thick. It stuck to her skin, reminding her of the honey she had been sent to purchase.

She stepped around a group of learned men, skilled in predicting weather. They had gathered near the city gates, pointing and murmuring about the clouds swirling on the desert horizon.

"It will reach us come evening," said a gray-bearded man with colorful cloth wrapped around his head. "Warn those in the city and bazaar to seek shelter early."

Saina looked over her shoulder. She had seen those circular clouds before, a harbinger of strong winds. Perhaps even a dreaded sandstorm. But there was still time to complete her purchase before she must hasten her return to the caravanserai.

She pulled harder on the lead rope, urging the donkey to move faster through the narrow streets flanked on each side by rows of two-storied homes and shops. The mud-brick walls gave way to painted wooden doors and rich tapestries draping the edges of flat rooftops, where families would gather in the cool of the evening.

Ahead, an old man, slumped and wrinkled with age, sat on a narrow step in front of a turquoise door cracked open behind him. He puffed on a clay pipe, blowing out smoke between his thin lips. The tangled voices of children spilled from his home, but he seemed content where he sat.

The road opened into a large courtyard. In the center, children dipped their toes into a shallow pool beneath the marble glare of a bubbling fountain. Women congregated in the shade of the inviting garden, beneath green vines fat with clusters of sweetly scented flowers.

Saina stopped for a moment in the shade and looked across the courtyard where men gathered in the crowded *chaikhana*, sipping tea and eating shashlik. Did the weaver and Narisaf also gather in the teahouses of their homeland, discussing the matters of men? How strange that she, a lowly servant girl, longed to know that part of their lives.

The thought was cut short when Umida, the midwife and healer, stepped outside the door of her apothecary. Saina watched the motherly woman, whose long, gray hair fell unbound around her shoulders. She seemed to be scanning the courtyard for something. When Upach stepped out of the crowd, Umida smiled wide and drew the young woman into her arms, then leaned close and spoke in Upach's ear. When she pulled away, Upach was laughing.

Saina was glad Upach had found a friendship outside Ning Po's harsh authority. Still, her delicate friendship with Upach had been damaged, and she did not want to be seen. She put her head down and walked past them.

"My time is short," Upach said, her voice carrying to where Saina walked a short distance away. "Ning Po insisted she come to the city with me. She is purchasing new fabrics and furnishings for her bedchamber while I retrieve her medicinal herbs."

Umida clicked her tongue. "Then let us not waste what time we have. Come, I want to show you my fresh delivery of *rhodiola* root and tell you of its properties."

Saina slowed. Was it true? Ning Po was in the city? She gripped the donkey's lead rope tighter and, turning onto the narrow road that led to the old town, quickly left the courtyard. It was unlikely that she would see her, but still, she must use caution.

Ahead was a strip of storefronts where a salt merchant was arranging several baskets of the valuable preservative. Another merchant was selling oak galls and yellow orpiment for dyestuffs. Beneath the awning of a fabric seller, a woman dressed in red, layered silk, her back turned to the road, was pointing at a colorful brocaded coat. Just beyond the shops stood the honey merchant, exactly where Vandakk said he would be.

When Saina was leaving the caravanserai earlier, Vandakk had warned her, "The honey merchant is named Issik, and he hails from the northeast. His stature is imposing, his demeanor is gruff. Do not be alarmed." But his warning could not have prepared Saina for the sight.

His skin was pale, his hair a fiery mane. The furs of wild beasts were draped over his cart. Behind him were pallets of clay honey jars, etched with the same strange carvings Saina had seen on the jars in Bao Li's khana. She had used the delicacy inside them countless times to sweeten Bao Li's tea.

She left the donkey and shuffled forward, but as she approached, he stared at her, his face like stone, unmoving. Saina swallowed down her discomfort. Vandakk had told her to expect this. "I have come to purchase five jars of honey."

"Have you now?" Issik said. He put his hands on the makeshift table between them and leaned closer. "My honey is highly desired and fetches a high price."

"I know the price," Saina said. She set the five coins Vandakk had given her on the table. "Five jars."

The large man took the coins and placed a single jar of honey on the table, then stared at her with hard eyes, as though daring her to make a move.

Saina frowned. Who was this man that Vandakk had sent her to? "You are dealing dishonestly. I have given you enough money to purchase what I need."

His eyes moved from her face down her body, and Saina stepped back, repulsed at the scent of stale sweat and the knowledge of his yearning.

The merchant smirked. "If you cannot afford the full price," he said, lowering his voice, "then you can pay me another way."

Saina hated how her hands trembled. Why must she give herself away in this manner? Still, she could not stay here and fight off his advances. Vandakk would understand.

The sound of a woman's laughter cut through the air, startling Saina. It was sharp and cruel and pricked her skin with warning.

Saina cautiously turned around to see Ning Po approaching

her, glaring with eyes lined in kohl, her dark hair pulled into a tight bun. She was draped in a red silk dress tied at the waist by a white ribbon and was holding a stack of colorful fabrics.

It did not matter to Saina that Ning Po looked upon her with open disdain. Indeed, she had come to expect it. Just not here, alone, in the far corner of the city. She looked down the empty street, her stomach tightened.

Ning Po sneered, then looked to the honey merchant. "Is this filthy slave cheating you out of your labor?"

It was a bitter insult, but Issik laughed, as though pleased he had found someone just like him.

"He is dealing falsely," Saina said, flaring with anger. Was it not enough for Ning Po to destroy her reputation with Bao Li? Must she continue to humiliate her even now? She turned to the honey merchant. "My mistress will not be pleased with your actions."

"Bao Li is *not* your mistress any longer," Ning Po said.

Saina flinched. The words, true as they were, struck her as though she had been dealt a physical blow.

A sudden gust of wind snapped awnings, toppled baskets, and swirled dust stung Saina's eyes. She turned away and shielded her face.

When the wind settled, Issik looked into the sky and growled. "There is no time. I must seek shelter before this storm arrives," he said, then threw the coins at Saina's feet. "Take your money and leave."

Saina's eyes burned with tears as she gathered the coins into her satchel. She yanked the lead rope, setting the donkey in motion. From the corner of her eye, she saw Ning Po approach the honey merchant.

"You seek shelter?" Ning Po said.

But Saina could not hear what Ning Po said next as the cart's wheels lumbered along the ground, drowning out her voice.

Saina stared into the empty courtyard. Vandakk stood quietly at her side.

Overhead, circular clouds had merged together and began to swirl. Reports of violent weather to the west had slowed the arrival of caravans. Only a few sojourners had trickled in throughout the day.

"What will we do without the honey?" Saina said.

Vandakk shook his head. "Purchase from a local seller instead. Bao Li will be disappointed, of course. She intended to pack some on her trip to Penjikent, as she has every year. But she is leaving in a few days, and there is no time to consider another source."

"I should have searched for honey elsewhere." Saina said. "The coming days are busy, and now you must bear the burden of searching it out."

"You did well to return early. I would not want you caught in this storm," he said. "If that is how Issik has chosen to conduct business, so be it. Sooner or later, he will eat the bitter portion of his greed. It is the way of all things."

The sycamore tree began to sway wildly, bowing to the strength of the gusting wind. A livestock handler rushed from the stables, ran across the courtyard, and shut himself in his room.

Saina looked up. Beyond the caravanserai walls, the horizon had turned the color of saffron.

"Come, let us seek shelter in the storeroom," Vandakk said, pointing toward the sky. "The storm has arrived, and look, it carries the desert with it."

Tucked away in the kitchen, Saina tended fires beneath the clay ovens while Vandakk filled dough with seasoned lamb and potatoes.

The sandstorm raged the remainder of the afternoon, followed into the evening by a deluge of rain.

"A simple meal of *samsa* will suffice on a night like this,"

Vandakk said, bending over the oven. He pulled out the steaming pastries and set them in prepared baskets. "Take these to the merchants. When you have finished, we will share a meal together."

Saina smiled. She had come to appreciate Samarkand's rare storms for many reasons, but most of all, she favored the opportunity to eat a slow meal with Vandakk free of the press of chores gnawing on either of them.

She took the leather cape off the hook by the door and draped it over her shoulders. With several baskets in hand, she walked into the courtyard.

Through torrential rain, she saw the outline of a man huddled at the gates, speaking to Makh. How miserable to be caught in a storm such as this. It would be no trouble to show him to a room and offer a hot meal before tending to the other merchants. She skirted the edges of pooling water and walked toward them.

Drawing near, the man's silhouette became a hulking figure. She studied the furs draping his shoulders, his drenched red hair, and the cart full of honey jars being pulled behind his donkey.

The honey merchant? Saina stopped suddenly. *Why is he here?*

She dropped her head, not wanting him to see her face. What should she do? Bao Li was protective of her servants. If she knew that the honey merchant propositioned Saina in exchange for honey, he would not be welcomed. Saina must tell her.

With her head down, Saina approached Makh and pulled him aside. "Do not give this man shelter until I speak with Bao Li," she said, her voice firm. She had never spoken to Makh with such authority and hoped he understood the urgency.

Makh glanced at the honey merchant and gave a slight nod, then returned to the gates.

Saina gave the baskets of samsa to two servants who had come from the stables. "Take these to each of our guests," she said. "Do not delay."

Relieved of the chore, Saina approached Bao Li's khana. She

no longer held the status to walk freely through these doors, but she must risk the consequences. This matter could not wait.

Inhaling a deep breath, she opened the door and walked inside.

The khana was quiet; its thick walls deadened the pounding rain. In the vaulted receiving room, Bao Li sat at her desk, her head bowed over her scrolls. Saina glanced around the room, relieved the stable girl was not there.

Bao Li looked up. "Saina?" she said, her back straight, brows pulled together.

Saina fixed her gaze on the ground. Had she made a terrible mistake?

"I...I know I am not welcome in your presence," Saina said. "But a man...has come..."

"Speak clearly, Saina" Bao Li said, standing.

Saina swallowed, trying to calm herself. "Vandakk sent me to fetch your honey today, but the merchant dealt deceitfully. He wanted to charge me five times the asking price, unless I...I paid him another way." She shook her head.

Bao Li stepped around her desk, her face reddened. "Did he touch you?"

"No," Saina said. "I left. But now he has come seeking shelter."

"He dares come here now?" Bao Li said.

"Perhaps he does not know that I serve in your caravanserai." The memory of Ning Po asking if the merchant sought shelter flashed in Saina's mind. Why had she not considered that he would arrive here? She glanced up, but Bao Li was already at the edge of the room, wrapping her thin coat around her shoulders. Saina rushed toward her, taking off her leather cape.

"My lady, the rain pours hard. Wear this instead." She draped it over Bao Li's shoulders. "It will keep you dry."

Bao Li looked at Saina, her eyes glistening. "Thank you," she said.

Bao Li rushed out the doors, and Saina followed closely

behind. By the time they reached the honey merchant standing at the gates, the rain had soaked through Saina's tunic. A chill settled on her skin, but it was her nerves that caused her body to shake.

"You are late seeking shelter," Bao Li said. There was no kindness in her regard.

Issik's eyes darkened. "I am lucky to be alive after getting caught in this sandstorm," he said. "And now this rain. I only need to stay for one night. Just long enough for the storm to pass." He reached into his satchel and pulled out a handful of coins.

Bao Li peered at the coins in his hand then shook her head. "What you offer is not enough."

The merchant scowled. "Not enough? But I was told this is the going price." He looked at Saina, his mouth dropping as recognition washed over his face. "You?"

Saina stood firm. She would not be intimidated here. Not with Makh and Bao Li at her side.

He pointed a sharp finger at Saina. "You know the woman who told me to come here. She was standing behind you in the city. Tell her I am here!"

"Do not speak to my servant," Bao Li said. "You have harassed her and now the consequence will be on your head." She motioned to the cart of honey behind him. "If you cannot afford to pay the cost, I will consider a trade. One crate of honey for a single night's stay. I am certain you understand the situation."

"Your price is too high," he barked.

"Agree to my conditions or leave."

He looked out at the unceasing storm, and his shoulders fell. When he turned around, his lips were curled back. "Take the honey," he said, his teeth clenched.

"Very well," Bao Li said. She stepped toward Makh as he unloaded a single crate of honey and placed it on the ground. "Set a guard outside his room for the night. I have it on good authority that he cannot be trusted."

Saina watched them leave. Out of the corner of her eye, she

thought she saw someone dressed in red standing at the entrance of the hallway leading to the storeroom. But when she turned, nothing was there but the flickering glow of the oil lamps.

Left alone, Bao Li approached Saina. "He should know better than to kick the hive and disturb the queen," she said, the hint of a smile raising the corners of her mouth.

Saina warmed at Bao Li's confidential tone—the trust she had shown in Saina's judgment. She longed to return to those days of favor.

"See to it that the honey is taken to the storeroom. I will retrieve my portion from Vandakk tomorrow," Bao Li said, then walked away.

Saina counted the jars and laughed into the dark night, the sound drowned out by the pouring rain. She cradled two jars in her arms and ran through the courtyard. Vandakk would be pleased to know that his search for honey was over, for Bao Li had managed to secure ten jars of the delicacy after all—twice what Saina had been sent to purchase earlier.

Chapter Eleven

The storm passed in the night.

At Bao Li's orders, servants rushed through the courtyard in the dim glow of torchlight, collecting rainwater in pots, and pouring the contents into deep cisterns placed throughout the caravanserai.

It was tiresome work but when morning light arrived, Saina marveled at the sight. All cisterns were full to the brim, not a drop more could be added. The sun had risen just enough to set fire to the lingering clouds above and be reflected in the still water that had puddled on the ground. By midday, the parched desert would reclaim any water that was not put to use or carefully stored away.

Though wearied by the long night, duty beckoned. In this harsh environment, no one could afford to be stagnant without consequence.

Saina pulled down the sodden drapes that flanked the entrance to the hallway and carried them toward Sapan, who approached with his donkey and cart. He was gathering soaked carpets and woven cloths to be taken outside the southern wall where they would be wrung out and set to dry in the hot sun.

Saina dropped the drapes in the cart as he passed by, then

turned to see Vandakk setting a bowl of yogurt on the serving table. He looked up and called to her.

"Retrieve a jar of honey from the storeroom," he said. "It will go well with the porridge and yogurt."

Saina slowed. "Now? But the honey merchant is still here. What will he think?"

Vandakk tilted his head. "Should we concern ourselves with his offense? He chose his lot."

She recalled the merchant's advances. He did not care that his vulgar conduct made her skin crawl. How many other women had he mistreated in the same way? "You are correct," she said, grinning at Vandakk. "I will not make his offense my own burden."

"Go quickly," Vandakk said, pointing to the handlers who emerged from the stables with their teams of camels. "They will expect food by the time they cinch goods on the backs of those beasts."

Saina rushed into the hallway but stopped suddenly when Bao Li's new servant walked out of the storeroom, carrying two jars of honey.

The stable girl's eyes widened in surprise before she quickly looked away.

"I had planned to bring Bao Li her honey later in the morning," Saina said. Just last night she had sensed Bao Li softening toward her. She had hoped to gain her favor by tending to the chore.

"I was asked to bring them to her," the girl said quietly.

"Yes, of course," Saina said, her chest tightened.

"I do not want this job," the stable girl said, her voice thick with emotion. "And I know I displease Bao Li. Everything I do is measured against you. I cannot compete." Her eyes welled with tears. "I was content working in the stables...not waiting upon her in that khana. How silent and dreadful the boredom is."

Saina was struck by the stable girl's admission. It had not

occurred to her that she might be miserable too. She took a cloth from her sash and dried the girl's eyes. "Perhaps the work will change soon...for both of us," she said, offering a weary smile. What more could she do than encourage her with a thin strand of hope, delicate as it may be?

The stable girl bowed her head, her eyes holding a distant confidence. "Sometimes Bao Li calls me by your name. She does not catch herself, but I hear it plainly," she said. Shifting the jars in her arms, she brushed past Saina and walked into the courtyard.

Saina leaned against the cool wall and stared at the torchlight dancing on the wall. Was it true? Had Bao Li missed her in the same way? She had barely let the thought take root when a servant began sweeping the hall, reminding her of her own chore and Vandakk who was waiting for her.

With honey in hand, Saina returned to the courtyard where Issik was dishing up porridge. She glanced at Vandakk and the guard standing nearby, relieved at their presence. At her approach, the merchant glowered, dark lines etched across his forehead. Dry clothes and a warm night's sleep had not changed his countenance.

She set the honey on the table and stepped back.

Issik fixed his gaze on the jar, his face growing as red as his fiery hair.

"Try it," Vandakk said, the glow of mischief in his eyes. "We received it just last night. It is not often we have such a fine delicacy to serve our guests."

The merchant glared at Vandakk. "Do you mock me?" he said through clenched teeth. The guard stepped forward, but Issik thrust out his hand. "Leave me be." He slammed his bowl on the table, rattling the dishes and serving utensils, then walked away.

Saina watched him enter the stables, but the sight seemed to pull out caution from within. Had they just poked a beast they would be wise not to disturb?

Vandakk leaned toward her. "Why are you downcast? As I said, he has reaped the bitter portion of his greed."

"I do not deny the satisfaction of swift justice," Saina said. "But I fear we have kindled something greater..." Her voice trailed off.

Moments later, while Saina filled the handlers' cups with tea, Issik returned to the courtyard, pulling his donkey and loaded cart. He did not look up or to the side as he walked out of the gates.

Saina was glad. She hoped to never see him again.

———

After the night's storm, servants were pulled in all directions, and Saina fell into the rhythm of her chores. She spent the early afternoon cleaning the vacated rooms in anticipation of a large string of arriving guests whose travels had been hindered by the tempest.

Almost finished with the final room, Saina picked up the refuse pot in the corner and carried it out to the pushcart, relieved the chore did not fall to her very often. The stench churned her stomach. How could one ever grow accustomed to its foulness?

The first time she was sent to empty the pots as a young girl, one slipped from her hands and shattered on the ground. Embarrassed at the mess and sickened by the smell, Saina hid outside the back gate of the caravanserai until Vandakk came in search of her.

"Do not lose heart, child," he had said, kneeling beside her. "In life we are faced with many difficult tasks. Such things cannot be avoided, but we can find ways to overcome them."

"How?" Saina asked, her eyes filled with tears.

"By setting our minds on that which brings us joy." A long silence stretched between them. When he finally spoke again, his voice was choked with emotion.

"When I was a boy, I was tasked with caring for an orphaned lamb from my father's flock. I loved that lamb. I named her Jamuk. Always by my side, she was a faithful companion, until the day she caught the attention of hungry traders passing through our village."

Vandakk sighed. "My heart broke when my father agreed upon their price. I protested, begged him to choose another, but he would not give ear to me. He said that Jamuk was always meant to lay down her life, that I must accept it.

"And I did. I had no other choice. She died in order to bring sustenance to those hungry men." His eyes brightened. "When hardship falls upon me now, I think about the way she used to call to me from across the pasture or how she would run, jumping and kicking, when my attention was on the other sheep." He chuckled. "Sometimes it is in the loss of a thing that we realize its greater purpose."

Greater purpose? Saina shook her head, releasing the memory. How many seasons had the sycamore tree flowered and withered since Vandakk told her the story of his lamb? Yet nothing had changed. *Must I endure more losses before finding the greater purpose in it all?*

She pushed the unpleasant thought away and finished sweeping the floor. When she knelt to gather the sand blown in from the storm, someone stepped into the doorway, darkening the room.

Turning, Saina saw the broad shoulders of a man leaning against the doorframe. The sun was at his back, casting him in shadows. She saw the long knife tied at his waist and the familiar way he tilted his head.

"Narisaf?" she said, standing quickly. "You have come." She tried to sound calm, to not give herself away, but his open smile showed that he saw through her efforts.

"I waited for your return to the bazaar, and when I could wait no longer, I decided to come to you," he said confidently. "It worked well that my grandfather asked me to deliver a gift to Vandakk this same day." He stepped back, sunlight washing over him. "But first I have something for you."

Saina walked to the edge of the room as he set his satchel on the ground and reached inside. She looked out at the courtyard, which was empty of all but a few merchants. The hot sun pressed down from above, and the guards had taken their place in the shade of the wall just outside the gates. No one paid them any attention.

Narisaf held out a leather bracelet inlaid with indigo and gold thread, and Saina stepped toward him.

She ran her fingers along the braided threads. "Is this the thread you purchased from Renchou?"

"Yes, but only a small portion," he said. "Not the whole."

She searched his face. "This will fetch a high price in the bazaar."

Narisaf reached out his hand and gently took hold of her wrist. "It is not to be sold. I made it for you."

"For me?" Saina stepped back, suddenly aware of the grime on her tunic. "I cannot accept this. I am a slave, unworthy of such fine adornment."

"I do not perceive you that way," Narisaf said, tilting his head. "Who decided your worth that you believe them?"

Saina's stomach dropped at the offense she had caused. "No one... I..." Had he not noticed that she was covered in filth or that her position held no value? For her to be seen wearing such a thread would draw suspicion she could not afford. But neither could she bear to hurt him. "Your grandfather would not be pleased to have such fine thread wasted on me."

"You have learned the ways of my grandfather?" he said. "Not even I have achieved such a feat."

Standing in the shade of the room, Saina's face burned with shame. Why did he bring out such strong emotions in her? She stepped out from the shadows, and Narisaf took her hand in his.

Heat spread through her body. Her legs felt weak as he tied the bracelet loosely around her wrist. Looking up at him, she smiled, offering an unspoken apology. A soft laugh escaped her lips. "I have never beheld such a beautiful gift."

Narisaf laughed, too, but it was not the deep laugh Saina had heard before. It was gentle, calm, as though the whole of his body had found its rest.

A movement across the courtyard drew Saina's attention. She looked to see Vandakk carrying a long, flat basket of rising dough, his tunic covered in fine flour.

"Come," she said to Narisaf. "You can present Vandakk with your grandfather's gift."

Vandakk was setting the basket of dough beside the tandoor oven when they approached. He smiled, and his green eyes shimmered. "Narisaf, you have returned," he said, clapping him on the back. "How is your grandfather? Was he pleased with the meal I prepared for him?" Vandakk pulled rounds of camel dung from the pile beside him and set them beneath the oven, then turned back to Narisaf.

"How could he not be pleased? Your reputation is spoken of even in our homeland, and you did not fail him," Narisaf said. "He sent a gift to thank you for your generosity. He had hoped to join me in its presentation, but our journey to Samarkand proved hard on him. Even after a few days of rest, he has grown weaker." He pulled a rolled-up tapestry from his satchel and handed it to Vandakk. "My grandfather asked that you forgive his absence and accept this on his behalf."

Vandakk held it up, and as it unrolled, he gasped.

Saina studied the golden sun on the tapestry, shining over rolling hills in shades of green she had never seen before. A shepherd boy, with green eyes and flowing black hair, stood in the center. Beside him was a lamb nuzzling the boy's hand.

Her mouth fell open.

"Jamuk," Vandakk said as he stroked the white threads of the lamb. He pulled the tapestry to his chest, tears streaming down his face. He opened his mouth as though to speak, but no words came out. He shook his head.

Saina had never seen him at a loss for words. Her throat swelled as she considered him. She took great pride in knowing this man whose deep love flowed as strong and steady as the mighty Zarafshan River. If any person deserved such a touching gift, it was Vandakk.

"With this tapestry, my earliest memories have been pulled to the surface. It has touched the deepest part of me," Vandakk said. "How will I thank your grandfather for a gift such as this?"

"He expressed his desire to meet you in person and will send for you when his energy returns," Narisaf said.

Vandakk's eyes lit up. "It is possible you could hasten his recovery. There is a healer in Samarkand who is well known for curing many ailments. Her knowledge of plants and their properties is unmatched. I am certain she will know what ails your grandfather."

"I have heard mention of her name," Narisaf said, "and will seek her out tomorrow."

"The city is a dreadful maze," Vandakk said. "If you have not learned it yet, I will send Saina at first light to take you to the apothecary."

Saina straightened. Was he giving her permission to go to the city alone with Narisaf?

Narisaf smiled. "I accept your offer with gratitude, for the city is as you say. Twice I have entered its gates, and twice I have lost my way."

"It has happened to all of us," Vandakk said, chuckling. He turned his gaze back to the tapestry.

Narisaf leaned toward Saina. "I must return to my grandfather, but I will meet you near the city early tomorrow."

Saina stepped toward him, longing to reach out and touch him. "I will be there," she said, clenching her fist tight. It was all she could do to hold herself back.

"Narisaf," Vandakk said.

Saina shifted her weight and faced Vandakk, whose eyes still focused on the tapestry.

"How did your grandfather know about my young lamb?"

Narisaf seemed to ponder the question, then shook his head. "His mystery is like a deep well hidden within the desert sands. I do not know the spring from which it flows, only that it quenches the thirst of those who receive it."

———

Night settled over the land and the caravanserai grew quiet.

Saina returned to her room. She closed the door and slid the lock into place, then set the small candle on the floor beside her sleeping mat. She had longed to let her mind wander, to dwell on Narisaf and the fleeting moments she had shared with him. Like the parched desert soaking up the rare rains, her thirsty heart yearned for more time with him.

She pulled the bracelet off her wrist, drawing comfort from its beauty, the work of his hands. What did Narisaf see in her that convinced him she was worthy of this? Of him? She studied the vibrant indigo, the flash of gold woven throughout, and inhaled a deep breath. Dare she risk hoping for more? She was not free to love and certainly not to marry. The debt of her father's abandonment, paid through a lifetime of servitude, guaranteed it.

Saina shook her head. She did not want to linger in this cloud of dark thoughts. Not tonight, when she had barely glimpsed the shimmering edge of hope.

She pulled her clay vessel toward her and peered inside at the three colorful stones, a threadbare square of wool, and the tiny wooden elephant. She had collected these items over the years. Each one held a memory that was stored safely inside. But none were as treasured as the bracelet she held now.

She gently placed it inside the vessel and slid the jar back into the corner. Her mind drifted to Narisaf's kindness and the way his presence lit a flame within her.

Blowing out the candle, she studied the sliver of pale moonlight on the floor beneath her door. In the silence, she heard the quiet lowing of animals kept safely in the stables. She thought about Vandakk's cherished lamb, how its death brought him a vision of a grander purpose of all things. Could it be true of her as well, that her father's abandonment and Bao Li's rejection pointed to something far greater than anything she could have known? If so, what could it be?

She dropped the thought, recalling the man who appeared unexpectedly. "Narisaf," she spoke into the darkness, and his name was quickly absorbed by the jagged cracks stretching across the mud-brick walls that wrapped around her.

Chapter Twelve

S aina walked along the Silk Road, the morning sun casting a hazy, pink glow on the bank of thick trees and overgrown brush. The mighty Zarafshan River churned and roared just beyond them, its steady waters feeding the lush foliage, whose outstretched branches drooped with fat flowers and dew-covered leaves. Their rich, heady scent lingered in the crisp desert air.

She adjusted the satchel on her shoulder. Inside were several samsa left over from last night's meal that Vandakk had prepared for her.

"Eat before you leave," he had said when she entered the storeroom earlier in the morning. He placed the meal and a cup of tea on the table, but Saina shook her head. Her excitement at seeing Narisaf had chased away her hunger. She drank down the tea and wrapped the samsa in a cloth, promising she would eat on the way.

She passed rolling hills that dipped along the riverbank, until the outcropping of boulders in the distance signaled the road leading to the city. It was there she saw Narisaf leaning against the rocks, and the beat of her heart quickened. He stood and walked toward her.

"You are like the wind, appearing without warning," she said.

"Did you not expect me?" Narisaf said, his voice low, teasing.

"Not this far from the city. You have walked a long distance only to return where you started."

Narisaf wrapped his hand around her wrist, fingering her bracelet. "No distance is too far if it grants me more time with you."

Saina's legs weakened at his touch, but she glanced cautiously at the road behind her.

Narisaf laughed. "There is no one around. I have already looked."

"You are perceptive," Saina said. "What else do you know?" She hoped the lilt of her voice hid the uncertainty in her question. Could she chance loving a man when abandonment and servitude stood against her? Her heart was like a thread pulled taut, at risk of severing at any moment.

The glint in Narisaf's eyes faded, but he remained standing before her like an ancient tree, rooted deeply in the ground. "I know you can trust me," he said.

The words were like a balm to her bruised heart. She wanted to believe he was not like her father, that he would not run away when life became too difficult. Dare she let go of the fear that had kept her bound since she was a young girl? Her eyes welled with tears.

Narisaf stroked her face, drying her tears, and Saina did not pull away. The touch of his warm hands on her skin comforted her.

She knew so little about him, the grandson of the weaver, who emerged from the desert and captured her heart. Who was he, and what were his early years like growing up? Did he live in the crowded city or roam the countryside beyond its walls? And his parents, who were they?

These questions formed on her tongue, but the chime of camel bells rang out, drawing her attention to the winding road.

As a caravan approached and the grousing of the camels grew louder, Saina reached into her satchel and pulled out the samsa, still warm in the cloth. "I brought some pastries to share," she said, handing one to Narisaf.

The caravan passed by, and they set out on the road toward the city, eating while they walked. Peach and almond orchards lined the road, and a woman, her belly swollen with child, tended the young saplings.

Saina looked at Narisaf. "You were an infant once, born of a woman, but I have heard no mention of your mother. Did she die in childbirth?"

Narisaf slowed, and his countenance grew serious. She noticed the way he studied his surroundings, as though searching for words to convey deeply held emotions.

"Forgive me," Saina said, looking away. "It is not my place to ask such personal questions."

"I want you to know about her," he said. "I just...I have never spoken of her, of what happened to her," his voice trailed off.

Saina slowed, allowing him time to gather his words.

"My mother's name was Yena. She was a Sogdian, born in Samarkand." He turned and nodded toward the city. Smoke from cooking fires and smelting ovens rose above its walls, where it lingered in a thin haze.

"A Sogdian?" she said. "You and I share the same heritage. How did you come to live in the distant land of Merv?"

"My father was a Sassanian warrior. He was traveling through Samarkand when he saw my mother gathering water from the canal. She supplied his men and their horses with water, and upon his return to Merv, he told my grandfather about her. When the season of reaping came, they made the trek to Samarkand. They had waited at the well for many days when she came to fetch water, but it took two full moon cycles before my father was granted her hand in marriage." He looked into the orchard and grew quiet.

Saina twisted the indigo bracelet around her wrist. How fortunate Narisaf's mother was to have been granted favor and marry into a family of good men. She shook her head. If only marriage could come easily for her too.

Narisaf turned back to her as though she had spoken her thoughts aloud. "My father returned to his homeland with the woman he loved. My grandfather once told me that a high cost was exacted for my mother, but I was too young to know the details. He has not spoken of it since." His eyes searched Saina's. "I am not a child anymore."

Saina nodded, but sensing there was more he needed to tell her, she waited for him to speak.

"My mother was a kind woman," Narisaf said, his voice choked with emotion. "I remember her clearly. She cared greatly for my grandfather and me. Her laughter, her joy, was the light in our home during the dark days of my father's long absences in battle."

He grew quiet. When he spoke again, his voice sounded distant, hollow. "I hold this part of me close, for this was all I knew before I came to understand that evil men lurk in the shadows of the same land where good men must tread."

Saina understood the need to give words to unexplainable heartache, to release it in hopes that it would not come back and haunt without mercy. She remained silent as they walked through the gates of the city and down the narrow streets. She would not steal the opportunity for Narisaf to do the same.

"It was my mother's custom to bake honey cakes and provide fresh water for my father and his horse upon their return. We trekked to the spring hidden in the rock mountain near our city, but the narrow path was blocked by a rockslide. The donkey could not pass through the rubble." Narisaf closed his eyes and shook his head.

"I wanted to help my mother. I told her I would fetch the water. It was late in the day, and the shadows of the mountain seemed to crouch along the ground, a fearsome, dreadful thing. But I swallowed my cowardice, convinced myself I was brave, just like my father.

By the time I returned, dusk had settled over the land. I called out for my mother, but her voice did not return to me. I found her a distance away, her body cold, motionless. Her clothes were torn, her mouth was filled with sand."

His mouth twisted, and Saina saw the deep torment of this memory in his eyes. Her chest ached with his pain.

"I removed my clothes and covered her," Narisaf said, "then lay down beside her and wept until my tears dried up and my tongue clung to the roof of my mouth. Looking upon the violence that stole her life, I had no other hope but for death to take me too." He grew silent. "Night blanketed my mother and me, its blackness so still and resolute that I began to fear its grip.

"I awoke to cold hands pressed against my naked back and my grandfather kneeling beside me, weeping. My father cradled my mother's body to his chest, then threw his head back and cried out with the unceasing anguish of a battle-weary warrior. He had seen all the cruelties the world offered, but my mother's violent death broke him." Narisaf's voice quaked.

On the side of the empty road, Saina's eyes pooled with tears, blurring Narisaf's face. "I am sorry," she said, choking out the words. She wrapped her arms around him and pulled him into her embrace, not caring that she took a great risk in doing so. He was all that mattered in this moment, and she was honored that he trusted her to hear his burden.

In the full light of morning, Saina held him until the tension in his body released. When he finally pulled away, she searched his eyes. How bright and vibrant they suddenly seemed.

"How do you carry such strength in spite of the difficulty you have lived?" Saina said.

The words had barely left her mouth when a bird's raspy caw rang out. A large, black bird came to rest in the canopy of the tree beside them.

The bird turned its head, and Saina noticed that one of its eyes was clouded over and a deep crack ran the length of its yellow beak. Feathers were missing where a scar streaked down its neck. What gruesome past had this bird experienced?

"When I watched my father lower my mother into the grave, the disrupted earth cradling her body, I begged them to bury me with her. I could see no way out of that tremendous pain. But my grandfather would hear none of it. He held my face between his hands and looked into my eyes. He told me that although our laughter may cease for a season, it will not remain hidden forever, and though my eyes have looked upon terrors, one day they will look upon love." Narisaf paused. "The pain was so great that I did not know how it could be true, but I trusted him. There was no other choice for me."

Saina sucked in her breath. Like dry brush consumed by flame, she was struck with a fierce understanding of the price all creatures must pay to live among the dust of the land.

The bird spread its wings, pushed off the branch, and flew away. She looked again at Narisaf. *He is like the bird, refusing to let his scars keep him from soaring.*

Narisaf wrapped his hand around Saina's. "My grandfather was correct. I am grateful death did not take me when I begged it to, for my eyes have finally looked upon you. At last...I have found love." He looked into her eyes and bringing her hand to his lips, kissed her.

Saina melted into him, aware of the ease of her breath and the pulse of a slow burning fire within her.

She wanted to stay in this moment the remainder of her days, but the distant sound of rolling cart wheels brought her back to herself. Narisaf seemed to take notice too. He let go of her hand and smiled. "We should go," he said. "I do not want to cause you trouble."

They meandered through the maze of roads until they came to the main courtyard where a potter was setting out stoneware beneath the awning of his storefront and a baker prepared pastries for the workers who passed by. At the opposite end, Umida stood outside her apothecary. Her long, gray hair hung loosely at her shoulders. Her arms were crossed, and her eyes narrowed, but there was a hint of a smile at the corner of her lips.

"Come in," Umida said. She glanced at Narisaf, and Saina saw her smile broaden.

They walked inside, and Saina inhaled the musky scent of herbal tinctures and aromatic cedars. Jars of fine powders lined the walls and nets of gnarled roots hung from the ceiling of a shop that felt peaceful and calm. She understood why Upach came here often.

Umida closed the door behind them. "Have you come for Kang Dahan's tea this early in the morning?" she asked. She pulled two jars from the shelves and set them on the table. "Has he returned already?"

"Not yet, but it should not be long now," Saina said. "As you know, Vandakk wants to be prepared."

"Of course." Umida dropped a spoonful of tea leaves on the bronze scale, then looked up. "And Bao Li, is she prepared?"

Saina shook her head. Umida and Bao Li had been friends for many years; she knew how Bao Li felt about Kang Dahan. "Her mind is divided with many troubles," Saina said. She did not want to admit that she had caused Bao Li's recent pain and that her actions made Kang Dahan's return far more complicated. "But she is leaving for Penjikent soon. Perhaps the trip will soothe her."

"It always does," Umida said, but she quickly waved her hand, brushing away the comment. "Upach was here two days ago. The girl has a gift of healing. At such a young age, she holds a knowledge of herbs and medicines that I have not seen in learned people three times her age."

"I saw her when I was sent to purchase honey," Saina said. "She looked happy."

"She is free to be herself when she is with me," Umida said. "If only she was not a slave in Kang Dahan's household, I would take her in with my family." Her eyes suddenly widened, and she

116

covered her mouth. "Oh, I am sorry, Saina. I did not intend to gossip."

Saina shook her head. "I am not offended. Bao Li's servants are treated justly. But Ning Po is not like Bao Li."

Umida frowned. "I am concerned for Upach's safety. And still, she takes on her mistresses concerns as her own. Just the other day she came seeking a remedy to ease the crying that keeps Ning Po up at night." She shrugged. "But we are not miracle workers. We cannot concoct a tea to take away grief. One can only walk through its darkness and hope to see the light again."

Saina pondered her wisdom, like the weaver's when he spoke life to Narisaf upon the death of his mother. How beautiful and true it was.

"And you?" Umida said, looking at Narisaf. "Have you come to seek healing or just to enjoy the company of the beautiful young woman at your side?"

Narisaf's eyes widened; his face grew red. "No...well, yes..." he cleared his throat.

Saina laughed at the banter but felt the need to defend him. "Narisaf recently came from Merv, but his grandfather is suffering from the arduous trek. Vandakk is confident you can prepare a healing tincture and asked me to bring him to your apothecary."

Umida raised her brow. "It was Vandakk's recommendation?" she said, a teasing lilt in her voice. "And that is the only reason you two are together?"

Narisaf looked at Saina and winked. "It would have been foolish of me to turn down Vandakk's offer."

Heat crept into Saina's face.

Umida grinned. "I can see that. Just use caution. Eyes are everywhere in this city, and so are rumors. Take care that none are spread about Bao Li's head servant."

"I would never dishonor her."

"Good," Umida said, giving Saina the pouch of Kang Dahan's tea. "Now, tell me about your grandfather."

The sudden change of subject caught Narisaf off guard once

again. He seemed to search for words in the stretch of time before he spoke.

"My grandfather and I made the trek from Merv, but since our arrival, he has complained of feeling dizzy and exhausted. Even though his body longs for rest, sleep does not come."

"I know this well," Umida said, taking another jar off the shelf. "Many sojourners come to me after their travels through the desert. The drying sand and physical exertion take their toll, especially on the aged." After counting out several handfuls of dried mushrooms, she placed them into a pouch filled with fine powder and weighed it on the scale.

"Boil the reishi mushrooms with a pinch of powder in the morning and evening, and serve as a tea. You must ensure that your grandfather drinks it all down. The tea will be bitter on his tongue, but it should help restore his energy."

Umida tied a leather cord around the pouch and gave it to Narisaf. "If in three days' time he is not feeling better, bring him to me."

When Narisaf took it, she gripped his arm, stopping him. "My knowledge is vast, and my remedies have cured countless ailments, but I must warn you that nothing can return an aged man to his days of youth."

"We do not expect it," Narisaf said. "But my grandfather's greatest joy is to work at his loom, and it is my greatest desire to provide that for him."

Saina watched Narisaf straighten with resolve. How he loved his grandfather. His loyalty was apparent to anyone who cast their eyes upon their bond. How could it be that a man with such deep affections would feel the same toward her?

"Come," she said, wanting to linger with him a little longer. "I have been granted a portion of the day with you. Let us spend it preparing tea for your grandfather, that he may feel well again."

Narisaf smiled down at her, as though she had done him a great kindness by her offering. He opened the door, and Saina stepped into the light of the morning.

The city was awake. People had congregated in small groups, talking and laughing, while others set out to work, weaving through the courtyard with their pack animals and push carts. Saina looked at Narisaf and smiled. For the first time, she felt like she belonged, as though she was now a part of something far greater than her past.

Chapter Thirteen

As they left the city gates, Saina walked close to Narisaf but left enough space between them to not draw curious eyes. Their steps were slow, their conversation lingering until they had walked deep into the bazaar, where extended awnings and makeshift stalls spread out around them.

Narisaf turned to her. "Do you recall your father's face? The sound of his voice?" he asked above the din of bartering voices and lowing pack animals.

Saina searched the expanse of azure sky overhead, hoping it would reflect long hidden memories, but none came. Neither could she command them to appear, for they emerged without warning, and she was seldom prepared for the force with which they struck.

"I remember his essence, hints of who he was when my mother walked the earth. At times I am reminded of the way he would tilt his head up and split the air with his laughter." Saina cherished the memory. She held on to it a moment, a welcome glimpse into a distant time. "But when I think about his eyes, the shape of his nose, or whether his skin was firm with youth or wrinkled with age, I cannot recall him clearly. For that part of him is like the shifting clouds above, having changed shape and faded long ago."

Saina had never felt free to speak of her father in this way. Her mother's death had cracked him open, his deep grief a valley he could not escape. And so, she held these things close out of respect for the vague memory of a good man. She could not bear to hear the judgments spoken of him by those who had never walked such depths.

"My mother used to say that I was a tender child, easily bruised by an unkind word. She would stroke my back at night, telling me I must learn to quiet the thoughts that troubled me so. If only I had learned to master them before she died. I did not know how to deal with it, except to carry the guilt of her death and the death of her child that never came to be."

"You are not to blame," Narisaf said. "All women heavy with child know the risk that comes with giving birth."

Saina remained silent. She had not told him about Ning Po's stillborn baby whose lifeless eyes would never see the colors of the earth. Neither had she spoken of Ning Po's accusations. Her poisonous words still echoed in Saina's mind. But it was Bao Li's anger, which still burned hot against her, that hurt more than anything else. She had been bound to the consequences not once but twofold.

"I carry the consequences, nevertheless," Saina said. "I lost the freedom to wander the hills of my youth, to feel the wind upon my face and dream about my future. It was taken from me before I had ever known the weight of its importance."

"Perhaps one day Bao Li will release you," Narisaf said. "And you will be free to"—

Saina sighed deeply, shaking her head.

—"free to marry me," he said, undeterred by her protest.

Saina spun on her heel, her mouth dropped open, but she could not find words to speak.

He slowed.

"You want me to be your wife?" Saina finally said. He was

teasing her in the same way he teased his grandfather, but his shy smile creased the corners of his mouth, and a hint of pink crept up his face, sending a flush of heat through Saina's body.

"Yes." His admission was simple and honest. Her stomach fluttered as though a flurry of butterflies had been loosed within.

Their future flashed before her, and she glimpsed a home filled with their young children. It brought a smile to her face, a peace she never thought she could attain. She wanted to remain in the comfort of these thoughts, but her smile faltered. She could not let Narisaf think it was possible.

Forcing herself to hold his gaze, she summoned the courage to speak honestly, for that much he deserved. "I wish marriage was an option for me, but it is not. My duty is to Bao Li and the caravanserai. This is the life that was forced upon me, the debt I must repay." Would the words bring an end to their relationship? Her throat constricted.

Narisaf lowered his head to meet her eyes, his intense focus set upon her. "I commit myself to the challenge. Soon you will be my wife."

His sure response filled Saina with cautious hope. She laughed. "You are certain of my future then?" she said, allowing herself to imagine living with Narisaf in the city of Merv, the city of his father and grandfather. But how could she picture it in her mind? She knew nothing of the desert place he was from.

"I am like my father and grandfather, men of great courage, wisdom, and tenacity. Their blood flows through me," he said, finishing with a bark of laughter that drew the attention of two women passing by. The women looked over their shoulders, scowling in displeasure, but Narisaf paid them no attention. "I can see in your eyes that you doubt me."

"It is not you I doubt but the willingness of the people I am beholden to."

He shook his head and smiled, undeterred by her reasoning.

"Perhaps what you say is true, that one day we will marry,"

Saina said. She had heard awe-filled whisperings among the merchants that the weaver of Merv possessed the gift of a seer. She considered the weight of their words. A common man would not travel such a great distance to find his son a wife if he did not hold certainty of the outcome. Could the same be true for his grandson?

"Is there truth in what has been said about your grandfather?" Saina asked, squinting into the sunlight. "Is he a seer?"

Narisaf slowed. He seemed to consider the question thoughtfully. "It is a reasonable conclusion, for many are drawn to the allure of his mystery. It is something that even I cannot understand."

They walked past the perfumer's stall where open vials were placed on high tables, scents of musk, cassia, and rose wafting into the air.

Ahead, the tentmaker stood outside his stall, rolls of red and white felt piled at his side. His countenance alight, his words dripped with honey. "Come and see the finest tents to be found in all of Samarkand," he said, his eyes locked on Saina's. He motioned for them to draw near. "A beautiful tent for a beautiful woman?"

But Saina remembered the way he had abused his servants with a sharp tongue. Averting her gaze, she pressed herself against Narisaf's side as they entered the weaver's tent.

As night is different from day, so the welcoming sight of the weaver's stall contrasted to that of the tentmaker. His striped awning extended over shelves and baskets filled with brightly colored tapestries and other woven pieces. Inside, the weaver sat before his loom, his back bent like a bow.

Narisaf walked up behind the weaver and squeezed his shoulder. Kneeling down, he kissed him gently on the cheek.

The weaver slowed his shuttle and smiled, then turned and motioned toward Saina. When she approached, he cupped her face in his hands. She felt the thin bones beneath his skin, but she felt strength within him, as well.

Narisaf searched the stall, pointing to a low table that was beside the loom. "Did you pull that over here?" he asked.

The weaver nodded. "I needed my threads closer to me. It proved easier to drag the table closer to my loom than to constantly expend the energy getting myself off this stool."

"You should have waited until my return," Narisaf said. "Your impatience will slow your recovery."

The weaver clicked his tongue. "It is not easy to grow weak in front of the boy I was charged with raising up not so long ago. But I am still sharp of mind and perceptive in my understanding."

"Are you now?" Narisaf said, teasing.

"Did I not tell you that you would soon find the woman you would love?" he said, looking from Narisaf to Saina. "You are like your father, following your heart."

Narisaf leaned forward, his eyes full of mischief; a thought seemed to occur to him. "You are correct. It is no wonder your reputation as a seer has preceded you."

Narisaf winked at Saina, and she shook her head. She held an even greater admiration for the weaver as she considered the years he had put up with his grandson's humor.

"A seer?" The Weaver chuckled. He waved his hand, dismissing the comment. "Perhaps it is true. I did not know where you had gone when I awoke this morning and saw the morsel of bread and suzma beside my bed, but I knew exactly who you were with."

Saina stepped forward. Her years of serving under Bao Li demanded she give an account of her day's work, and she felt compelled to do the same for the weaver. "When Vandakk learned you have suffered exhaustion from your journey, he asked that I show Narisaf where to purchase medicinal tea for you."

"Is that so?" The weaver looked at Narisaf. "You try to force youthful vitality upon my aging body, but it is going the way of all living creatures. Nothing can stop it."

Narisaf leaned forward. "I should have been more cautious

when you demanded we make the arduous trek across the desert. I fear you hastened your decline unnecessarily."

Taking a bundle of thread off the table, the weaver turned on his stool. With shaking hands, he wove the thread through the warp. "Tell me, grandson," his voice was soft, worn down by the dust of the land and toil of years packed within his thin flesh. "Do you regret that I brought you to Samarkand?"

His question hung in the air for a moment before Narisaf inhaled deeply, setting his gaze upon Saina.

Her breath slowed as the colorful tapestries blurred into one, becoming a faded backdrop behind Narisaf. In that sliver of time, flecks of dust were set aflame by the beam of sunlight piercing the shaded stall. It was Narisaf's gentle eyes—the boy lurking just beneath the flesh of the man—and the kindness held within him that sent an awakening through Saina's body. There was no question. She loved him.

His eyes softened. He took a small blanket and draped it over the weaver's thin shoulders. "How could I regret that you brought me back to the land where I belong, to the woman I love?" Narisaf said, unwavering.

The weaver raised his brow as though he had known it all along. "Neither do I regret having spent my body to bring you here." He returned to his loom, his agile fingers moving freely.

A sense of belonging washed over Saina. So certain she was of her place within their small family that had they asked her in that moment, she would have left with them. She would have lived in Merv, as the wife of Narisaf, no matter the consequences.

The clack of the shuttle picked up speed. Saina's eyes lifted to the tapestry of the warhorse, her thoughts melding with the rhythm and carrying her into a distant time. She stood on the packed earth of her home, watching her father pull her mother into his arms. He kissed her tenderly, then walked out the door, but Saina ran after him. "Please, Father, stay with us," she called out.

He turned and smiled, the rising sun casting a golden crown

upon his head. When she came to him, he knelt down, and his breath was warm upon her face. "A storm came in the night and scattered the horses. I must gather them before winter descends from the mountains."

Saina placed her hand on her father's cheek, felt the prickle of his beard on her tender hands. She searched the rolling hills, their grasses bowing to the wind, giving way to peaks so rough and jagged, they seemed to split the sky. "How will you know where to find them?"

"I send out my voice, and they respond. With a little guidance, even the horses will return to where they belong."

Saina could not recall if her father was successful in gathering the horses all those years ago. Perhaps he endured a great search and, having found most of the beasts, left the few to face the fierce winter alone, just like he had left her.

"What weighs upon your mind?" the weaver said, his voice bringing Saina back to the stall where she stood. His hands were stilled, his shuttle silent.

She slumped back, feeling their eyes upon her. "I recalled something my father said to me when I was young, and I am left to wonder why, after lying dormant all these years, does the memory return to me now?"

The weaver's face softened, and his gaze fastened on her father's hanging garment. "You remember because there was truth hidden within that you are finally ready to know." His cerulean eyes bore into hers.

Saina looked away, letting the words hang in the air. If it was a statement meant to be responded to, she made no attempt to do so.

"Now, where is this medicinal tea you speak of?" the weaver said, rubbing his hands together.

"I will prepare it for you," Saina said, eager to set her mind upon useful work. She walked to the corner of the tent where she found the kettle of water sitting over hot coals and poured it over the tea.

When she returned, Narisaf was reclining on a thick rug, his hands tucked behind his head.

"I must warn you, the tea is bitter," she said, placing it in the weaver's outstretched hand.

Putting the drink to his lips, he coughed and sputtered. His hands shook as he set it down. "Did my grandson put you up to this?"

Saina looked at Narisaf and saw he was trying to hold back his laughter.

She shook her head. "I do not claim his humor as my own, but I share in his concern for you. It is possible your ailment can be cured with this tea, but first you must suffer the drink."

"Come now, Grandfather," Narisaf said, sitting up. "It will serve you well."

The weaver tilted his head, his eyes softening. "Saina, you have gained my grandson's favor, and for that I will drink it down, for it is rare to find a woman who would tolerate a man with his disposition."

Laughter escaped Saina's lips. She cupped her hands over her mouth, feeling, for the first time in many years, as though her longing had found its resting place.

———

The moment Saina entered the storeroom, she saw that Vandakk had been waiting for her.

He spun around from the table, a knife in one hand, a potato in the other. "Bao Li came in search of you this morning," Vandakk said, swallowing down the morsel in his mouth. "She requested that you bring her tea."

"This morning?" Saina stepped toward him, surprised at the sudden rise of guilt. "But that was long ago! Has she waited for me all this time? I would have returned immediately if you had sent someone to fetch me."

Vandakk clicked his tongue, silencing her. "I told her you had run an errand in the city. She assured me there was no hurry, that she would wait until you returned."

"Even this late in the day?"

"Yes," Vandakk said, his voice strained. "But I cannot speak for Bao Li when she learns that you failed to tend to her immediately upon your return." He raised his eyebrows.

Saina strode across the room and set Kang Dahan's tea on the shelf before pulling out Bao Li's jar. It was no longer the beautiful vessel she carried the night Ning Po gave birth. Now it was a simple earthen jar, plain in color and form. Bao Li deserved something far grander. She resolved to search for something more suitable when time allowed for it.

As she lifted the lid, the scent of tea leaves brought a swell of emotions. Her mind flooded with thoughts of Narisaf and the weaver and how much had changed since she was last tasked with preparing the drink. What had caused Bao Li's heart to soften toward her now?

She selected a handful of plump figs and a round of warm onion bread, then set them on the tray beside the tea. Picking it up, she inhaled a nervous breath.

With a glance at Vandakk, she walked past him and left the storeroom.

———

Saina walked through the khana and into the vaulted room where Bao Li sat, her parchments unrolled and spread out before her.

"My lady?" Saina said, hoping Bao Li did not hear the nervous quiver in her voice.

Bao Li looked up, her eyes searching, her expression unreadable.

Saina swallowed hard, feeling like the desert had made its home within her throat. She stepped forward, wondering if Bao Li had held on to the memory of a night long since passed when Saina had run into the desert, calling after a man she thought was her father. She had run until her feet were as cracked as the earth and her voice had grown hoarse, only to realize it was not a man but a shadow that could not be grasped.

Crushed in spirit, she returned to Bao Li who stood outside the walls of the caravanserai, her head held high, the setting sun burning crimson in her eyes. When Bao Li lifted her hand, Saina drew back, her face pinched tight. She expected to be struck, to feel the sting of a blow across her face, but none came.

Instead, she felt Bao Li's soft hands stroking her wet cheek with the tenderness of a mother's touch. Saina's breath hitched, her face burned with shame when she looked into her eyes and saw the same depth of loss, the finality of failed hope, staring back at her.

Looking across the vaulted room now, Saina blinked away the tears blurring the giant mural of Kang Dahan and Bao Li's wedding day. She fixed her gaze on the peasant boy standing alone.

She placed the tray on the table and with a slight bow stepped back. "Forgive me for being late," she said. "I have only just returned from an errand in Samarkand."

"It is a small matter," Bao Li said. She pushed away from the table and stood slowly. "I have requested your presence for more pressing matters." Her silk slippers brushed along the rug as she drew near to Saina and looked at her with the same motherly tenderness she had many years ago.

"Your absence has been a void within my khana. You understood my needs and tended to them before they were uttered from my mouth. It is not the same with the young stable girl. My expectations go unfulfilled." She shrugged. "Of course, it is understandable. These things take time to learn, and for that I offer her grace."

Bao Li blinked and placed her hand on Saina's cheek, her eyes softened. "I regret that I did not do the same for you when my judgment was clouded with accusations contrary to your charac-

129

ter. As such, I have requested that Vandakk release you to my service for a portion of your day."

Saina could not move, her body suddenly heavy. She thought of Narisaf, of their time together and the peace she felt when she was with him. What would happen now? She searched for words. "And the stable girl?" Saina asked.

"She will return to her work in the stables," Bao Li said, her voice softening. "I sense she is happier there."

Saina remained silent. What was she to make of this request? She had wanted to be reconciled with Bao Li. The strain in their relationship had grieved her deeply. Indeed, Bao Li's admission brought a flood of relief. But in the days since being cast out of her presence, when she felt untethered in purpose, it was Narisaf's love that had anchored her. Now it was Narisaf's love she desired more than anything, impossible as it seemed.

A sigh escaped Saina's lips. Her life had expanded beyond the walls of the caravanserai. The realization sent a sharp pang through her body. She looked away.

"Speak of what troubles you," Bao Li said.

Saina suffered a smile. "Thank you," she said, and she meant it. But she could not deny the tightening in her chest as she considered Narisaf. Would she see him again now that a double portion of her time would be demanded from her?

She pressed her lips together, binding up the words that threatened to spill from her mouth. She could not risk offending Bao Li now and losing everything.

Chapter Fourteen

S aina pulled off her sandals and stood at the edge of the Dargom Canal. With a bucket in each hand, she walked down the sloped bank, then stepped carefully out into the flowing water, feeling a thin layer of silt press up between her toes.

She closed her eyes against the sun's glare and inhaled the scent of damp earth, of tall grasses and trees sinking their roots at the water's edge. She allowed herself the simple pleasure of feeling the lap of cool water against her legs.

There was a deep peace in the quiet moment, stolen from the day's harried press of chores. After spending the morning preparing Bao Li and her khana for a host of midday visitors—the wives of dignitaries from the city—she had returned to find Vandakk rushing through the courtyard.

"I need water for the cauldrons," he had said, taking the yoke from the wall and placing it on Saina's shoulders. "Fetch it from the canal, or the meal will be late."

Saina had not eaten anything since earlier in the morning and had hoped to have a small morsel between chores. But she swallowed her hunger and obeyed Vandakk's command. Perhaps there would be time to eat when she returned.

Dipping the buckets into the water, she filled them to the

brim. She had stepped toward the bank when the faint laughter of a child gave her pause. Searching, she saw a dark-haired boy push through the tall grass. He climbed over the mangled roots of the chinar tree, then stooped to pick up a stone.

Behind him a woman stepped into the clearing. She glanced at Saina and stopped, her eyes registering surprise. "Come, Uta," she called after the boy. Her long, black hair was braided down one side, her plain tunic and wool shawl were simple homespun.

"I am not hungry, Mama," he said. He threw a stone into the tall grass, sending a flurry of birds flying into the canopy of leaves above. He was a striking boy with dark eyes, wavy hair, and a restless energy that seemed to both amuse and try the patience of his mother.

"You have grown thin from our travels," his mother said. "Eat a small amount, or you will float away like a feather in the wind." She sat in a patch of sunlight and pulled out a small loaf of bread. The boy reluctantly joined her.

The roll of their tongue indicated they were not from Samarkand. Were they alone? Saina searched the banks but saw no sign of any other people. If she had traveled alone, even for a single day's journey, she took great risk in doing so. Goaded by curiosity, Saina approached them.

The mother pulled a small feather from the hem of the boy's tunic. "See?" she said, clicking her tongue. "Already you have started to grow feathers. It will not be long before there is nothing left of you."

His eyes widened. He looked at Saina as she drew near, then smiled shyly at his mother, exposing pink gums in the gap where young teeth had fallen out. Taking a handful of torn bread, he returned to the shade of the chinar tree.

Saina wondered at the mischievous glint in his brown eyes. Is this what Narisaf was like as a child? Three days had passed since she had seen him, and she was overwhelmed by the desire to be with him again, but she pushed the feeling aside and smiled at the woman.

"Have you come to work in the orchards?" Saina asked, pointing to the trees across from where they stood. It was common to see farmers and orchard workers pulling water from the canal.

The mother shook her head as she pulled the threadbare shawl closer to her body, her shoulders sagging. "We just arrived from Khiva," she said. "We will not be in your way. Tomorrow we will finish our trek to Penjikent."

"Does your husband travel with you?" Saina asked, looking around.

She shook her head. "My husband left two years ago to trade goods along the Silk Road. He never returned. All this time I have waited, but the charity of my neighbors has run dry. With a life of begging at our doorstep, we had no choice but to return to the home of my father in Penjikent."

"You have traveled all this way alone?" Saina said, stepping closer.

"No," she said. "A Sassanian merchant allowed us to travel in the safety of his caravan. We had journeyed well into the desert before I understood that his kindness came with obligations." She looked away. "Uta and I have remained at the back, putting a great distance between us and the caravan. But now his handlers have threatened to leave us, insisting that we have slowed them down."

"Are they staying in the caravanserai?"

She nodded. "We were not permitted to join them, and neither could I afford to stay there. It is for the best. I saw the relief on their faces when the head merchant demanded we stay out here, away from him and his men."

Saina straightened. "They have no authority to decide who stays in the caravanserai and who does not."

"Who am I to speak against them?"

Saina knelt down, put her hand on the woman's arm. "I am a servant of Bao Li, the head mistress of the caravanserai. If she knew you were left alone outside those walls, her anger would be kindled against the men who left you and against me for not offering you a safe place." She stood and lifted the yoke onto her shoulders, the water buckets swayed on each end. "Come with me, for tonight you will eat a full meal and sleep in peace."

Relief washed over the woman's face. She pressed her palm to her chest and sat up. "Thank you," she said. "I am Miunai, and this is my son, Uta. Yours is the first kindness we have experienced in many moon cycles. We are indebted to you."

Ducking under low hanging branches, Saina led them away from the water's edge and up the worn embankment. They approached the caravanserai, where a caravan waited outside the gates. Several handlers sought shade beneath the karagach trees lining the outer wall.

Uta went before them, carrying his uneaten bread. Saina walked slowly with Miunai, the weight of the water buckets pulling on her shoulders.

In the distance, a horseman approached at great speed, the dust of the desert billowing up behind the rider and his horse.

Narisaf? Saina strained to see. In the sliver of anticipation, the weight of the yoke no longer pulled on her. The hope of seeing him made her burden light.

But the moment fled as the horseman drew nearer and she saw clearly his pointed red hat and leather boots. It was not Narisaf, but a courier sent on official business.

His horse had not yet come to a full stop when he dismounted the beast and pushed his way to the front of the waiting caravan, where guards were standing at the gates.

The courier motioned to the satchel hanging from his shoulder, and Makh straightened, his countenance growing serious. Saina watched as Makh rushed the courier through the gates. A prickle of unease crept up her spine.

"Stay close to me," Saina said. Miunai took hold of Uta's hand, and Saina led them through the gates, where grousing camels and the voices of men barking orders grew louder.

Servants and handlers rushed through the courtyard, hauling goods to their rooms and leading animals to the stables. At the far end, a group of merchants suddenly stopped laughing. Saina felt the change in the air. Their cold eyes were fixed on Miunai. From the center of the group, a finely dressed man stood up and scowled.

Saina turned to Miunai. "Do not worry yourself over him," she said. "You have protection here for the night."

Miunai's eyes glistened, her body rigid. "What will happen tomorrow when I must join myself to these men again for the final trek to Penjikent?" she said.

Her question hung in the air, the thought becoming more troublesome as Saina contemplated the answer. What could be done now? Had her efforts to help only caused more trouble for Miunai and her son?

The thought was interrupted by Vandakk calling to her. "Hurry, Saina," he said. "Water brings life to the land, but it cannot bring itself to the pot."

Saina shook her head. She would think upon it later, surely something could be done. She quickly joined Vandakk and was followed shortly by the mother and her son. He greeted them with a curious glance, then took the buckets from the yoke and dumped them into the cauldron.

"Miunai and her son, Uta, traveled from Khiva with the caravan bearing oak galls and yellow orpiment," Saina said, motioning to the men at the far end of the courtyard. "But the merchants left them alone by the canal for the night."

"That will not do," Vandakk said, his eyes softening as he looked toward the mother and son. "We are not full tonight. You can sleep there," he pointed to the room over his shoulder, shut behind a carved wooden door. "The night guards keep watch over the courtyard. You will be safe and comfortable there."

Saina opened the door, then left them to unpack their few belongings inside the room. She returned with heavy wool blankets and a small candle to burn when night fell. "The evening meal will be served later, but I brought you a gift from the kitchen while you wait," she said, kneeling down and placing a dish of dried apricots, pistachio, suzma, and drizzle of honey between them. "We reserve this small meal for our most important guests."

Uta looked at his mother and then to Saina. A wide grin spread across his face.

"I cannot recall the last time we ate such fine food," Miunai said, tousling Uta's hair. "Thank you."

Saina returned to Vandakk in time to see the courier following Makh out from Bao Li's khana. Having accomplished his task, he walked slower, his hand no longer protecting the contents within the leather satchel.

Saina turned back to Vandakk. "I wonder what news the courier brought."

Vandakk slowed. "Who can know? Couriers are as common as the swarms of flies that accompany the caravans." He turned his attention to stoking the fire beneath the cauldron.

Saina stared silently into the courtyard. Vandakk was correct, couriers arrived daily, sometimes more often than that. But this knowledge did not lessen her unease. "It seemed a matter of great importance, that is all," she said, her voice sounding hollow in her own ears.

"There are many matters within the caravanserai that are not made known to us," Vandakk said as he slowly stood up. "It is not worth our time to focus on them and neglect the job that has been entrusted to us." He lifted his eyes, his forehead creased as he tilted his head toward the kettle of tea boiling beside them.

His command was understood. Saina prepared a pitcher of tea and walked to the courtyard, offering the drink to their thirsty guests. With great reluctance, she made her way toward the Sassanian merchant and his men who sat in the arched doorway of his room. The door was open behind them. Inside, the walls were lined with crates of silverware, brass vessels, and large sacks of oak galls. With their legs outstretched, they made no move to ease her path through the tangled group as she filled their cups.

Saina thought of Miunai and what she must have felt at night, alone in the desert, surrounded by these men.

She felt the Sassanian's eyes on her, and when she turned to face him, he worked his mouth into a smirk. "Do you know what happens when you treat feral dogs with kindness, giving shelter and food to such thankless beasts?" he said, his words dripping with disdain.

Saina swallowed. She knew he spoke about Miunai and her son, but it was a bold question, nonetheless.

"You create a nuisance that begs the hand and bites the heel," he said to the laughter of the men around him.

Saina clenched her jaw. Men like this saw Narisaf's mother as a dog to be mistreated. They were the same kind of men who stole Miunai's dignity, a woman with no other choice but to risk her own life in the hopes her son received better.

She narrowed her eyes. "And what should be said about the loathsome man who takes advantage of a desperate woman?" she said, her voice low. "He is a snake in the grass, the lowest of all creatures. Even dogs stand taller than him."

Saina's boldness sent her heart beating wildly within her. With a trembling hand, she gripped the pitcher tighter and spun around, leaving the men to stare in silence.

———

The sun had set, and cressets were lit throughout the courtyard. Beneath their dancing light, merchants reclined on rugs, waiting for the evening meal to be served.

A musician had taken his place under the sycamore tree. His mouth grazed the lip of the ney as he soothed the weary merchants with its wind-like sound. Sojourners who had not already taken their place in the courtyard stood in the doorways of their rooms, listening.

Vandakk pulled blistered rounds of bread from the tandoor and set them on top of a mounding tray to cool in the brisk night air, then he looked up at Saina. "I have a dish to delight your mouth and satisfy your appetite." He wiped the sweat on his brow with a thin cloth before spooning a ladle of pilaf into a bowl. "Eat quickly," he said, handing it to her.

Saina took the bowl and found a quiet spot against the wall and inhaled the pleasing aroma. She pinched the pilaf between a strip of torn bread, her hand hovering near her mouth as she scanned the courtyard. It was Kang Dahan's rule that servants were not allowed to eat in front of guests, but she had not eaten since early this morning, and no one seemed to pay any attention.

Each bite she took soothed the burn of hunger in her belly. With the bowl empty and the final morsel in her mouth, she looked up in time to see Bao Li walking toward her, her mouth set in a hard line, determination in her step.

Saina choked on her food. She began to cough and covered her mouth. Chewing quickly, she tried to swallow down the pilaf. She had betrayed Bao Li's trust yet again. What would be her reprimand? Saina thought of the caged birds, silent and still.

"I have received word that my husband has arrived in Chach," Bao Li said, clutching a scroll. She shook it in the empty space between them.

Saina frowned. That was why the courier arrived in haste, the reason for her unease.

Bao Li continued. "Upon completion of his business, he will make the last leg of his journey home. We are to expect him within the moon cycle."

Saina looked into the sky where the moon hung silently, casting pale light upon the caravanserai. She had anticipated Kang Dahan's arrival and knew it would be soon, but such knowledge did not lessen the dread settling within her. The pilaf, which satisfied her moments before, turned sour in her stomach.

Kang Dahan's caravan had trekked east late the previous summer with camel teams finely dressed in gold-and-silver-threaded saddlebags, their sturdy backs piled high with bulging sacks of saffron, indigo, sugar beets, and asafetida, a resin coveted by dignitaries and wealthy families, which fetched a high price.

The weight of the goods on the camels' backs had caused the

sacks and crates to groan and creak, and the chime of the bells hanging from their necks rang out as the camels shifted their weight. Saina had watched from the upper balcony as the caravan lumbered through the gates and onto the Silk Road. She had never grown tired of the magnificent sight.

Not long after his departure, Bao Li had received a letter from Kang Dahan, confessing that the trip had already proven to be more harrowing than he had anticipated. Their misfortune started little more than a fortnight into their journey when his lead puller, a man who Kang Dahan had loved like a brother, fell while securing goods on the back of a camel. His only consolation was that his handler's final, terrible breaths were cut short by Kang Dahan's merciful hand and the blade of his sword.

Upon the puller's death, the gates of their suffering were thrown open. With the body still fresh in the grave, mountain-sides gave way to the pounding of heavy rains, forcing the caravan to frequently alter course. Kang Dahan admitted his suspicion that their trip had been cursed. 'Burn incense in my name in hopes of our safe return,' he wrote. 'For I fear this journey is demanding a portion of our souls every day.'

Saina had waited for Bao Li's orders to purchase incense from the city, but the orders did not come.

Several moon cycles had passed before Bao Li received another letter informing her of his delayed return. His caravan had crested the Pamirs, but they were chased down the eastern slope by an early winter storm. After skirting the edge of the dreaded Takla-makan Desert and mourning the untimely deaths of three more handlers in the caravan—a tragic event that he was still too shaken to speak of—they arrived in Kashgar with a weariness that had slowed their step. In all, they had lost fifteen camels, eight yaks, and four handlers but had retained their most valuable goods, and to that end, the trip was a success. He asked nothing of her this time, only stating that they would remain in Kashgar until the spring thaw reopened the mountain passage.

The letters had ceased, and the land became still as the trees dropped their leaves, sleeping naked beneath silver, paper-thin clouds. The caravanserai quieted as it often did in winter, when trade was left to the hardiest of men, those whose reticent strength lay in the thickness of their blood and the silence of their suffering.

Kang Dahan believed he was such a man, but arrogance had gripped his heart. He had refused to acknowledge the suffering he placed upon Bao Li when he brought a second wife into their home.

Saina had felt the tension immediately, but in the hollow span of his absence, contention had festered between his two wives. The question was, which wife would Kang Dahan believe upon his return?

Bao Li stood rigid before her, a sheen of sweat on her brow.

A chill rippled through Saina's core. "What will happen if Ning Po accuses us before Kang Dahan?" She swallowed hard. "Of murdering his...heir?"

Bao Li's eyes bore into Saina's, but she seemed to look through her, her thoughts far away.

"My husband is a foolish man," she finally said, her lips pursed, her mouth whiskered by thin lines of age. "He is like a tree whose roots have been planted in shifting sand, easily uprooted by the slightest wind of deceit." She cleared her throat, her eyes narrowed as she studied the faces in the courtyard.

Was she searching for Ning Po?

"He took that woman as his wife, but her tongue is split like a serpent's. No truth can come from her. It is a shame he cannot see it."

At this Bao Li paused, choosing her next words carefully. "But it is an even greater betrayal to expect me to live with it." Bao Li crumpled the scroll in her fist, her knuckles turning white. She threw it into the glowing embers beneath the cauldron of pilaf. The scroll twisted and curled in on itself.

"Kang Dahan will expect a feast upon his return," she said, her voice sharp as though her words could cut him from the letter and rid him from her memory altogether. Saying nothing more, she spun on her heel and walked away.

Saina stared after Bao Li until her mistress was swallowed up by the press of merchants. When she looked back, the scroll was gone. The fire had consumed it.

Chapter Fifteen

Saina pulled the silk blouse and long wrap from Bao Li's gold-leaf wardrobe and held them up. "Shall I pack your favored *ruqun*?" she said. Even after many years of living in Samarkand, Bao Li refused to wear anything but the traditional clothing of her homeland behind the Great Wall.

Bao Li looked up from the jewelry box opened before her. "Yes," she said slowly, her eyes distant, as though sifting through a tangle of thoughts. She pulled the folded square of mulberry paper from the silk-lined base of the box.

Saina yawned and blinked away the burn in her eyes. A night servant had awakened her long before the sun rose with news that Bao Li was leaving for Penjikent this morning, three days earlier than her scheduled trip. The sudden decision sent Saina scrambling, and she had not slowed since.

She folded the long wrap and set it inside the trunk with Bao Li's other garments, an embroidered waistcoat, and pointed leather shoes. "And these?" she asked, holding the ivory comb and hairpins.

But Bao Li did not respond as she unfolded the letter and slowly ran her fingers over the faded symbols.

The letter was written in the language of Bao Li's homeland;

Saina did not know what it said or who it was from. She had seen Bao Li read it on days such as this, when melancholy darkened her countenance. And although the letter drew great emotion, it seemed also to soothe a deep ache within her.

Bao Li turned to Saina, her eyes wet. "Look through my trunk again. Ensure that everything I require is packed. My husband's arrival has forced me to hasten my trip. With my sudden departure, I fear I am forgetting something." She dropped her hands to her sides, the letter held delicately between her fingertips.

Saina placed the comb and hairpins inside the trunk and stepped toward her. "Do not allow such thoughts to trouble you," she said. "I trust you will complete your business in Penjikent and return before he arrives."

Bao Li's jaw tensed. She pulled the letter close to her chest. "It is not as simple as you say, Saina. There are many things you do not understand." She looked away.

Silence hung between them. Saina searched the pained expression on her mistress's face, waiting for her to speak.

When she did, her voice was quiet. "I am not traveling to Penjikent for matters of business," Bao Li said, lifting her face to meet Saina's. But her skin was pallid, her eyes heavy as though pulled down by a great weight.

Saina swallowed, her throat thick with dread. She waited for Bao Li to say more, but no explanation came. Garnering strength, she asked the question whose answer she feared. "Are you leaving us?"

Bao Li shook her head slowly. "I will return, but only because there is nowhere else for me to go."

A rush of relief flowed through Saina.

"Nothing from my old life remains for me," Bao Li said, then paused, as though it was her turn to find the strength for what would be spoken next. "You must know that I had no other option but to be the wife Kang Dahan demanded of me. I swallowed my love for Chen Tien and tried to bury reminders of my beautiful life before coming to this distant land. For a long time, I fooled myself. In duty I succeeded. With Kang Dahan's constant absence, I kept his caravanserai running," she huffed. "Thriving, even."

Saina looked at the gold perfume bottles lining the wall in Bao Li's bedroom, the painted murals, carved wooden furniture, and fine rugs. Truly this was a life of opulence. She turned back, but Bao Li's eyes were set upon her like black stones.

"Do not think that I was fooled by these things," Bao Li said sharply. "My happiness was not bought by their hollow gifting."

"Please, my lady, I would give no such thought to—"

"None of it could satisfy the longing deep within me," Bao Li said, cutting Saina off. "My only regret is that it took so long to peel back the bitter layers of my heart. For at its very center, I found that Chen Tien had remained there all along." She shook her head.

Bao Li turned around, and Saina was struck by the light in her eyes, the youthfulness in her face. Her secret no longer held sway over her.

"In a moment of weakness, I scrawled a letter to him confessing my abiding love. With trembling hand, I sealed it up and sent it out. But when I did not receive word in return, I gave up hope, convinced myself I had been foolish." A faint smile creased her mouth. "Until the day a letter arrived, bound with the familiar braided grasses that grew along the riverbanks of my homeland."

Bao Li's eyes watered as she held up the mulberry paper with the faded words. "I did not have to open it to know it was from Chen Tien. I remember clearly our first kiss hidden in those tall blades of grass, the flowing water tickling our toes." Through her tears, her face was lit with mirth.

"The letter was written in his brother's hand, for Chen Tien had never learned to read or write the ancient symbols. He admitted it brought him great shame, but it did not matter to me. I used to read him stories written on scrolls taken from my father's house. They were an entry into worlds we did not know, setting loose our imaginations.

He shared that he had watched from the cover of the trees the day I was married to Kang Dahan, and his heart shattered into a thousand pieces that could never be reassembled. To him, his future had become like the stories in my father's scrolls...he could not know it, could not imagine it, without me by his side."

Bao Li looked longingly at the letter. "He took ill shortly after receiving my first letter. I consulted the apothecary, sending all manner of medicine. I paid a handsome sum for a nurse from his village to care for him, but my efforts were in vain."

Saina could not pull her eyes from Bao Li. Who was this strong woman she had served faithfully all these years, yet knew so little about?

"As autumn waned and the cold winds were pulled down from the north, a final letter arrived." Bao Li folded the paper and held it up. "Just a few unadorned symbols, scrawled in the hand of a dying man. These I have committed to memory. Chen Tien died in peace knowing that I loved him still. His heart was whole once again."

Bao Li stared off into a long, straight silence.

Finally, she slipped the paper into the silk lining and inhaled a shaking breath. "I am going to Penjikent to meet Chen Tien's brother and bring gifts for his family, as I have done the past four years." She crossed the room to where an intricately carved box had been set out.

Shocked by Bao Li's admission, Saina followed silently.

Bao Li turned and faced Saina, studied her for a moment. "I see you are troubled, but do not worry yourself. There is nothing between us but the shared love for Chen Tien. Visiting his brother has brought me back to myself, a reminder of who I once was." She shook her head. "This trip is to be his last. The trek has become too great for his aged body." Bao Li looked up, her eyes hard. "But Kang Dahan's arrival has forced me to hasten my journey. Now I can only hope that Chen Tien's brother arrives in Penjikent before I must make my return home."

"What if you are found out?" Saina said.

Bao Li shrugged. "I have not been unfaithful." She picked up a silver flask and packed it in the carved box along with a satchel of flower seeds purchased from Samarkand's famed gardens, a bolt of fine silk, and three jars of the honey Bao Li had secured from the honey merchant.

Closing the lid, Bao Li picked up the box. "If my trip goes as planned, I will return within ten days."

Saina lowered her gaze. "And if Kang Dahan returns before you do?" she said, the thought twisting her stomach.

Bao Li stilled. "Do not worry yourself over such matters. I will not leave you to face him alone."

Saina pressed her lips tight. She trusted Bao Li's word, but traveling the Silk Road was dangerous. Even with highly skilled guards, safety was guaranteed to no one.

Outside Bao Li's bedroom, the scrape of rushing footsteps drew near. The stable girl appeared in the doorway and bowed her head.

"Your camels have been prepared and brought out to the courtyard. If you are ready, I will send the men to load your trunk." She looked anxiously around the room. "I urge you to depart quickly, for already the courtyard is packed with merchants preparing to do the same. Soon the road will be crowded, and your journey will be slowed."

At the stable girl's warning, Saina remembered Miunai and Uta, a sense of urgency gripping her. Why had she not thought of them until now?

"My lady," Saina said. "I welcomed a woman and her son to stay in the caravanserai last night after the men they traveled with told them to stay alone by the canal." Saina swallowed. "They, too, are going to Penjikent. I implore you to allow them to travel with you in the safety of your caravan, for I fear the abuse she will receive if she is forced to continue with such men."

Bao Li furrowed her brow. "A woman traveling alone invites trouble," she said with a curt nod. "You did well by her."

For the first time since Saina walked into the khana this morning, Bao Li seemed occupied by a different thought.

"A woman and young child would be a welcomed distraction in my caravan. But they must not slow me down. Tell her she will be safe in the company of myself and my guards if she wishes to come along."

Saina drew her hand to her heart, grateful for Bao Li's kindness. She turned to leave, excited to give Miunai the news.

"And Saina," Bao Li said, stopping her.

Saina spun around.

"If they choose to travel with me, ensure that Vandakk packs enough provisions for their trip as well."

———

Saina knocked softly on the door and was met with Miunai's voice on the other side. It sounded as thin and worn out as the homespun shawl she had draped over her thin shoulders when Saina first saw her walking along the banks of the canal yesterday.

She stepped inside and saw the worried lines in Miunai's tired face. Uta lay beside his mother, wrapped in a thick blanket, his head resting in her lap.

Miunai smiled quickly at Saina, but her eyes were deeply troubled. They darted to the courtyard where the Sassanian merchant and his men had gathered, preparing their camels for the day's trek.

"Do not let your heart be troubled, for I come bearing good news," Saina said kneeling down, her heart light. "My mistress is leaving for Penjikent this morning. She has welcomed you to travel in the safety of her caravan."

Miunai's eyes brightened as she sat up. "Both Uta and myself?"

Saina nodded. "You would do well to accept her offer. She will ensure that you are fed and treated with kindness."

Relief washed over Miunai's face. She leaned her head back against the wall and wept.

Uta stirred. "Mama?" He tilted his head back and looked long at her, but she pulled him to her breast, holding him tightly.

"Do you remember how I told you not to fear, Uta?" Miunai said, her eyes glistening in the candlelight. "God of heaven has provided us safe passage, just as I trusted he would."

Uta yawned, pushing away from his mother. "But I am tired," he said, rubbing his eyes.

"Will you travel with us?" Miunai said, her eyes searching Saina's.

Saina shook her head. "My duty remains in Samarkand, but I take comfort knowing you will return to Penjikent safely." She turned to Uta and tousled his hair. "Come, we will fetch your provisions, but we must move in haste. Bao Li's caravan is leaving soon."

Uta eyed her suspiciously, but at his mother's urging, he stood up and slipped his hand into hers.

Saina helped gather their simple belongings and led them to the storeroom, where the scent of spiced meat and cooked bread greeted them.

Vandakk took no notice of them as he rushed along the shelves, pulling down spices and tea leaves.

"Look, Mama," Uta said, his eyes wide as he walked toward the shelves stacked with goods. He ran his fingers along baskets heaped with walnuts and pomegranates, pine nuts and apricots.

Vandakk spun around at the sound of Uta's voice, and smiled. "The boy has good taste," he said, the lilt of laughter playing on his tongue.

"Yes, and it is with great fortune," Saina said. "They are joining Bao Li's caravan to Penjikent. We have come on orders to ensure enough food is provided for their travel as well."

Vandakk clapped his hands together. "This is welcomed news, but I require your help if we are to be ready in time."

Saina nodded and stepped forward, but Uta called out, stopping her.

"What is this?" Uta said, approaching them. He held out a large, stuffed vine leaf in his small hand.

"Uta," Miunai said, stepping toward him. "Do not touch the food. We must not be a burden." She turned to Vandakk, her face red. "I am sorry, my son, he does not—"

"No, no, let him," Vandakk said, clicking his tongue. "Nothing in my kitchen is too fine to deny a curious child a taste." He smiled at Uta. "This is dolma. Vine leaves stuffed with spiced meat. Try it."

Vandakk's face softened, as though youth, having long since slipped away, returned to him. Saina smiled. Vandakk was a gentle man, his rough edges smoothed long ago by the winds of hardship. If given the chance, he would have been a good father. Saina was certain of this.

Uta took a cautious bite, pushing the dolma around in his mouth. He took notice of Saina watching him and smiled with a shyness that reminded her of Narisaf.

"Do you like it?" Vandakk asked. When Uta grinned, Vandakk motioned for the boy to follow him. "Come, you can help me finish the last of the preparations for your trip."

Saina handed Miunai a basket and pointed to the shelves at the far end of the kitchen. "Fill your basket with the hard-crust bread which has been prepared for your long journey. It will be your sustenance once the fresh provisions are eaten."

Miunai returned as Saina filled two more containers with dried fruit and salt meat. She set the basket of bread on the center table and gripped Saina's hand tightly. "I must confide that I had lost all hope this morning," Miunai said, her voice barely a whisper. "I said I trusted God, but each passing moment became more desperate. During the evening meal, I sought out other merchants who were traveling to Penjikent, begged them to allow us to travel with them, but they all refused my pleas. I could not sleep last night, fearing what would become of my son and I." Her eyes glistened in the storeroom's candlelight. "But I resigned myself to this duty and hoped they would not mistreat me again."

Saina embraced Miunai. "You will be safe now," she said. "Bao Li's guards are good men; her livestock handlers are full of knowledge. Do not fear the return to your father's home."

"I will remember your kindness," Miunai said, squeezing Saina's hand.

From across the room, Saina studied Uta's childish face, his soft skin, and the way he searched Vandakk with wide eyes. Relief flowed through her. Uta would not experience the same fate Narisaf did, his mother's abuse seared like a brand in his memories.

Vandakk worked quickly, stuffing the vine leaves and folding them together. Wrapping the dolma in a cloth, he placed them in a basket and gave it to Uta as they approached.

"Eat the dolma first or it will spoil," Vandakk said. "The rest will keep the length of your trip."

Together they walked out of the storeroom, Vandakk and Saina carrying several large baskets filled with food for Bao Li, her guards, and the livestock handlers.

When they reached the open air of the courtyard, Uta ran ahead. Vandakk clicked his tongue and called after him. "Slow down, Uta, or you will startle the animals." He shook his head, his voice full of concern. "You are like a sandstorm coming from the west. One must not take their eyes off you."

Miunai stopped to scold her son, and Saina turned to Vandakk. "Did you ever long for children?"

"Oh, yes," he said without hesitation. "But it was not to be, so I found my joy in a different way." He tapped the food in his hand, his eyes softening. "But on the rare occasion that a child visits the caravanserai, I feel a twinge of sadness at what I have missed all these years."

Saina slowed. Would that be her fate too? Childless? The thought opened a familiar sadness deep within.

She pushed the thought aside and searched the courtyard. The Sassanian merchant and his men had cleared out. In their spot was Bao Li's colorful caravan, with towering camels dressed in finely threaded saddlebags, braided harnesses, and painted bells strung down their long necks.

Saina looked for Bao Li through the crush of animals and saw her emerge from her khana holding the gift box close to her chest. Two servants followed, carrying her trunk on their shoulders. They shuffled beneath its weight.

"Put it here," she said in a rush, pointing to the ground beside the rear camel where several handlers worked quickly, cinching down the supplies with thick leather straps.

"This will remain with me," Bao Li said, handing Makh the wooden gift box. When she turned back, her eyes fell on Miunai and then Uta, and she smiled. "I see you have taken up my offer," she said.

Miunai bowed her head slightly. "We are indebted to you, but I fear we have nothing to give in return. Perhaps my father will have a way to pay you when we reach Penjikent."

"Do not speak of it," Bao Li said. "You traveled this far at the mercy of unprincipled men. That is hardship enough. I will not heap another burden upon your shoulders." She motioned for Saina to follow and walked to the front of the caravan where her camel waited.

"You have done well, Saina" she said as Makh helped her into the shade of the howdah on the camel's back. He handed her the box, then at his urging, the camel stood, rising up from the dust of the courtyard. Bao Li leaned down, the sun shining on her face. "I trust you and Vandakk will keep the caravanserai in order during my absence."

"Yes," Saina said. "And we will work to prepare the feast for Kang Dahan's arrival."

Bao Li offered a stiff smile. "You are to me like a child from my womb. I do not know what I would do without you." She looked away as the lead camel began to walk, setting the caravan in motion.

By the time they ambled through the courtyard, a knot had formed in Saina's throat, tears stinging her eyes. Bao Li had treated her with every undeserved kindness. It was an honor to be trusted with her mistress's deepest held secrets. She would not let her down.

She watched as the unforgiving desert seized the distance between them, blurring their sharp lines, until one by one, Bao Li and her caravan faded away.

Chapter Sixteen

In the three days since Bao Li's departure, all the servants had begun the great task of preparing for Kang Dahan's arrival. New paint was applied to faded doors, and wine was brought from the vineyards. Rooms tucked deep within the inner corridors were cleared of their stored items and replaced with silver ewers, wax candles, and bed mats for the townspeople that would join in the celebration.

Vandakk was most affected by the weighty obligations. With the exception of serving morning and evening meals to their guests, little had been seen of him. As usual, he buried himself in the task of taking stock of goods and planning a feast that had demanded more of his energy with each passing year. So, when Saina found him asleep at the back of the storeroom, beside the shelves of warming stones and rising bread, she took the cleaning paddle and set out to the courtyard.

She poured a bucket of water into the cauldron and stared hard at the charred remains of the morning meal. Meat cakes, rice, and sticky pomegranate sauce had baked like clay to the rounded sides. Soon, the coals smoldering beneath the cauldron would bring the water to a boil and help loosen the food from the walls.

With the wooden paddle in hand, Saina bent over the cauldron and began scraping. Steam billowed in her face. She marveled at the speed at which Vandakk could complete this task. He would have been finished by now.

In the monotony, she fell into a rhythm, her mind occupied with thoughts of Narisaf and the way he appeared when she least expected him. Time quickly passed in this way, the chore bringing its own sort of comfort. Perhaps he would do the same today, surprising her with his sudden arrival and bringing news of his grandfather's health. It had been seven days since she last saw him, and each passing day her longing burned greater. Something had taken hold of his time and kept him away, but what?

A movement at the gates drew Saina's attention. She set the paddle in the cauldron and looked up expectantly, but instead of seeing Narisaf dismounting his horse at the entrance, she saw a single sojourner entering with his horse, nothing behind them but the vast desert.

She closed her eyes and tilted her head back, the sun warming her face. How foolish of her to hold such hope.

When she opened her eyes again, Vandakk was approaching.

He peered into the cauldron, then looked at her. "I meant to lay my head down for only a short time." He yawned.

"You needed rest," Saina said.

"I did not intend for you to take on this task," he said. "But since you have done such a fine job, perhaps you can add it to your daily chores?"

Saina put her hand to her hip and shook her head as he chuckled.

After a moment Vandakk's smile faded. "I know you are busy, Saina, but I must make one more request of your time. I have a few items to secure at the bazaar, and I ask that you join me."

Saina straightened at the unexpected news.

"It has been a long while since we went together, and I could use your help with the donkey," he continued. "You know she is too difficult for me to handle alone."

"I would be glad to join you."

"Very well," he said, taking the paddle from her. "Prepare the donkey while I finish cleaning this mess."

Saina stepped away and walked toward the stables, excitement swelling at the turn of events. She would not have to wait for Narisaf to come to the caravanserai. She would go to him instead.

———

Children gathered at the fringes of the bazaar, their high laughter drawing Saina's attention. Like bees in a hive, they swarmed around the ice merchant who stood proudly beside his yak-drawn cart, his hand resting on top of the layers of wool and fur blankets that covered the contents.

He was the same leather-faced man Saina had visited in her youth. Though his hair had since become gray, little else about him had changed.

Twice a year he came down from the high country selling the season's first offering of sour cherries and fish pulled from clear springs, but it was the ice he packed to keep his goods fresh that drew the children to him.

"It was a long trek from the mountain passages near my home to Samarkand," the ice merchant said as he stretched out his hand, his sharp finger drawing circles around the white peaks in the distance. "I sold all the goods that I set out with, but my yaks are weary and do not want to pull the ice back to the mountains. Will you take this burden from us?" He pulled back the blankets, exposing a block of ice as translucent as the clear crystals sold in the bazaar.

Squeals of delight filled the air. The eager children pressed closer to one another as the merchant broke off small chunks with his mallet and placed them into outstretched hands.

Saina turned to Vandakk, "Do you remember the first time you brought me to see the ice merchant?"

Vandakk grinned. "How could I forget? The moment he

placed the ice in your hand, you cried out and dropped it on the ground."

"I thought it burned me," Saina said. "But the other children did not seem bothered, so I picked it up and put it in my satchel. I thought I could show it to my father when"—she stopped, surprised at the sudden remembrance—"when he came back for me."

Vandakk's eyes shimmered. "Oh, how my heart ached when we arrived at the caravanserai, and you told us of your plans. You tried to show it to Bao Li, only to find it had melted. You wept to learn that it could not be brought back."

Saina was silent for a moment. "I did not know that this desert land, with all the beauty contained within, was not meant to sustain such a thing," she said quietly.

"Every person who walks the dust of this land long enough will come to know this truth," Vandakk said. "But it is how we react to such knowledge that defines us. We all have a choice."

Did anything of value ever last? The cruel thought haunted Saina, but she vowed to keep it to herself for fear that her babbling would expose her weakness. She must choose to press on, to be strong and remain loyal to Bao Li and her work in the caravanserai. Lowering her head, she fell into step beside Vandakk as they continued to the bazaar.

Colorful banners snapped in the breeze beside a merchant selling kingfisher feathers, tortoise shells, and rabbit pelts. Smoke from meats cooking on long grills swirled into the walkway, their scent a welcomed distraction that helped loosen the fetters of the unpleasant memory.

Ahead, Zimat pushed bread into his oven as the sharp fragrance of za'atar spice wafted from his stall.

When he straightened, his eyes flashed with surprise. He rushed toward them. "Vandakk, you have been gone for so long I thought the desert had swallowed you up," he said, pulling Vandakk into his big belly. After a moment, he stood back, holding him at arm's length. "Tell me, where have you been, my friend?"

"Cooking day and night," Vandakk said, laughing, but Saina saw the weariness in his eyes. "The caravanserai is bursting with guests, more than I have seen before."

"You would have it no other way, my friend," Zimat said, clapping him on the back. "Perhaps with reports of fewer attacks on caravans and small bands of sojourners, hesitant travelers are willing to risk the journey. I am certain Kang Dahan is glad for it. There are rumblings around the city that his return is soon."

Vandakk nodded. "It is for this reason we have come today. Arrangements for his feast are being made now, and I need your help to purchase the finest rye flour and prepare the bread. Our ovens will not accommodate so many loaves. You will be paid a handsome sum."

"Of course, I would be honored to help," Zimat said, bowing his head. "The caravanserai is alive with excitement at the looming celebration, yes?" He looked at Saina and nodded, as though expecting no other answer.

"There is much to do in preparation," Saina said, offering a quick smile. She hoped this gesture would seem agreeable, but the dread of Kang Dahan's arrival lurked just below the surface. It would do no good to offer an opinion to the contrary.

"As it should be," Zimat said, turning back to Vandakk. "Grand feasts require grand preparation. But for you, I will do anything to help lighten your load."

At Vandakk's acknowledgment, Zimat leaned close, his voice lowered. "My heart grew heavy the other day when I saw Saina walking through the bazaar with a man other than yourself. I feared Bao Li had replaced you with a younger, far more handsome cook." Zimat sent a bark of laughter into the air.

Saina feared the suspicion his observation would cause and stepped forward. "That was Narisaf of whom you speak," she said quickly. "Vandakk sent us to purchase medicine for his grandfather, the weaver."

Zimat's eyes widened. "Ah, yes, Narisaf." He was thoughtful for a moment as he walked back to his stall and took the long, wooden paddle off the shelf beside his oven. "I have not yet met him but have heard he is a man of fine character. And rumor has spread that he caught the eye of the perfumer's daughter." He slid the paddle into the oven and pulled out two loaves of bread.

Saina's heart sank. Is that why Narisaf had stayed away? Had he found someone else? After all, she had nothing to offer him, not even a single lamb or donkey to her name. Her legs felt heavy, as though the earth was pulling her down into its dust.

Zimat did not seem to notice; his voice grew distant in Saina's ears as he continued. "The perfumer approached the Weaver, so I was told, offering his daughter to Narisaf in marriage. He even presented them with a handsome dowry and the promise of lavish living. But they *denied* his offer," he said, his eyes wide with astonishment.

Relief flooded Saina, a sudden release from that which threatened to draw her away, but it was replaced by a different thought. Had Narisaf turned down the request because of her? She lowered her head, hoping her relief would not be too evident.

"Few men would turn down such an offer unless he already had his heart set on a woman," Vandakk said.

Zimat shook his head. "But there has been no sight of another woman nor mention of her name. Why else would he come all this way if not to marry?"

Saina studied the steam swirling up from the bread. It spread out beneath the covering of his awning. "Narisaf's mother was a Sogdian, born in Samarkand," she said. "Perhaps he came only to see the city where she once walked and to learn the ways of the people who inhabit the land."

The answer seemed to satisfy Zimat. He nodded slowly. "There may be truth in what you say. A man must know his roots in order to know himself." He motioned toward the bread.

Vandakk pulled coins from his purse, but Zimat waved him off. "Not today, old friend. Take it and enjoy."

They forged through the crowds purchasing extra sacks of wheat and rice, braided garlic, walnuts and currants. With each stop, the cart creaked and sagged under the added weight. The sun had long moved past its midpoint when Vandakk stopped. "There is one more stop we must make," he said. "When Bao Li left, she requested new tapestries be purchased and hung throughout the caravanserai..." he paused, his statement lingering in the air. "Should we see what the weaver has to offer?"

"Yes," Saina said, trying to control the excitement building within her. "His tapestries are finer than any other I have seen. You will be pleased."

"Then we should go before the day grows old," Vandakk said, smiling at Saina. "I trust you know the way."

———

From the end of the walkway, Saina spotted Narisaf tenderly stroking the long neck of his tethered horse. Beside him a stable boy, with sleeves too short for his long arms, laid alfalfa in the trough.

Deep in conversation, they seemed unaware of Saina and Vandakk's approach.

"What happened?" the boy said, pointing to the jagged scar on the horse's belly, raised up from its flesh like the spine of the cragged mountains cutting across the sky.

"Battle wounds," Narisaf said. "She was bred to charge fearlessly into flying arrows and bellowed war cries. Though she's too old for such feats now, courage still courses through her blood."

Saina smiled. How true that trait was of Narisaf, too, a man of courage and honor.

As though suddenly aware of her presence, Narisaf looked over his shoulder, his gaze falling on her. His face brightened. Without saying more, he left the boy and drew near, his eyes holding Saina's.

For a moment, the colorful stalls and bustling people filling the walkway faded. Only Narisaf remained. Saina reached out to greet him, but Vandakk's voice brought her back.

"You are popular among the youth," Vandakk said.

Saina stopped suddenly, pulling her hand back.

"It seems that way," Narisaf said, glancing over his shoulder at the boy who had begun pouring water for the horse. "For three days now, Lushan has met me at the stables, asking to feed her. His persistence has left me with no other choice."

"That is a sign of a good man," Vandakk chuckled. He walked along the outer edge of the stall, pointing to several hanging tapestries. "Is all this your grandfather's work?"

The weaver shuffled toward them. "Most were completed by me," he said, extending a warm smile. "Narisaf set his hand to a few of them. He has an eye for fine threads, the careful hands for such delicate, masterful work. But he is like his father, preferring to ride on his horse than sit at the loom all day."

"Horsemen are highly sought after," Vandakk said, his playful gaze on Narisaf. "Perhaps that is why you have caught the eye of the perfumer's daughter?"

Narisaf's face reddened. He looked at Saina and grimaced. "Her attention was unwanted; her father's offer of marriage even more so."

"We have heard," Saina said.

"Two elders of the city meddled in the affair, telling us we were foolish to deny such an offer." He groaned low in disgust and shook his head.

"Take no offense. *They* are the fools for growing old while concerning themselves with matters that do not pertain to them," Vandakk said.

"You speak the words of my heart," the weaver said. "I am preparing tea. Will you join me?"

"Of course." Vandakk followed the weaver into the stall. "But first I would like to conduct a matter of business."

Saina remained with Narisaf, grateful for the moment alone.

"You have been busy these past days," she said, her voice light, teasing.

A shy smile pushed up the corners of his mouth. "The perfumer's daughter was only a distraction for the townspeople." He took her hand in his and gently stroked it. "Be assured, my days have been filled only with thoughts of you."

Saina tilted her chin up. "It is the same with me." Then she peered at Vandakk as he walked through the stall with the weaver, looking at the tapestries. "I was glad when he asked me to join him today, but I do not know when I will return. There is still much to do before Kang Dahan arrives."

"I will come to you, but I must heed Umida's warning. I do not want to cause you dishonor in any way."

"I understand," Saina said, her heart sinking. "If only things were different."

"It will not be this way for long."

Saina nodded and searched his eyes. How could he speak with such certainty?

"Did you make this warhorse garment?" Vandakk said, his voice carrying from inside the tent.

The garment. Saina quickly pulled her hand away from Narisaf's and looked toward them.

The Weaver nodded. "It is my creation. Many layers of history are tucked within those threads, but only two men have ever worn it. One was my son who fought on the battlefields of nations." He paused and looked intently at Saina. "The other was a man who fought the battle within his own mind."

Saina understood that he was speaking of her father. She shrank back, sensing there was a story he wanted her to know. She looked at Narisaf, then at his horse and the raised scar running along her belly. Another memory slowly unfolded, building on itself until the remembrance became clear.

She was standing with her father outside the stables while he stroked the pearl-colored neck of a warhorse. He was speaking to a man with leather-wrapped wrists and a bow and quiver of arrows drawn over his back. When the man turned to Saina, he smiled, and his dark brown eyes were as warm as spiced clove.

She looked once again at Narisaf's warhorse, a knot forming in her throat.

Was this the same horse her father had trained all those years ago? She studied its face, then closed her eyes, inhaling the familiar scent of dust and sweat and muscle. She thought of the ice she had saved for her father. Though it melted long ago, could it be that a part of him had finally returned?

She pinched her eyes shut, trying to hold on to the vision.

"Saina?" Vandakk's voice lifted the fog of her memory.

The vision disappeared. She could not call it back. Saina opened her eyes.

"Are you well?" he said, his face creased with concern.

"Yes," she said, her voice barely a whisper. She turned to Narisaf, seeking the comfort only his presence brought, and saw in his eyes a reflection of the warrior in her memory.

She was ready to learn the truth about her father, about the garment, and the men from Merv who tied them together.

Chapter Seventeen

K neeling along the edge of the Dargom Canal, Saina dipped the last bucket into the flowing water. The pulse of the water rushed over the brim, adding to its weight as she pulled the bucket onto the bank and stared out across the canal.

Orchards extended as far as her eyes could see. Hidden beyond the rolling hills and the workers tending endless rows of peach and almond trees was the city of Samarkand. The bazaar. And Narisaf.

Saina craned her neck, searching the road. She had been expecting Narisaf's arrival since leaving the bazaar with Vandakk the other day, when the weaver assured Vandakk that he would complete the final tapestry and have Narisaf deliver it in two days' time. She hoped to catch sight of him, but all she saw was a caravan so distant the camels looked like the tiny figurines hawked in the bazaar.

The day rolled out slowly, as it often does when a highly anticipated event lies on the horizon. But the sun was now setting on the second day, and he had not arrived.

"Has he been delayed?" Saina said out loud, but the only creatures there to receive her question were the finches flitting in the scrub brush along the opposite bank, and they offered no consolation.

Heaving the yoke onto her shoulder, Saina left the canal and walked toward the mighty karagach trees lining the outer walls of the caravanserai, their long, finger-like shadows spreading across the desert in the setting sun. Caravans and sojourners alike lined up in their shade, waiting to be granted entry through the gates.

With one last, longing glance over her shoulder, Saina entered the courtyard behind a group of traveling musicians who offered to ply their trade in exchange for food and shelter. These requests were common enough that a small room had been reserved near the stables for such casual entertainers.

She was glad for the distraction of the men with their thick beards, threadbare robes, and flaxen cloth wrapped heads. They were not men of great means, not even a beast of burden accompanied them, but Saina was drawn to their tranquil nature.

"I will take them to their room," Saina said to the guard as she unburdened herself from the yoke and gave the buckets to waiting servants. She led the musicians through the courtyard. Their eyes were wide, their steps slow as they pointed to the upper balcony where merchants gathered, and colorful banners swayed in the breeze.

The smell of livestock grew strong as they drew closer to the stables. Saina pushed open the door to the room and stepped back, allowing the men to walk inside. The small chamber hummed with swarming flies, but the musicians seemed unbothered.

The elder man in the group, with his graying beard and deep-set eyes, went quietly to the ewer set in the corner. Wetting a cloth, he washed his face and hands, while the younger men laid out their belongings. They unrolled bed mats and carefully propped their leather-wrapped instruments against the wall, all the while speaking to one another in a language Saina had never heard. The smooth cadence of their voices was broken only by their soft laughter.

Setting the cloth beside the ewer, the elder musician approached Saina and spoke in broken Sogdian, the language of her people, and the common language of the Silk Road. "My sons and I have come from a land far beyond the Karakoram mountains, to see with our own eyes the golden city of Samarkand and to play our instruments for the people who are staying within the walls of this caravanserai." He swept the room with a glance. "Both have great renown and are spoken of in distant places, but nothing could have prepared us for such grandeur." He closed his eyes as though savoring the moment.

"It is the master's expectation that all traveling entertainers are well cared for with fine food and safety," Saina said.

"I trust you will relay our gratitude." He smiled. "I assure you; such generosity will be rewarded when we play for your guests tonight."

"As is customary for entertainers such as yourself, a meal will be set aside for you to partake of once all merchants have bedded down for the night. Until then, I will see to it that you are given a morsel of bread, fruit, and cheese to satisfy your hunger from the journey."

"Of course. It is our duty to earn our keep," he said, bowing low.

Saina left the musicians and walked through the courtyard, where broth, seasoned with cumin and allspice, boiled in the cauldrons. Unable to find Vandakk through the maze of merchants unloading their goods, she went in search of him in the storeroom.

Vandakk was hunched over a basket, pulling out fresh mint and cilantro when Saina entered. He straightened, and with slow, heavy steps he crossed the room and set them on the table already piled with bowls of cut vegetables and measured lentils and rice.

"Soup tonight?" Saina said, approaching the table.

"Of course," Vandakk said, his voice gravelly.

In the years Saina had worked under Vandakk's guidance, she had learned that this soup came from roots bound in the history he had shared with the only woman he ever loved. Vandakk once told her that he would prepare the soup whenever he was overwhelmed with longing for his wife, but Saina had come to recognize that as the anniversary of her death approached, the soup was eaten often.

"Shall I season the suzma," she said, knowing he preferred to eat the tart, herbed yogurt with the flavorful dish, just like his wife had served it.

"You know me too well," Vandakk said. A thin smile of distant remembrance spread across his face. He picked up the bowl of vegetables and faced Saina. "Join me in the courtyard when you have finished chopping the herbs. The meal is simple, it will come together quickly."

Savoring the rare moment of solitude, Saina finished chopping the mixture of herbs from the garden, then unwrapped the muslin cloth and emptied the suzma into a shallow bowl. As she made a paste from the fresh picking, she saw the flash of gold thread on her leather bracelet peeking out beneath the sleeve of her tunic and smiled.

She remembered the way Narisaf's fingers lingered when he first placed it on her wrist, the strength in his calloused hands. Her longing to see him again had settled like an ache deep within her bones, but such hope proved too painful.

Even if he had come today as promised, their love was hindered. The obstacles between them seemed too great.

———

The sinking sun set the clouds ablaze in the fiery sky as servants lit cressets throughout the courtyard. Merchants filled the empty spaces, lulled by the soothing sounds of the musicians' stringed instruments and flutes carried by the quiet beat of the drum. The hearty scent of soup and hot bread baking in the clay oven grew thick in the night air.

With her back turned to the courtyard, Saina was arranging

the last trays of food on the wooden platform, when she heard the smooth scrape of leather shoes on the stone ground behind her.

"The meal will be served shortly," she said, setting out the honeyed walnuts and dates to be eaten after dinner.

"It is not a meal that I seek," Narisaf said. "Only to look once again upon the woman I love."

Saina spun around, her body suddenly light. "You have come," she said, unable to hide the lilt of surprise in her voice. She looked at the bundle in his hands, plain cloth tied together with a single strand of rope. "And you brought the tapestry. Vandakk will be glad."

"And you?" Narisaf said.

Saina's face reddened. "I have awaited your arrival since morning broke, but my confidence waned as the day grew long."

"You doubted me?" Narisaf's eyes were dark, teasing. He gave the bundle to Saina, his fingers brushing against hers.

It was a moment before her breath returned and the thrum in her chest slowed. She was struck with an intense desire to touch Narisaf, to feel the warmth of his body, the strength held within his flesh, but she held herself back.

She pulled the bundle close. "I feared your grandfather had not finished the tapestry in time," she said, lowering her voice. "And that another day would pass before I saw you again."

Narisaf leaned his hip against the platform. He reached for a date and put it to his mouth. "My grandfather has never been late in completing his work. The tapestry was finished late last night."

Saina straightened. "Yet you waited until the day was nearly over to come?" She offered a quick smile, trying to hide her disappointment.

"I have my reasons," he said, mischief flickering in his eyes.

Vandakk appeared before Saina could inquire more.

"Narisaf, we have awaited your arrival with great anticipation," Vandakk said, eyeing the package in Saina's hands. "May I open it?" He took it from Saina and untied the rope. The tapestry unfolded, exposing finely woven rich colors.

Vandakk looked at the upper balcony outside Saina's room and smiled. "I know just where to hang this to catch Bao Li's eye upon her return."

Stepping back, Vandakk gripped Narisaf's shoulder. "Saina will dress a room for your stay tonight. As you know, it is too late in the day to make your return home. Such travels would be unwise."

Narisaf's shoulders relaxed, as though his well-laid plans had been realized. "I had planned on it."

"Very well," Vandakk said. "I have prepared a special dessert in anticipation. The three of us will share it later tonight."

Saina watched Vandakk fade into the hallway, then she slowly turned back to Narisaf. She shook her head and laughed. "You are far more clever than I believed you to be."

He winked. "I gave you my word."

———

The musicians played quietly as the meal extended long into the night and coals from cook fires cooled beneath the cauldrons.

When Narisaf learned that a group of merchants had arrived from his village of Merv, he sought them out near the sycamore tree, reclining with them around their small warming fire.

Saina passed by often, refilling tea and lingering long enough to hear the shared stories of their travels and news of their city. But it was Narisaf's voice she listened for above it all. Though at times he spoke in the language of his homeland, the soothing tone felt as familiar to her as her own breath.

What would it be like to sit among this crowd, to savor her food and drink her fill with Narisaf by her side? The pitcher grew heavy in her hand. Her desire to be free had set loose a restlessness within her even though her longing could never be satisfied. She could not lay claim to a man's love without great consequence to herself.

Narisaf's deep voice pulled her from her thoughts. He was

sitting up, his soft gaze set upon her. Firelight danced in his clove-colored eyes. "Does enough wine remain in your pitcher to slake my thirst?" he said, holding out his cup.

Saina smiled. Each step that drew her closer to Narisaf helped to ease the uncertainty that had wrapped itself around her. In that moment, it would be enough to serve him.

When the last pitchers of wine and *chal* were finished, the merchants retired to their rooms. One by one, the flicker of golden light beneath their doors was snuffed out. The musicians packed up their instruments and took their leave, carrying with them the plates of food that had been set aside as payment.

All was silent when Saina finally motioned to Narisaf, who was waiting beside the last coals of the small warming fire. Together they made their way to the storeroom to seek out Vandakk, but they found him asleep against the wall, a thin wool blanket pulled up to his shoulders.

Saina glanced toward the kitchen at the back of the storeroom where the evening meal had been cleaned, the kettles scrubbed. The only chore that remained unfinished was to make the bread dough for their morning meal. Saina sighed. Vandakk had worked himself too hard.

She reached down and touched his shoulder, watching the slow rise and fall of his chest. "Vandakk?" she whispered. She regretted having to wake him, to disturb him from the sleep he so badly needed.

His deep breathing broke, his eyes fluttered open. He groaned and sat up slowly. His hand trembled as he pressed his palms to his face. "Have I slept long?" he said, his voice heavy with weariness.

"Do not worry yourself. Night has long set in, but we have only just returned," Saina said, as Vandakk yawned, his shoulders slumped against the wall. "Take your leave while I complete the bread. Daybreak is short in coming."

"I will not burden you with more work," Vandakk protested. "Your days are as long as mine."

Saina glanced quickly at Narisaf as he stooped down and helped Vandakk stand.

"With my help the work will be light," Narisaf said. "I was taught to make bread by my grandfather. My hands are capable."

Vandakk shook his head, but Saina continued. "If you do not rest, you will be overcome with exhaustion before Kang Dahan makes his return. I cannot prepare his feast without your help." She walked to the shelf at the back corner and took a warming stone. Returning to Vandakk, she wrapped it in cloth and gave it to him. "Take this to keep you warm."

He stilled for a long moment, his green eyes searching Saina's. "I am convinced but only for this night. Come the first light of morning, I will fire up the ovens to feed the men who are expecting me," he said defiantly. He turned away and slipped past the leather flap, the patter of his steps fading in the hallway.

Saina placed a large bowl on the table, then walked along the shelves. Pulling down leaven and sugar, she set the ingredients beside the bowl. She looked at Narisaf as he carried a sack of flour from the shelf and set it at her feet.

"Does a beloved cook such as Vandakk make his bed among the servants?" he whispered.

Saina glanced at the small dish of pistachio halva sitting in the center of the table and thought of Vandakk's earlier excitement at partaking of the rich dessert when they returned. She regretted not offering it to him before he left.

"He has a room of his own, similar to mine, with little space for more than a bed mat and a few simple items." She frowned. "But it is nothing compared to the grand room he once had."

She slid the dish of halva between them, and as Narisaf took one, she continued. "As a highly favored cook, Vandakk used to make his bed in the finest room within these corridors. With fine rugs, carved furniture, and all manner of beautiful adornments, it was a symbol of great honor and respect. But when Bao Li refused to share her khana with Kang Dahan's new wife, he demanded that Vandakk's room, and everything within it, be given to Ning Po."

Narisaf's eyes darkened, he shook his head. "He is not owned by the masters of this caravanserai but is here of his own free will. Why did he choose to stay?"

"His greatest treasure was his wife," Saina said. "And death had already taken her. What more could be taken from him in which the sting would be greater?"

Narisaf pressed his lips together, thoughtful.

Saina took a bite of halva, savoring the dense dessert, its sweetness a distraction from the bitter memory. Vandakk deserved better.

She began to measure out the flour and sugar, mixing them in a large bowl, along with the lard Vandakk had set out earlier. "Will you fetch the water?" she said, pointing to the cistern in the far corner.

Narisaf returned with a small pitcher, pouring slowly as Saina mixed the wet dough with her hands.

"One day I will watch you make bread in the home we share together," he said, his voice confident.

Saina paused, feeling the smooth dough in her hands. Narisaf's dark eyes seemed to shimmer with a delicate hope. Her heart sank. She could not expect a future with him, but neither could she bear to take it away from him. Not now.

"I thought your grandfather taught you to make bread," she said, teasing. "Will you leave the chore to me in our home?"

"I will help." Narisaf laughed. "When I am not busy tending to our land and animals."

"Who am I, a simple servant, to deserve your love?"

Narisaf furrowed his brow, ran his hand tenderly along Saina's neck. "Why do you think so lowly of yourself that you do not deserve to be treated well, to be loved?"

"But I am treated well," Saina said. "I have certainly been treated fairly."

He shook his head. "But they cannot love you the way that I

love you," he said, his voice thick with emotion. "Love does not keep a person bound; it sets them free."

He gently pulled her to his chest, kissing her softly.

Saina's chest thrummed, like a thousand running horses had been set loose within her. In the stillness of the storeroom, while the caravanserai slept, Saina slipped loose from the chains of abandonment that had snaked around her heart. She let go of her servitude and the fear of being seen and imagined the life they would share together. Freely she returned Narisaf's affection. She wrapped her arms around his body, allowing herself to be caught up in his embrace.

How long had Saina remained there with him? She could not recall. The passing of time was only a distant thought until the scrape of footsteps on stone, the faint clatter of pottery, sent a shock of alarm through Saina's body.

She pulled away from Narisaf and looked toward the doorway, where Upach was clutching a small tray, her mouth open.

"Upach?" Saina said. Ning Po's vengeful eyes flashed in her mind. "Why have you come?"

Upach did not respond.

Saina moved away from Narisaf. "I beg of you, speak of this to no one..." Saina said, her throat tightening. She struggled to choke out the words. "It was a mistake."

Upach stared, her amber eyes penetrating, as she knelt down and slid the tray on the floor. She stood without speaking, without offering a hint of assurance, and left the room as quietly as she had entered.

"Saina, I am sorry," Narisaf said, drawing close, his face was troubled.

But Saina held up her hands, stopping him. "You do not understand," she said. She closed her eyes, trying to push aside her fear and focus on what must be made known to him. "I have enemies within these walls...and I...I have been careless."

Narisaf shook his head. "You cannot take the blame for this. I will make it right."

"You should leave," Saina said, looking through a blur of tears. "Return to your sleeping quarters."

"No," Narisaf said, reaching for her.

But Saina stepped back and shook her head angrily. "Go now, or my suffering will be even greater."

He began to walk away, then looked back at Saina. The hurt in his eyes, the weight of grief drawing in his shoulders, fractured Saina's heart into pieces.

She turned away, unable to bear it any longer. She had dared to think that she would be free to love him but had only hurt him in the end. When she looked back, Narisaf was gone.

Perhaps she was just like her father, after all.

Dropping her head in her hands, Saina wept.

Chapter Eighteen

S aina set the basket of dirty tunics on the bank by the canal and looked toward the city. In the distance, mountains split the azure sky with their cragged spines, but Samarkand and the vast desert surrounding it seemed nothing but an empty expanse now, an uncrossable chasm between her and the man she loved.

Four days had passed since she turned Narisaf away in the storeroom, and she was right to have done so. They could never really be together; she was a slave after all. But the anguish on his face, his faltering steps, burned afresh in her mind's eye. The memory returned to her often, like the pulsing waters of the canal. She could not rid herself of its torment.

Tears pooled in her eyes, blurring the desert terrain. With a long sigh, she set to washing her tunics.

The rhythm of the chore was a soothing balm. For a time, Saina lost herself in its temporary relief until a rustling in the tall grasses drew her attention. She looked over her shoulder and straightened when Upach stepped into the clearing, carrying a basket of clothes.

Saina stilled, her eyes locked on Upach, but the young servant girl was first to break the silence.

"I would not have come if I knew you were here," she said, clutching the basket to her chest.

Saina looked away. What could she offer in response, even as the weight of unspoken things swelled between them?

She rushed through the task, her hands shaking as she wrung out the tunics. From the corner of her eye, she saw Upach had not moved.

Saina's jaw tightened. Why must she continue staring and cause more discomfort? Her anger flared, and she spun around. "You did what you had to do," she said, throwing the tunic into the basket. "And I have resolved myself to the consequences of my actions. There is nothing left for me to lose."

Upach did not flinch, did not look away. "I did not go to the storeroom on my own accord. Ning Po sent me because she suspected you. And she had every reason. Your love for that man is obvious to everyone."

Saina's mouth fell open. She slumped on the bank and dropped her head in her hands. The damp earth soaked through her tunic and stuck to her skin. "I risked my standing to help you deliver Ning Po's baby, and because of my foolishness, I stand accused of murder." She looked up at Upach. "Must you also seek to do me harm?"

Upach's face reddened. "Your view of me is unwarranted," she said, stomping her foot in the mud gathered on the water's edge.

Saina drew back.

"I did not tell Ning Po what I saw in the storeroom," Upach hissed. "She questioned me often, but I refused to speak the truth. Because of it, I bear the weight of her mistrustful eyes and the dreadful sense of her plotting." She spun on her heel and stormed away.

Saina stared after her in silence, trying to make sense of what she heard. Was it true? Upach had not told Ning Po? The understanding built slowly as she awakened to the faint trilling of birds in the brush. Her assumptions had been wrong.

Saina stood quickly. "I am sorry," she called out. But there was no response, not even the sound of footsteps. Upach was gone.

Saina dropped her shoulders and stared into the canal where a leaf tumbled this way and that, seeming to struggle against the strong current that carried it onward. Had Narisaf felt the same way, tossed about in her gauntlet of fear and hopelessness? He never wavered in his loyalty, and still she turned him away, like she did with every good thing.

She was certain he had given up on her now. Tears stung her eyes. How could she mend the unraveling?

"Saina?" a voice called from down the canal.

She spun around, quickly wiping her eyes with the back of her hand. A young man with large eyes and a long, narrow face stood in the shade of the chinar tree. His arms hung at his sides, extending far beyond the sleeves of his threadbare tunic.

"Lushan?" Saina said, recognizing the boy who had tended Narisaf's horse in the bazaar. She stepped toward him and searched the overgrown banks. "Has Narisaf come?"

He shook his head. "I am alone."

Saina frowned. She understood the reasons for Narisaf's absence. "What news do you bring me that I must bear?" she said, planting her feet. She had stood in the desert and watched her father leave. She would stand for this too.

Lushan walked into the sun and shaded his eyes. "The weaver requests your presence tomorrow. He desires to speak with you about a matter of great importance."

"He wants to speak to me?" Her stomach tightened. Did he wish to tell her how careless she had been with his grandson?

She looked toward the city and the drab haze that had settled around it. With Kang Dahan's arrival expected any day, Vandakk would not consent to her leaving the caravanserai, even for a small portion of the day. She shook her head. "I cannot be certain..." she said.

Lushan nodded. "It is understandable. But if you choose to

make your way there, Narisaf will wait for you along the southern road." He turned to leave.

"Narisaf?" Saina said, his name flowing from her mouth without intention. Had he not turned his back on her after all? She was struck by the depth of color that suddenly returned, of the bright sky, the russet earth, and the clear water. Did the embers of love, of hope, still smolder between them?

"Tell him I will be there," she said firmly. It mattered not that it would be an impossibility. "I will find a way."

———

It happened simply enough. Upon Saina's return to the caravanserai, Vandakk greeted her in a panic, frustration heavy in his voice.

"The sheep I ordered for Kang Dahan's feast were not delivered today as promised, and now I must remain here tomorrow to ensure we receive the choicest animals. I had planned to purchase the last of the food from the bazaar come morning, but now you must go in my stead. There is no one else I trust to do it."

Saina smiled. "I will complete the task."

He walked away, and Saina felt as though her heart leaped within her. She could not have imagined it would happen this way, but Vandakk's misfortune had provided her opportunity.

Beneath the heat of the late morning sun, Saina hitched the donkey to the cart, and set out through the caravanserai gates, marveling at the ease in which she found herself walking to the bazaar, alone, just as the weaver requested.

The road stretched out long before her as a battle ensued between Saina's desired pace and the donkey, whose stubborn strength dictated otherwise.

With her gaze firmly on the path and anticipation growing stronger, Saina took little notice of the karagach trees at the edge of the oasis. The huddle of dense, dark shadows was a peripheral thought, until a movement on the other side of the path drew her attention. Narisaf stood up from where he sat against the trunk of an old, twisted tree. He offered a shy smile, but his eyes held a measure of sorrow and regret.

Saina's steps faltered.

"You have come," he said, moving toward her. But he stopped short. "I was not sure if you wanted to see me."

Were they alone? She glanced at the path extending out beyond him.

"Forgive me, Saina, for what I caused," Narisaf said, his voice breaking. "I have not slept or eaten these past few days."

Saina approached him but stopped an arms distance away. She dared not come any closer. "I knew the risk I took and chose it anyway," she said, then looked away. "But I regret that you were hurt because of it."

Narisaf shook his head. "It was selfish of me to put you in that position. It will not happen again."

She longed to wrap her arms around Narisaf and press her ear to his chest, to hear the smooth cadence of his beating heart resonating with her own, but she gripped the donkey's lead rope tighter. In that moment, it was enough to behold the mending between them. A gift of great value had been returned. No matter the cost, she would not lose it again.

Saina looked him in the eyes. "Suspicions are growing, but for now, no word has been spoken of it. We must take care to keep it that way."

"Of course," Narisaf said, stepping back.

They walked this way, a distance between them, talking until the city and bazaar came into view and the shared moment between them was swallowed up by the crowds. Slowly they pressed through the tangle of people who had gathered around baskets overflowing with the season's first fruits of crimson pomegranates and purple-fleshed eggplant.

Before Saina left the caravanserai earlier, Vandakk had insisted that she search for the season's first melons, and she found the melon seller exactly where Vandakk told her he would be. She paid the large sum while Narisaf loaded a dozen green and white striped melons, each one the size of a donkey's head, into the cart.

"Do you purchase this much food every day?" Narisaf said, sweat dripping down his forehead.

"The melons are reserved for the feast being offered upon Kang Dahan's arrival," Saina said, as they continued through the press of people. "We have filled the storeroom with the finest flavors to delight the mouths of the dignitaries who will welcome him home. With the addition of these highly sought-after melons, our preparation is complete."

Saina's throat tightened with dread at the mention of Kang Dahan's name. Ten days had already passed since Bao Li left for Penjikent, and there was little time left. Would she return as promised or leave Saina to face Kang Dahan alone?

"Come, taste the finest pistachios in all the land," a young man's voice called out.

Saina looked up to find they had walked into a quiet corner in the bazaar, where a pistachio seller was standing in his stall. The crowds remained in the main walkway a distance behind them, but no one else had come this way. They were alone.

The pistachio seller locked eyes with them and held out a pouch of nuts. "There is a proverb from the land of my youth that says if a man wants to prove his love to a beautiful woman, he will present her with a handful of pistachios every day."

Narisaf chuckled as he drew near. "And will it guarantee the woman's favor in return?"

The seller glanced between them, a slow smile building on his face. "What does a proverb benefit a man if there is no truth behind it?"

"Then give me two," Narisaf said. "Perhaps today I will prove to the woman I love that I am worthy of her." He looked at Saina and winked.

"Perhaps," Saina said, then turned away to hide her smile.

When they had walked a few stalls down, Narisaf gave Saina a handful of pistachios.

She smiled. "You seek to secure my love with these, but I assure you, there is no need," She cracked one open and held it up. "Nonetheless, I am grateful for the clever merchant."

"Clever?" Narisaf stopped and turned to Saina, his brows raised.

She nodded. "Merchants in Samarkand have a keen eye for lovestruck men and will take advantage if given the opportunity," she whispered. "Their tactics are as ancient as the dust on these cobbled streets. It is men like you who increase their wealth."

He smiled proudly and leaned toward Saina, taking the donkey's lead rope from her. "If there is truth in the pistachio seller's words, then I would gladly give my riches away if it guaranteed your love for the remainder of my days."

"True or not, these things cannot be bought with pistachios."

Narisaf threw his head back and filled the air with his deep, contented laughter. The sound drew the attention of the perfumer and his daughter. They peered out from their stall, then looked at each other and shook their heads.

The weaver shuffled out from the shade of his tent, leaning heavily on his twisted walking stick. "Even with these tired ears of mine, I will always know the laughter of my grandson," he said, his eyes shining.

Saina approached him while Narisaf hitched the donkey outside the tent.

The weaver smiled at her. "After watching his silent days of affliction, my heart is glad to see his delight return to him."

Saina's heart fell at the weaver's admission, and she dropped her head. "It was not my intention to hurt him. I should not have reacted so harshly."

"You were right to do so," the weaver said.

Saina looked up.

"As a man, Narisaf bears the weight of responsibility in the matter. It is his duty to exercise control."

Her face grew hot. "But we did not—"

"I know," the weaver said. "But as a woman and a slave, it is *your* honor that will be questioned. The consequences will fall upon you alone. Narisaf understands that now."

How had he come to hold such understanding, to speak the words that could soothe her weary mind? A thickness built in Saina's throat. But Narisaf soon approached, and Saina's heart swelled with gratitude. Who was she to stand in the presence of these two men?

The weaver pointed to the pouch in Saina's hand. "What have you got there?"

She held up the pistachios and smiled. "Your grandson had his first lesson on the cunning ways of Samarkand's merchants."

"That is partially true," Narisaf said, looking at Saina as though she had given away a secret. He cleared his throat. "The merchant took the last of my coins but gave me the assurance of something far greater in return."

The weaver chuckled. "It seems we all have much to learn." He paused, his eyes searching Saina's. "That is the beauty of life, yes? Every day is a new opportunity to discover what others have come to know before us."

Saina looked over her shoulder, and her gaze fell upon the warhorse tapestry inside. She contemplated the deeper meaning lingering in the weaver's words. "Are you speaking of my father?" she said. But she already knew the answer to her question.

Time slowed to a crawl. In that long, drawn-out moment, she resolved the matter in her heart. She must be willing to hear the truth, regardless of what was revealed.

She lifted her eyes, searching the weaver's face.

"Do not fear," the Weaver said. "Freedom is found in the knowing, and the time has come for these things to be brought to light." He turned, motioning for her to follow. "Come, join me in the shade of my tent."

———

The weaver sat across from Saina and placed the warhorse garment on the table between them. "Do you remember the first day we met, when you asked how I came to have this?"

Saina looked at Narisaf beside her. Time had not dulled her emotions. She stared at the tapestry now as she had that first day, still unable to reconcile her yearning to know the truth with the dread of what that knowledge would tell her. Both weighed upon her in equal measure. The silence in the tent swelled, became a heavy, burdensome thing. She drew a breath and nodded.

"Indeed, I asked the same question of your father the day he arrived at my home holding this garment in his hands," the weaver said. "When I asked who he was, he told me he was a Sogdian, from Samarkand. He called himself Turghar."

Turghar. The name punctuated the still air. Saina straightened. Hearing her father's name spoken out loud put flesh on the bones of her memories.

The weaver continued. "Long before your father ever took possession of this garment, I presented it to my son, Arash, on his wedding day. He wore it proudly in the years that followed, warming his wife's shoulders with it and wrapping Narisaf in it the day he was born. Countless beautiful memories are tucked within those threads." He paused, as though searching for something that lay deep in the past.

"That is why I was greatly troubled to see it in your father's hands two years after I had buried my son. But I sensed a sufficient answer would be provided, so I held my tongue. Before me stood a man with lifeless eyes, his shoulders drooped like spent wax. I perceived that his face was a reflection of my own. That he too grieved a terrible loss."

He grieved a terrible loss? Saina shifted where she sat, her jaw tightened. Was the weaver defending her father? The thought sparked a dark turmoil in her heart, sending it into an erratic beat. But in the burning moment, when she was certain she could not hear more, Narisaf wrapped his hand around hers. His touch grounded her, gave her courage to remain sitting.

Saina swallowed her dread and nodded for the weaver to continue.

"Your father stayed long enough to share a simple meal and answer the question that burned upon my lips. But it was the thread running through his story that captivated me. Indeed, the same thread is what drew us out of the desert and brought us back to Samarkand. Back to you."

Saina leaned forward.

"Born the son of a shepherd, your father told of spending his childhood grazing his family's sheep in the hills north of here. The seasons were long and the work unceasing, but the days were softened by the horse he rode, and the friendship of a girl named Yena."

"Yena?" Saina said, curiosity pricked her voice. "That was not my mother's name."

The weaver continued. "Early one spring, your father waited expectantly for Yena to appear at the top of the hill beyond his home, like she did often. By then, he was no longer a boy in need of a playmate, but a young man with a different yearning. But Yena did not come. A short time passed, and he went in search of her. Her uncle said her father had died suddenly, but when Turghar inquired about Yena, her uncle shrugged and walked away.

Seasons faded into years, and your father buried himself in his work, becoming a highly regarded trainer of heavenly horses. When he met your mother while bartering in the city, she awakened love in him once again. And then you were born. His life was full. His joy complete."

That could not be. Saina shook her head, but the weaver pressed on.

"One day, my son, Arash, came to Samarkand to acquire a warhorse from your father and to put the grief of his wife's death to rest. Their bond was immediate. But when Turghar invited my son to stay in his home, Arash declined. He told your father that he preferred to sleep in the open fields where his late wife, Yena, roamed as a girl."

Saina stared, unmoving. The threads were coming together, a fractured design emerging. Slowly, she looked at Narisaf. "Yena was your mother?" Her voice trailed off.

Narisaf smiled shyly but did not seem surprised by the news.

"Your mother and my father were childhood friends?" She let go of his hand. "My father loved your mother. Why did you not tell me about this?"

"I only learned of this recently," he said.

Saina looked into Narisaf's eyes, struck with the depth of love she felt for him. She considered her father. Had he looked into Yena's eyes and felt the same? How unbearable his pain must have been to lose such love not once, but twice, upon her mother's death.

The weaver leaned forward. "When Narisaf returned from the caravanserai sick of heart, I knew it was time to tell him. For it is in the revealing of Yena's story that both of you will find hope.

"After Yena's father died, her uncle sold her into servitude in the home of an orchardist in Samarkand. She remained under her slave master's heavy hand until Arash saw her retrieving water at the well and pursued her."

Slave. That was all Saina heard at first. Bound to the word, like a prisoner to chains, Saina envisioned Narisaf's mother at the well. She was certain that Yena had felt the desperation of the years extended out before her, in servitude to people above. Always people above. How wearisome it was.

Narisaf turned to face her. "Did you hear that, Saina?"

She blinked.

He was smiling at her, his eyes hopeful. "My mother was freed."

Until now, Saina had never heard of a slave being freed. Was it even possible? She fixed her gaze on the garment that bound their families together.

The Weaver continued. "When Arash departed, he left the

garment in your father's care. My son sensed that he would not survive the coming war and preferred it be kept with Turghar rather than be trampled upon the battlefield and divided as a spoil of war. Turghar had it in his mind to return the garment one day, but your mother's sudden death thrust him into despair. He loved you greatly but could see no way forward."

"No," Saina said, her voice quivering. "I have replayed his leaving countless times in my mind. Each memory as terrible as the one that came before." Bitterness swelled in her heart, poured out of her mouth. "He blamed me for my mother's death, bound me to Yena's fate. How can I believe he felt anything but hatred toward me?"

The weaver's eyes glistened, his chin trembled. There was a long silence before he spoke again.

"I will never forget the well of deep sorrow held in your father's eyes. His grief had laid him bare. Unable to care for you, his only consolation was knowing that Bao Li was a good woman. You would be safe with her. But regret had consumed him ever since. After our shared meal, he shoved the garment into my hands, then turned away, mumbling that soon his bones would be covered in the dust of the earth, and he would have finally found his rest."

"My father is dead?" The ground seemed to shift beneath Saina. How was she to make sense of this simultaneous upheaval and bringing together of things?

The weaver shrugged, his eyes holding great sorrow. "I never saw him again."

His answer was not a confirmation, but it was enough. Deep down she knew it was true.

"Why did you wait all these years to come?" Saina finally said.

The weaver glanced at Narisaf, then back to Saina. "Everything in its perfect time."

Saina studied the large hands and kind eyes of the man she loved sitting next to her, a thought forming in her mind. Had the weaver planned their meeting all along?

The weaver continued. "The day Narisaf and I came to Samarkand, I set out the garment. I knew that if you should find us by way of these threads, then it was the God of heaven who had sent you."

Why would the weaver be willing to trust such a god after suffering the deaths of his son and his son's wife? This god had been cruel enough. Saina opened her mouth, tried to put words to her swirling thoughts, but came up empty. The weaver had come to free her, but were his efforts too late? Did she even have a chance?

"How can it be?" she finally said. "I am a slave, sold to a life of servitude." She searched their faces, wanting badly for them to understand. "It is not an easy task to procure freedom, and there are complications you do not understand. I do not see a way..."

"If God has provided a way, nothing will stop the plan that was set in place," Narisaf said, kneeling before her. "Do you not see how the threads of my mother and your father and of this garment are coming together?"

Saina bit her lip.

Narisaf took her hand in his. "I love you, Saina. I desire to spend my life with you. But that same love compels me to respect your decision if you do not want the same."

A light breeze drifted through the tent, carrying with it the faint scent of the melons and the unwelcome reminder that Vandakk was expecting Saina's return. Her throat felt gritty as she looked from Narisaf to the melons, then back. More than anything, she wanted to marry him, but to say those words aloud would open her up to another shattered dream in the future. "How do I hope for such a notion when my circumstances will not allow it?"

"It is my burden to bear," Narisaf said.

Saina looked away. Could she risk losing everything for a small glimmer of hope? Dare she put her trust in this God of heaven, delicate as it may be?

She swallowed down the knot forming in her throat, the

vibrant hues of the weaver's tent fading away. She clung to Narisaf's hand as though it was the only life-giving thing. "Yes, I want to marry you. But you cannot let me down; I have everything to lose."

Relief washed over Narisaf's face as a smile creased his mouth. He took the garment off the table and placed it in her hands. "Then I will find a way," he said, pulling her into his embrace. "Trust me."

Chapter Nineteen

S aina pulled aside the curtains in Bao Li's bedroom and pushed open the dark shutters, flooding the room with warm sunlight. She set a porcelain dish of fresh rose water on the windowsill. A murmur of voices flowed in from the courtyard where a band of sojourners gathered to toss stones. The sharp rise of their laughter reminded her of Narisaf, and she smiled. Lately she recalled him with such ease it seemed a part of him had always lingered at the edge of her thoughts.

Even with the khana closed in Bao Li's absence, the desert dust was so pervasive that a thick layer had settled over every surface. She pulled out her cloth to begin cleaning, then paused. On the small writing desk below the window, Saina wrote Narisaf's name in the gathered dust, feeling the curve of each letter on her fingertip. Unpracticed as she was, the movement felt natural, and she was grateful Bao Li had insisted that Saina learn to read and write from her earliest days of servitude.

She studied his written name for a moment longer, then took out her cloth and carefully wiped the desk clean of dust. If she truly believed that Narisaf and the weaver would succeed in seeking her freedom, then Bao Li would learn of Saina's love in due time. Until then, she must remain cautious.

After pulling the cover off Bao Li's bed, Saina replaced the blankets and straightened the embroidered pillows, putting forward in her mind what it would be like to tend the home she shared with Narisaf. How strongly that desire took hold of her and swept her up in its temptation. She would fix their bed every morning, just as she did now, pulling aside the curtains to let in the light and closing them each night to shut out the world. His voice would fill the walls of their home, and she would receive him freely.

Time passed quickly as Saina left Bao Li's room and worked her way down the hallway, sweeping the stone floors. Slipping off her sandals, she walked into the vaulted greeting room and set out another bowl of rose water on the low table in the center of the room. Every year Bao Li had requested the scent be placed throughout her khana to help ease the low mood that always seemed to darken her countenance upon her return from Penjikent.

Saina's steps slowed when she neared the mural of Kang Dahan and Bao Li's wedding day. As she took careful regard of Chen Tien standing alone, holding the basket of fish, a pang of sadness wrenched her heart.

She closed her eyes, trying to unburden her thoughts of the hidden story in the mural, but a dark question took form in the recesses of her mind. Seeing Chen Tien's brother would remind Bao Li of all she had lost—and the false life she had been living. What reason would she have to return to Samarkand, knowing contention and false accusations awaited her?

Would Bao Li abandon Saina too? Saina was wearied by the thought that seemed to come regularly now.

The silence in the khana affirmed the very real possibility. Saina shook her head, then quickly finished her preparations for Bao Li's arrival, hoping her sharp attention to the duty would ensure her return.

By the time she left the khana, the sojourners had finished their game of stones and were sitting in the sun outside their room. In the lull of the day, traders filled the empty spaces, combing wool or resting in the shade of the sycamore tree while others fixed worn and broken tools or fashioned leather harnesses for their animals.

Saina continued to the storeroom to help Vandakk prepare samsa pastry for the evening meal.

She pushed through the leather flap and saw Vandakk grab a handful of onions from a large basket. He smiled at her, his face and tunic dusted with flour. "We have guests," he said, motioning to the center of the room.

Saina turned to see Narisaf leaning against the center table, his eyes holding hers. The weaver sat on a stool beside him. Her heart beat faster at their unexpected presence.

"You have come," she said, unable to hide the pleasure in her voice. She walked toward them and scanned the table where a small kettle of water and three half-empty cups sat. "And you have been here for some time."

"We brought the tea for Vandakk," the Weaver said. "But he insisted we stay awhile and share it with him."

Vandakk joined them, setting the onions beside a dish of black sesame seed and prepared samsa dough on the table. "I was delighted to learn the tea was made with ground rhodiola root harvested in my homeland," he said. "It was my honor to share the flavors of my youth with them."

The weaver chuckled. "It was not my intention. I only inquired of the apothecary for an herbal decoction that would restore his endurance for the long days ahead."

Vandakk reached for the kettle of water. "More tea?"

"No, no," the weaver pointed to the dough. "I see you are busy, and this meal will not make itself."

"It is a small matter," Vandakk said, brushing away the weaver's concern. "With Saina's help, it will come together quickly. There are only a few items to retrieve from the garden and all will be set."

Narisaf tilted his head. "You have a garden?"

"Of course," Vandakk said, pouring two cups of tea. "What good is a cook if he does not have a garden to pull fresh produce from?" He took a shearing blade from the wall behind them and gave it to Saina.

Narisaf seemed perplexed. "With all your responsibilities, how do you have time to tend it?"

"Between Saina and I, we manage to get it done," Vandakk said. "You are welcome to join her while she fetches a few handfuls of basil and dill. I trust you will be pleased with all that we have accomplished."

Surprised at Vandakk's invitation to Narisaf, Saina turned the blade over in her hands. He had made a practice of keeping the garden private from the view of their guests; indeed, even the other servants in the caravanserai were not allowed inside. It was their one place of respite, where demands were not made of them. But Vandakk's suggestion revealed the inner desire of her heart. Truly Narisaf was the only other person she wanted to share it with. How strange that she had not considered it until now. And with the garden in full bloom and vines ripe with fruit, the timing was perfect.

Saina turned to Narisaf and grinned. "Come with me." She took the key from the notch in the wall and led him deep into the inner corridors.

"The beauty of this caravanserai has been rumored in distant lands," Narisaf said, his voice echoing off the narrow walls. "But I never heard mention of its garden, not even from you."

"It is not widely known," she whispered.

They neared the end of the hallway, and Narisaf's steps slowed. He pulled gently on Saina's hand, turning her around. With her back against the wall, he leaned close. "It seems there are many secrets within this place."

Saina smiled, studying the shadows lining his face. "There are only secrets that time has not yet revealed."

He closed his eyes and pinched his lips together, as though a battle was waged within. Then he shook his head and pushed away from the wall.

Saina slid the key into the iron lock and opened the door. Metal scraped against metal as the door swung on its hinges. Light flooded the hallway, carrying the heady scent of honeysuckle and night-blooming jasmine on its golden rays. She stepped aside as Narisaf walked into the garden.

She never grew tired of the changing light that filtered through the leafy canopy and spilled onto the colorful flowers below or the way dark corners were brightened with painted tiles fashioned by artisans and arranged on the surrounding walls.

Saina paused. Was the splendor only in her own eyes? Perhaps in Narisaf's homeland, there were even more beautiful gardens. She was struck again by how little she knew of his life outside of Samarkand.

Narisaf stood perfectly still, his mouth open, his eyes focused. Saina approached him, drawn by the perfection of his form. Pride swelled within her. He was captivated by the garden just as she was.

She led him along the stone path, past the small orchard of almond and peach trees.

Narisaf looked out across the garden then turned to Saina. "How did you come to have ownership of this?"

"Bao Li gave it to Vandakk and me," Saina said. "It was a gift far greater than any room or fine furnishings could ever satisfy. But we did not inherit the garden in this form. Long neglected, it required great effort to bring it back to life."

Narisaf seemed to consider this as he walked to the edge of the pond where lilies floated in the still water, their blossoms opened to the azure sky. "It rivals those I have seen in the city. What fortune you have been given to work within it." He swept a thin strand of hair from her face, his smile fading. "But I am not surprised by this, for you have found favor in the eyes of all who know you."

Saina looked away. "Bao Li and Vandakk have been good to

me. They have treated me with kindness and taught me many skills. But this garden is where I came to learn that with time and careful tending, even things once dead can rise again."

Concern crossed Narisaf's face. "Are you willing to leave a place of such beauty and deep bonds for me?"

Saina studied the sun's reflection in the pond. How beautiful it seemed, glistening within the confines of the water. But its true, brilliant source came from higher up and farther out, untethered by man-made cords. She reached for his hand. "Yes. You have taught me to hope for greater things and offered me life beyond these walls." She paused. "But there is one request I must make."

Narisaf shifted.

"When we marry, I want to live in a house in the hills with a small garden to tend."

A smile of relief slowly spread across his face. "You have been thinking about it."

Heat crept up Saina's neck and spread across her face. "How could I not? The open land is in my blood as surely as it is in yours...in your mother's. Do you not perceive that such a foundation has already been laid for us?"

"I perceived it the moment I first saw you."

She leaned closer. "Do you desire it?"

"I desire to marry you above everything," he said. "But if we must wander the desert in order to be together, then I will be satisfied."

Saina smirked. "Am I a camel that you should force me to wander the desert and live among tents?"

"My love," Narisaf said, stroking her hand, one corner of his mouth raised in amusement. "If life should demand that I reside on the back of a camel in order to spend the rest of my days with you, I will do it without complaint."

Saina narrowed her eyes and stepped back. "You are teasing me. And you have given yourself away. No man who has spent a day's journey on the back of a camel would agree to such a notion."

Narisaf laughed deeply. Saina stilled, finding solace in the depth of his voice and the strength his presence exuded. She ached to be held by him. Ached to be free.

His laughter quieted. A muscle twitched in his jaw as he cleared his throat and let go of her hand.

Saina turned away, fearing that if she allowed herself, she would fall headlong into his arms, without restraint, before their time had come. The flush of his skin told her he felt the same.

Seeking to distance herself from the pull between them, Saina led him through a grapevine trellis and circled around to the herb garden near the entrance. "Vandakk grows the herbs used in our meals," she said, grateful for the distraction. "When we first began our work, he insisted that the herbs be the first to be planted. Since then, he has sought the knowledge of seed merchants from far and wide, each addition contributing to new and varied flavors."

"He has succeeded," Narisaf said. He knelt down, pinching a small dill frond between his fingers, then stood. "But is this enough to sustain all the meals in the caravanserai?"

"Not all. Most of the food grown in this garden is reserved for Kang Dahan, Bao Li, and any guests that come to see them." She lowered her voice. "But whenever Vandakk prepares their meals, he sets aside extra to be shared between the two of us." She searched his face and smiled, unable to hide her delight at sharing their secret.

Narisaf turned the bracelet on Saina's wrist. "And you trust me with this information?" he winked.

"I trust you completely, I..." she hesitated, recalling the night she held Ning Po's baby in her arms, her chest constricting at the memory that returned to her often. The time had come, she must tell him the truth of what happened. "But if you want to marry me, I must be completely honest with you about what I face. What *we* face."

"Tell me," Narisaf said, his tone serious, his earlier teasing suddenly gone.

Saina could barely breathe, the weight of what must be spoken pressed upon her severely.

She trained her eyes on the door to the garden and saw that it was cracked open. She stilled, creased her brow. After all the years of heeding Vandakk's warning that she keep the door closed, had she forgotten to shut it? But the task before her flashed in her mind, and she shook her head, turning back to Narisaf. If she did not tell him now, her resolve would flee.

"Since the day Bao Li first took me as a servant, she treated me more like a daughter than a slave. But it took me a long while to soften toward her...toward this life forced upon me." Saina sighed.

"During that time, she showed me many kindnesses reserved for one's own kin. This garden is only one of them," Saina said. "My unwavering loyalty to Bao Li was built from this foundation. I was the child she was unable to bear in her womb, and I vowed to never let my faithfulness falter...until recently." Saina paused, trying to find the words that would come next, hoping Narisaf would understand.

"When Kang Dahan's second wife was found to be with child, his only heir, the contention between Bao Li and Ning Po became unbearable. Ning Po hid herself away, refusing to allow anyone to lay eyes upon her. The baby was not expected for another moon cycle, so when Ning Po went into labor, even her midwife had been called away to the high country, to the home of a birthing mother. With no one else to turn to, Ning Po's young servant sought my help." Saina shook her head.

"At first, I denied her. I could not betray Bao Li, my barren mistress. But neither could I bear to burden Upach, barely a woman herself, with the task of delivering Ning Po's baby alone." Saina stared silently for a moment. "As you know, I was a child when my own mother..." her voice faltered.

"I understand," Narisaf said. Saina was grateful she did not have to explain herself more.

She inhaled a deep breath. "The thought of denying Upach's

request filled me with wretchedness. I resolved to help her; there was no other choice."

She stared at the fat-blossomed flowers and pregnant buds preparing to bloom in the garden. Even the canopy of leaves seemed to announce the fullness of the season in which they lived, but this was a season Ning Po's baby would never know.

"The moment the baby was born, there was no life in her," Saina said, her voice quaking as she recalled the baby's translucent skin, her pale lips. Her eyes welled at the haunting memory. "There was nothing I could do to change it."

Narisaf shook his head, his dark eyes unreadable.

"Please, do not think lowly of me," Saina said. "I am not skilled in midwifery—"

"Lowly? I have no such thoughts toward you. You were put in an unfair position. Your choice was an honorable one."

"Ning Po saw no honor in my actions. She accused me of murdering Kang Dahan's heir and vowed revenge," Saina said. "When Kang Dahan returns, she will convince him of such. Even now, she is searching for every reason to make her case against me." She hung her head.

"But there is no case to be had."

Saina snapped her head up. "It was Ning Po's servant who saw us embracing in the storeroom. She had been sent to observe us."

Narisaf straightened, his face suddenly ashen. "But you said..."

"What I said is true. Upach did not tell Ning Po that she saw us that night. At least...not yet."

"And if Upach remains silent, what then?"

Saina swallowed. "It changes nothing. Ning Po is bent on revenge."

"Kang Dahan will not give ear to her lies," Narisaf said, anger rising in his voice.

"It is not about truth, but about what holds sway over Kang Dahan's mind."

"You have served Bao Li faithfully all these years. She will defend you," he said, as though trying to convince himself of such. But even Narisaf must have heard the rumors that Kang Dahan was an impetuous man.

"Bao Li cannot defend me if she does not return from Penjikent in time." Saina stepped back, saw the way his unfocused eyes were upon her, as though reliving a distant memory. His nostrils flared and his breath quickened with the steady rise and fall of his chest.

"I regret burdening you with such matters," she said quietly, hoping to give him some assurance. "But I could not keep it from you any longer, for I do not know what will happen to me upon Kang Dahan's return."

"I could not protect my mother when evil men took her life," Narisaf said, his words hot, as though fire burned within him. "I will not allow the same to happen to you. No matter the cost, I will protect you. I will find a way."

He reached out to touch her, but the hollow scrape of the garden door shocked them to attention. Narisaf pulled his hand back.

From the corner of her eye, Saina thought she saw a flash of red through the sharp beam of light shining in the hallway, just before it disappeared in the shadows.

Ning Po. A cold rush of panic coursed through her body.

"What is it?" Narisaf said, stepping closer to her.

The name was clear in Saina's mind, but she could not form a sound on her lips. Finally, her tongue loosened. "Ning Po was here. She was watching us."

Chapter Twenty

Beneath the pale light of dawn, Saina worked alongside Vandakk in the courtyard. The early morning air was unusually warm as she lit fires beneath the cauldrons and prepared the tandoor oven for the morning bread.

The chores were simple, and Saina was glad for it. She had slept little last night and felt unsettled, remembering the creak of the garden door yesterday and the dread that someone had been spying on them. Even now, she sought to convince herself that she had imagined the flash of Ning Po's red coat in the hallway, but it was a foolish task.

Saina sighed. How much longer would Ning Po remain like a coiled snake, waiting for the perfect moment to strike?

Vandakk set a tray of dough rounds beside her. "What weighs heavily on your mind at this early hour?"

Saina shook her head. Vandakk had enough on his mind, she could not bear to trouble him with this too. "Nothing."

He raised his brows and pointed at her hands. "Tell that to the cloth you are strangling."

She looked down, saw she had wrung it tightly, and dropped her hands at her sides. "It is a small matter...certainly not worth burdening you with."

"Is that so?" Vandakk said, suspicion in his voice. "Then it has nothing to do with the news the weaver shared with me yesterday...that a certain fondness has grown between you and Narisaf?"

"He told you?" She glanced quickly at the faint shadows in the empty courtyard, then at the sycamore tree still growing strong and steady as it always had. She looked everywhere but into Vandakk's eyes, embarrassed as she was with the revelation. But she was even more ashamed that she had not summoned the courage to tell him herself. He deserved to know.

Vandakk held up his hand. "He only confirmed what I had come to suspect. But I *was* shocked to learn that a secret betrothal was made between you and Narisaf in the weaver's company."

"I did not set out to fall in love with Narisaf," Saina said. The last thing she wanted was to hurt Vandakk, for him to think she had chosen Narisaf over the two people in the caravanserai she loved and cared for. Still, she could not deny the wholeness Narisaf's presence made her feel. "It just...happened."

"The heart loves whom it loves," Vandakk said, smiling weakly. "I was a young man once. I remember the way a fire was lit within me the day I first laid eyes upon the woman who would become my wife."

Saina stared, her mouth open. Was he giving her his approval?

Vandakk continued. "To have the love of a man like Narisaf is a benefit to you. There is no one finer. And I want more for you than to spend the rest of your days in this place, with its endless demands and constant servitude." He looked away. "But these things are not mine to grant, and Bao Li has much to lose..."

Saina's heart fell. She leaned against the table to steady herself, her mind drifting to a distant time as she considered the far-reaching consequences of her father's actions. All these years later she was still bound by the scroll. That terrible contract sealed her fate and denied any possibility of a life she had hoped to claim as her own. How tired she suddenly felt.

There was a commotion at the gates, the guards' voices began to rise. "Look there," one guard said, pointing into the desert. "A horseman is approaching swiftly."

"At this early hour?" another guard said, gripping the hilt of his sheathed sword.

Narisaf? Saina straightened, looking toward the gates as the guards positioned themselves. Would she know the cadence of his horse running at speed? When he left yesterday, he had promised to return as soon as possible. Could it be that he would come now? The pounding in her chest matched that of the hooves striking the dry ground.

"It is the courier, Zhentuo," the guard said, relaxing his hand from his sword.

At the mention of Zhentuo's name, Vandakk rushed toward them, and Saina followed quickly behind. She studied the courier's familiar pointed, red hat and dust covered boots as he dismounted his horse, the dust settling at his feet. She looked out beyond the gates, feeling as empty and barren as the desert landscape.

"I have been sent with a message by order of Kang Dahan and must speak with Bao Li," Zhentuo said.

"She is not present," Vandakk said, stepping forward. "But she is expected soon. If you have a message for her, her maidservant will ensure Bao Li receives it upon her return."

"Very well," the courier said, handing a small scroll to Saina. She turned it over, studied the wax seal stamped with Kang Dahan's signet ring.

The courier continued. "Send out word that Kang Dahan's caravan is camped one day's journey north of Samarkand. You are to expect his arrival tomorrow."

Saina drew the scroll to her chest, trying to still the tremble in her hands, then glanced at Vandakk who was already halfway across the courtyard. The success of the coming days hinged on his ability to pull endless amounts of energy from his aged bones. No matter how stocked the storeroom was or how many cooks were hired to ease the load, it never seemed to be enough.

Desperate for any reason to keep her mind from the dread of Kang Dahan's return, Saina ran to catch up to him. He was all she had left in the caravanserai, for it seemed Bao Li had abandoned her.

Word of Kang Dahan's arrival spread through the caravanserai as final preparations began to take shape. Couriers were sent to dignitaries in Samarkand announcing the day of the feast and servants were put to work, filling cisterns with fresh water and rooms with oil lamps.

Throughout the day, merchants arrived with carts of produce packed on ice from mountain caves. Soon the storeroom was overflowing with pomegranates, apricots, grapes, and peaches, as well as garlic, pickled onions, and rhubarb. Roasting fowl of all sorts were hung over open flames, and vessels of fermented drink were stacked wherever space allowed.

As the day drew on, night servants were pulled from their sleep to help bear the burden that did not cease even with the swarm of people toiling in the heat of the day.

Saina had spent the majority of her time in the storeroom with Vandakk, organizing and reorganizing baskets and crates filled with all manner of food. Stacked floor to ceiling, they lined a narrow path through the cramped space.

She had always been amazed at how much food was consumed during Kang Dahan's feasts. The work was toilsome, and sleep came little, if at all. In the past, a burning flame of excitement carried her through, but this time was different. Her wick had been snuffed out, and there seemed no fuel to light even a spark.

A servant entered the storeroom, searching, his eyes finally meeting Saina's. "I have been sent for Vandakk."

"I am here," Vandakk said, emerging from between the shelves carrying a basket of beets.

The servant gave a slight bow. "The bahkshi has arrived and seeks your attention."

Vandakk smiled wide, his green eyes flashed. "Ah, I have been expecting him." He set the basket at Saina's feet. "When you have finished blanching the hazelnuts and preparing the *tarator* sauce, take these beets to the grain closet. I have looked but there is not a shelf space to store them in here."

Saina watched him leave and then set to work, grinding the hazelnuts and garlic into a thick paste. She added yogurt, lemon juice, oil, and Vandakk's special blend of herbs. The aroma made her mouth water. She looked at the beets and green beans piled in baskets nearby and wondered which vegetable he would decide to drizzle the sauce over this time.

Wiping her hands, she picked up the basket of beets and was about to push through the flap when she heard the sound of footsteps in the hallway.

"Walk faster, Upach," Ning Po said. "You must act quickly if you are to reach the merchant and inform him of my plan before he leaves Samarkand." She was standing just outside the storeroom.

Merchant? Saina stilled, fixed her gaze on the stone floor. *What merchant?* With only the leather flap serving as a barrier between them. She dared not move.

"Please, my lady," Upach said, her voice weighed down with an unknown burden. "I beg of you, do not require this thing of me."

"How dare you speak against me," Ning Po hissed. There was a sharp snap of skin hitting flesh, and Upach cried out.

"I am the only person in this caravanserai who treats you fairly. No one else wanted you with your unkempt hair and ominous eyes, but I gave you a chance. And you betrayed my kindness by lying to me about Saina and that...that man."

Saina closed her eyes and pressed her back against the wall. Her suspicions were true. Ning Po *had* been standing at the garden door, watching her and Narisaf. Saina had let slip Upach's secret, and now Upach was paying the price.

Ning Po lowered her voice. "If you wish to save your life now, you will do as I say. Do you have the payment?"

"Yes."

"Then go. And do not return until you have accomplished what I have sent you to do."

Their voices faded, but Saina remained, pondering the fear in Upach's voice, how childlike she sounded. What dreadful thing had Ning Po planned, and did it involve her?

The thought remained with Saina the rest of the day. She could not rid her mind of it.

———

Saina walked through the dark courtyard, lit only by the low flicker of abandoned warming fires whose embers sent up thin wisps of smoke into the night sky. Like a dark blanket studded with golden light, the sky's covering seemed to extend forever. How great her vulnerability was within that vast expanse.

The sonorous sounds of men in deep sleep followed Saina as she climbed the stairs. Their sound rivaled the grousing of the camels that filled the courtyard earlier in the day, but the distraction was not enough to lift the sense of unease growing heavier within her, an unease that swelled the moment she stepped onto the landing, thickening the air around her.

From behind, she heard the scrape of movement, felt the faint flex of the wooden balcony beneath her feet. Every muscle in her body went rigid. She tried to turn around quickly, to face the threat behind her, but her body refused to move with the speed she demanded of it.

"Saina," Ning Po said, her name snaked low and slow from her mouth. Her head was tilted slightly to the side, light from the torch beside them cast sharp shadows across her face and down her red silk coat.

How foul Saina's name sounded coming from Ning Po's lips. Saina stepped back as Ning Po drew nearer. Then, with a swiftness she had not expected, Ning Po lunged forward and grabbed hold of her wrist. Her nails tearing into the tender skin.

Saina winced.

"Tell me, Saina," Ning Po said studying the bracelet on her wrist. "How does a filthy servant such as yourself acquire a fine piece of jewelry like this?"

Saina pinched her mouth tight. She would not give Ning Po the satisfaction of a response.

"You do not want to tell me?" Ning Po said. But she did not wait for a response. She knew one would not come. "It seems Upach is not the only servant who has kept secrets from me. Like her, you believe you have hidden it well, but the truth comes out. It always does." Ning Po smirked. "And so do the consequences."

"Do not touch me," Saina said, yanking her hand away from Ning Po's tightening grip.

Ning Po's eyes widened with surprise, her mouth fell silent. For an instant, she seemed more like a threatened dog backed into a corner than the wife of a distinguished man. But just as suddenly, her face hardened, simmered with anger.

"Have you forgotten that your place is to serve the meals and clean the refuse of people above you? Look at the rags draping your shoulders, the dirt on your soiled hands. What makes you think you deserve anything better when not even your own father wanted you?"

"You are cruel," Saina spat, tears stinging her eyes.

"Cruel?" Ning Po's lip curled back, her eyes turned black as stone.

Saina recoiled at the sight before her.

"It was *cruel* of Kang Dahan to promise my parents that I would be seated beside him as head of this caravanserai and *cruel* of Bao Li to refuse me my rightful position. But you, Saina, are the cruelest of all. You killed my baby and snuffed out the one chance I had to finally rise above your mistress and live with the honor and respect I deserve."

Saina's entire body shook. "What you say is not true."

Ning Po's eyes narrowed. "How can you claim to know what is true when even you have bought into the lies? You were foolish enough to believe that Narisaf, a man whose warhorse you are not worthy to touch, would love you." Her lips twisting into a sneer.

Struck silent, Saina could offer no reply.

Ning Po raised her chin. "You will pay harshly for what you did to me. And when Bao Li learns that you betrayed her once again and whored yourself to the weaver's grandson, your bitter portion will be doubled. Narisaf lied to you. He cannot protect you from what is coming." She spun on her heel and walked away, leaving the threat hanging in the air.

Saina watched her disappear into the shadow of the night. Like natural wool absorbing a droplet of dye, she swallowed the poison of Ning Po's words.

Tears filled her eyes as she walked to her room. She slammed the door and struggled to slide the lock into place. But nothing, not even a lock, would protect her from what was to come.

Kneeling on the floor, Saina wept. In a flash of anger, she yanked off her tunic and threw it in the corner.

She slipped off the indigo bracelet adorning her wrist and held it up, studying its delicate braids and fine craftsmanship. What care Narisaf must have taken in creating it for her. But she could not be seen wearing it again. Through tears, she buried it at the bottom of her clay vessel.

Saina pulled the warhorse garment out from beneath her sleeping mat where she had kept it hidden away since returning from the bazaar two days ago. Looking upon it seemed to spark something deep within. Unworthy as she was, it stood as a symbol of Narisaf's love, of their betrothal and something even greater. How impossible it seemed.

Wrapping herself in it, she was comforted by the memory of

the men whose lives were tied up within these threads. She inhaled the scent of sweat and toil, of battlefields and rolling hills. She could only hope the strength they showed would outweigh the evil that seemed to be closing around her. She pondered the thought, clung to its frail hope, until the faint cadence of a weaver's loom flowed through the room, lulling her to sleep.

Chapter Twenty-One

The faint sound of a woman's voice pulled Saina from her sleep.

She sat up quickly and listened. Had she dreamt it?

In the veiled moments between sleep and wakefulness, the small room seemed cavernous.

A donkey brayed, and a murmur of sound lifted from the courtyard. Out of it came the woman's muffled voice once again.

Bao Li? Saina yanked the warhorse garment to the side of her bed mat and stood. Had she returned? Relief washed over her. She pulled her tunic off the floor. Why had a night servant not been sent to wake her?

She dressed quickly and slipped on her leather sandals. As she turned to open the door, she saw the garment in a heap beside her bed mat. She paused, considered hiding it beneath her blankets, then shook her head. She would conceal it later when time allowed. For now, her duty was to tend to Bao Li.

Hints of morning light extended over the Pamirs, setting the jagged peaks, like royal crowns, on fire. But the courtyard below was wrapped in darkness. Everything was still.

Saina's jaw tightened. Had no one thought to light the way

upon Bao Li's arrival? She rushed down the stairs and into the courtyard, then stopped suddenly.

Bao Li's caravan was nowhere to be seen. She glanced at the khana behind her, it was still closed up. Bao Li had not come. Saina's heart sank. In an instant, her fragile hope had shattered, replaced by a familiar dread.

Torchlight flickered at the gates, and Saina saw a huddle of guards beneath the golden glow. Across from them stood Umida, her hands clasped, her face drawn tight with worry. Beside her stood her grown son, who served as her traveling companion whenever she was called away at night.

It must have been Umida's voice she had heard.

Saina looked at the cauldrons as she approached the gates. Fires had not yet been lit beneath them.

"Umida, it is early," Saina said. "The tea has not yet been prepared, but I can offer you *chal* from the storeroom. We have received a fresh supply of the fermented camel's milk for the feast later today."

"There is no time," Umida said, looking at the guards. They nodded, and she walked quickly through the gates, stopping in front of Saina. "I am looking for Upach. Have you seen her?"

"Not since early yesterday." Saina's mind flashed back to the storeroom, to Ning Po's taunting voice in the hall and Upach's pleas. She turned toward the guards. "Upach did not return last night?"

The head guard shook his head.

Umida's face fell. "She came to see me but was greatly troubled. When I inquired more, she refused to speak, saying only that she must find the honey merchant."

"Honey merchant?" Saina said, sharply. "Why...why would Ning Po send her to that man?"

Umida wrung her hands. "I have fretted for her since. I regret not sending my son to attend her and ensure she returned to the caravanserai."

Saina saw the motherly concern in Umida's eyes and felt

guilty for it. She had cowered in the storeroom while Upach pleaded with Ning Po not to be sent on the errand. And now Upach was in grave danger.

"You must find her, but do not go alone," Saina said, looking over Umida's shoulder. "Take your son with you."

Umida's eyes filled, as though Saina's urgency confirmed what she had suspected. "I sensed something was wrong. I should have stopped her. I should have..."

"Please, Umida, there is little time. You must go."

She nodded briskly, then returned to her son, who helped her into the horse-drawn cart and quickly left.

Saina watched them fade away, then fetched disks of camel dung to light a fire beneath the cauldron. Her body felt like stone. She would have done better to not involve herself. The last time she helped Upach, she had lost everything of value. What would happen when Ning Po learned that Saina had interfered once again?

But Saina could not help herself. Young Upach needed help, no matter the consequences.

———

The demands of preparing for Kang Dahan's arrival pressed heavily upon Saina, and she struggled to concentrate on her chores. A worry in her mind had been let loose, she could not stay focused.

Earlier in the storeroom, she had spilled a jar of oil while preparing a marinade for the lamb kebabs and later dropped a handful of quail eggs that were set aside to be boiled.

She had begun to clean up the mess when Vandakk placed his hand on her arm, stopping her. "Fetch some water for tea. I will clean this up and boil the remainder of the eggs."

Though embarrassed, she was glad to be in the fresh air, away from the dimly lit confines of the storeroom.

The courtyard hummed with activity, and bright sunlight

poured in from above. Saina filled the bucket with water and was reaching down to pick it up when a flash of green caught her eye. Looking up, she saw the watchman leading his horse from the stables and straightened.

A somber man, stout bodied with a thick, black beard, he wore a knee-length, green silk tunic and tall leather boots. All the servants around her stopped and watched in silence as he walked to the gates and mounted his horse.

Saina fixed her gaze upon the ram's horn hanging at the watchman's side.

It was a striking sound piece. Long and curved, it spanned the length of a man's arm and was beautifully formed in its natural state. When put to the lips of a master trumpeter, the horn produced a low, resonant sound that was felt in the chest and stirred all within earshot to a sudden alertness.

The watchman clicked his tongue, and the horse, strong and sure-footed, set out. They left, a delegation of one man and his regal horse, to greet Kang Dahan on the road and accompany him home.

It would not be long now before the horn would sound three times in the desert, heralding Kang Dahan's return. The thought wearied Saina, but there was no time to rest. Too much was at risk, a knot of troubles that seemed impossible to undo.

The dust from the watchman's departure had barely settled when servants were put to steady work outside the caravanserai walls, hauling water and driving pegs into the dry earth. Felt tents were stretched out, rising from the ground, and cooks, hired to ease the workload, poured in from the city.

Zimat arrived early in the day, along with a team of bread makers and several carts full of fine flours, fragrant spices, and dipping oils, and Vandakk ordered the ovens fired up. Saina returned to the kitchen with him, leaving the bakers to prepare the bread in the courtyard.

Contents inside pots began to steam and boil as the extra cooks worked furiously, their heads down and their brows set with intention. The air in the crowded room grew hot and sticky.

When Vandakk requested fresh dill from the garden, Saina left without delay, but as she walked out of the packed room, Vandakk stopped her. "When you return, bring the extra basket of beets in from storage."

Though the sun had moved well past its midpoint in the sky and the heat of the day pressed upon her, Saina appreciated the solitude of the garden. Nearing the herb bed, she bent down, pulled the knife from its sheath, and cut several fronds of dill.

Her mind drifted to Narisaf, his shy smile and the way he carried himself with confidence in spite of the uncertainty before him. Was it only two days ago that they stood here together as he offered her assurances that seemed impossible now? Her chest ached with longing to see him again, if only for the comfort his presence brought her.

She felt weak down to the marrow of her bones. There were so many questions, but no time to consider their answers.

Sliding the knife back into its sheath, Saina left the garden and returned to the corridor, feeling the weight of the narrow hallway consume her. She had entered the storage closet and begun sorting through crates of produce, searching for the beets, when a door further down creaked open.

"Where have you been?" Ning Po said, angrily.

"I...I did what you asked," Upach said, her voice flat, emotionless. "I delivered the message."

Saina straightened and walked to the entrance of the closet.

"He will be here soon then?"

Saina peeked down the hall and saw Upach standing in the doorway of Ning Po's room. She cupped her hands over her mouth to quiet her breathing, her heart thundered in her ears.

"Answer me!" Ning Po said.

"I do not know," Upach cried out.

A drawer slammed closed. "How do you not know? I told you to wait for his response."

"I did not stay. When I saw his eyes, I grew afraid. He is not a good man."

"You stupid girl," Ning Po said sharply. "Good men are not to be found in this land. It is better that you learn such things at your age. Return to him at once. Do whatever he requires of you to ensure he will be here tonight."

Saina was taken aback by Ning Po's request of Upach and the danger she was putting her in, but why was she surprised by it? And what was the reason behind such a demand? What plan had she set in motion?

"Please, my lady, I cannot go," Upach said.

"Do it!"

Upach's refusal had been brazen and would demand harsh punishment, but Saina could not let her stand alone. Not this time. She left the beets in the room and rushed to Upach's side.

"You?" Ning Po said, her eyes narrowed, her lip curled back.

Saina took hold of Upach's hand.

Ning Po fixed her black eyes on Upach. "You worthless slave. Your punishment will be severe. Go now, or..."

The low, ominous sound of the ram's horn rang out. It reverberated through the corridors, prickling the skin on Saina's neck. She covered her ears.

The sound of the horn dropped suddenly, leaving a deafening silence.

"He is here, and I am not ready," Ning Po hissed. "Your delay in returning from Samarkand has left me unprepared for my husband's arrival. Get my shawl. Get it now."

Upach did not move. Saina remained at her side, her body trembling.

The horn blew a second time.

Two male servants ran past them, laughing. Their voices swelled in the hall before fading to silence once again.

"My necklace. Upach, where is my necklace?" Ning Po said, panicking. "Do not stand there. Help me."

The horn blew for the third and final time, long and drawn out.

Saina could not think beyond the overwhelming sound heralding Kang Dahan's return and the revenge that would soon be wrought by his second wife. But she had made her choice, her actions had already incriminated her.

Ning Po grabbed her shawl and shoved past Upach. "Prepare my bed and draw a bath," she said, rushing toward the cheering, high voices in the courtyard.

Saina looked at Upach whose eyes were pooled with tears.

"Forgive me for what I have done," Upach said, her chin trembling.

Saina let go of her hand. "What is it? What have you done?"

"Ning Po sent me to deliver a message to the honey merchant, offering to avenge him for the humiliation he received on Bao Li's behalf." Her voice was a whisper, and Saina strained to hear through the cheers in the courtyard. "I was supposed to accompany him here and let Ning Po know when he had arrived."

"Why?"

"I do not know what she has planned. But..." Upach looked away. "It involves you."

"Me?" Saina said, her voice shaking. "How?"

Upach shook her head. "You should go. Your duty is to tend to Bao Li."

"She is not here," Saina said.

Upach closed her eyes, her shoulders fell. "That is what Ning Po hoped for." She turned and walked into Ning Po's room, then closed the door behind her.

Saina stared at the door and the line of light that spread out beneath it, just as it had barely a moon cycle earlier when she stood here the night Ning Po went into labor. So much had changed since she last walked through it. Her life was barely recognizable anymore.

Dread opened a pit in her belly, but Upach was correct. Bao Li was not here, and it was Saina's duty to represent her.

She left Upach and ran down the hall toward the light of the courtyard, the expectant servants, and Kang Dahan.

———

Saina shielded her eyes against the sun's harsh glare. She took in the blur of servants packed shoulder to shoulder, their gaze fixed on the gates flanked with colorful banners and now thrown wide open.

In the pregnant silence, the faintest chime of a camel bell was heard. A servant standing beside Saina pressed high up on his toes as a single chime became many, their song growing louder.

The guards shifted their weight and lined the entrance when Kang Dahan rounded the corner and came into view, sitting high atop his lead camel. His presence filled the entirety of the gates. A large man both in stature and girth, he held his shoulders high as cheers went up from the gathered servants. He scanned the crowd and smiled proudly, his lust for adulation well fed.

Both he and his lead camel were finely dressed. Kang Dahan wore a silk lampas robe and pointed shoes. His beard had grown thick, and his dark hair was pulled back with leather ties. He looked younger than his many years. His camel, draped in brightly colored saddlebags and gold-threaded tassels that shimmered in the sunlight, towered over all who were present.

Kang Dahan circled the courtyard while livestock handlers, with sand-worn faces and weary eyes, pulled teams of camels behind him. Bells danced below dyed-leather harnesses, ringing out as goods, piled high on the camel's backs, groaned and creaked with each step. The thick scent of sandalwood and musk, saffron and cinnamon lingered in the air.

Saina spared little attention for the lumbering caravan, her gaze trained on Kang Dahan. He stopped in front of Bao Li's khana and scanned the empty portico for his wife.

The courtyard began to spin. Saina gripped the arm of the servant beside her who pulled away from her. "Forgive me," she said, then she closed her eyes. When she opened them again, Kang Dahan's countenance was darkened, his proud smile had faltered.

He barked an angry command, and his camel kneeled. In an instant, his servant rushed to his side and helped him dismount.

The moment his feet touched the ground, he demanded that someone answer for Bao Li's absence.

Saina's heart raced. Why had Bao Li left her to carry this burden?

A surge of energy pulsed through her body. "Please move," Saina said, her voice quaking as she pushed through the knot of servants. "I must speak with the master." The crowd reluctantly gave way, and by the time she approached Kang Dahan, he was shaking his finger at the stableboys who had rushed to his aid.

"Put the saddlebags in my private stable. Do not let them touch the ground," he yelled. He straightened suddenly, as though aware of the tension in the courtyard, then gave a quick bark of laughter.

But Saina heard the quiver of agitation in his voice, saw how he struggled to regain his composure. He could not fool those who truly knew him.

Standing beside him, Saina saw his gaze fall on her. His face reddened. He opened his mouth to speak, but his servant tapped him on the shoulder.

"Master," he said, pointing to the crowd still gathered silently behind him.

Kang Dahan spun around, gazed long into their eyes, then raised his arms in the air. The courtyard erupted with shouts.

"Do not doubt that your reception is a welcomed sight for my weary bones," he said, speaking over them. "Not even from my days of youth have I experienced a journey so fraught with violent tempests and misfortune at every turn. But I am no fool. To choose the life of a caravanner is to choose a life of discomfort."

His voice faded, and his gaze grew distant. "I know it is my custom to entertain you with a story of my travels. Indeed, there are plenty. But I regret that I have been met with a matter demanding my immediate attention. Please, go about your duties, for the banquet is at hand and time is short."

Whispers erupted throughout the courtyard as the servants looked to one another for answers. Receiving nothing, they shrugged their shoulders and slowly dispersed.

Kang Dahan spun around. Taking three rapid steps toward Saina, he stopped, his face a hand-width from hers. "Why has my wife disrespected me in this manner?" he said through clenched teeth. "Tell Bao Li to ready herself, for I demand her presence immediately."

Saina opened her mouth, but her tongue became like molded clay. She could not fashion a careful response.

"Speak," Kang Dahan barked. "I have no regard for cowardice." His eyes bulged in a face grown fearsome.

Saina bowed her head, trying to bide time. "I beg of you, do not be harsh with your servant. My mistress is not here. She has traveled to Penjikent on a matter of business. It could not be put off."

"What business could take precedence over my arrival and force this humiliation upon me?" he snapped, beads of sweat showing on his forehead. "Was my letter not warning enough?"

Saina shook her head. She had promised not to reveal the true reason for Bao Li's trip, so she pressed her lips together and bound up the words in her heart. "Forgive me, but I do not know such matters," she said. From the corner of her eye, she saw him raise his fist. She closed her eyes, her body tensed, as she prepared to be struck, but Ning Po's voice cut in.

"Why worry yourself over such a simpleminded servant who *claims* to know nothing?" she said.

Saina slowly opened her eyes.

Ning Po walked up beside Kang Dahan, smiling, as though satisfied with the situation before her. "I watched Bao Li leave the day after learning of your pending arrival. Her actions were deliberate." Ning Po drew her finger across his chest and took her place in front of him. "But why should you trouble yourself with such

216

news on this day of celebration? Bao Li has made her decision, and this slave is not worth your anger. *Not yet.*" Ning Po looked over her shoulder and smirked, then turned back. "Tonight, after the celebration, I will tell you what has transpired in your absence."

A flash of concern crossed Kang Dahan's face, but Ning Po gave him no time to consider her words further.

"You have only just returned, and I can see that your travels have taken their toll on you." She leaned into him, the silk shawl falling from her bare shoulders. "Come, I have prepared a bath that you may wash yourself before your guests arrive. It has been a while since you have felt the touch of a woman."

Ning Po took his hand in hers, and Kang Dahan smiled, his eyes carrying him away. They brushed past Saina and walked toward Ning Po's room, the faint scent of her perfume lingering long in the air.

Chapter Twenty-Two

Saina set the dish of stuffed eggplant on the serving table beside the spiced carrots and salted cabbage salad, then straightened. Craning her neck, she looked past lamb kababs sizzling on long grills and musicians sending up their song to where Narisaf stood in the doorway of his room, looking out over the courtyard. His eyes met hers and he smiled.

Narisaf and the weaver had come earlier in the day, but aside from a few glances cast at each other, Saina had not had the opportunity to seek him out.

The weaver stepped out from the room and placed his hand on Narisaf's firm shoulder. Saina lingered a moment longer, comforted by their presence. The weaver pointed to the gathered guests, the dignitaries and artisans, men of noble rank and their finely dressed wives and spoke into Narisaf's ear. Narisaf tilted his head back and laughed.

Saina could just barely make out the deep sound above the low murmur of voices and instruments, but watching the ease of his movements, the pleasure on Narisaf's face, made her smile.

They left their room and walked into the courtyard, where several dignitaries had gathered, and Saina felt a sting of longing.

What was it like to be a part of a family, to be like a thread woven into a tapestry of stories that bound one person to another? She had no such ties. Her smile faded. More than anything she wanted to belong.

Vandakk appeared at the table holding a basket filled with hot bread. "I was delighted to see that Narisaf and his grandfather accepted our invitation."

Saina quickly arranged a spot on the serving platform for the bread as he continued talking.

"When Kang Dahan learned that the weaver of Merv was in attendance, he expressed great interest in speaking with him. But it is my hope he does not overwhelm him with his questioning." Vandakk looked around, then leaned toward her and lowered his voice. "You know how he can be."

Saina pursed her lips, startled by Vandakk's comment. He was correct of course. Kang Dahan was a prideful, tiresome man. But she had never before heard Vandakk express judgment of Kang Dahan's character.

For a moment Saina could not speak, but she bound his words in her heart, honored that he would speak so freely in front of her. If she had longed to experience the bonds of family, perhaps Vandakk's confidence in her was consolation enough.

"The weaver is a wise man and sharp in his observations," Saina said. "I am certain he can maintain his composure in the face of a braggart. Nevertheless, Narisaf would do well to remain at his side."

"Yes," Vandakk said, patting Saina on the arm. "But that is not where Narisaf desires to be."

Saina looked across the courtyard and saw Narisaf standing with his grandfather in a crowd. The wife of a dignitary was speaking to him, but his eyes were focused on Saina. Her skin flushed with heat as Vandakk walked away, chuckling.

Saina shook her head and looked out once more at the courtyard. Torchlight danced along the mud-brick walls while the pleasing aroma of roasted poultry over open fires and fresh baked bread grew thick beneath the copper sky. All that was needed to start the evening was Kang Dahan.

As if on cue, the music died down. Saina searched for the watchman and found him standing beneath the portico of the khana that Kang Dahan shared with Bao Li.

The watchman put the horn to his lips, and its low sound resonated deep in Saina's chest. The crowd grew silent.

All eyes turned toward the gilded doors from which Kang Dahan emerged, looking refreshed and wearing his brocaded silk robe. His hair had been loosed from its leather ties, falling at his shoulders. His beard, streaked with gray, was neatly trimmed. Ning Po appeared behind him and took her place at his side.

A murmur went up from the crowd as people cast sideways glances at one another.

Saina's body stiffened, and she stared hard at the spectacle. Why would Kang Dahan allow Ning Po to stand beside him? Did he seek to send such a brazen message?

Gone was his earlier agitation. He placed his hand to his breast, showing off thick gold rings set with lapis lazuli and carnelian. The fine jewels matched the striking necklace Ning Po was wearing.

"Friends," his deep voice bellowed over the guests standing in silence. "Words cannot express the pleasure I feel seeing you here tonight. As you can see, I have spared no expense and welcome you to partake in my offering."

His voice became a blur as Saina's attention was drawn to the familiar woman standing in front of her, shaking her head in disgust. A well-known dyer of fabrics from Samarkand, she was elegantly dressed in violet and red ochre layered silks. Her hair was held in place by a gold clip, her dark eyes lined with kohl. She leaned toward her daughter who was heavy with child.

"Where is Bao Li, and why is Kang Dahan's lesser wife standing in her place?" she said loudly, without regard for who overheard.

Her daughter shook her head. "I do not know, but Ning Po is too young to understand the responsibility of such a position."

"I am concerned," the dyer said sharply. "Bao Li has always assured me of the choicest indigo from the caravan delivery. Her knowledge is vast; her dealings are fair." She swept her hand through the air. "Look around at the craftsmen who have come for the same assurances. Why would Kang Dahan risk offending his most loyal customers in this way?"

Silence hung between them for a moment as the daughter placed her hand on her swollen belly. She bit her lip. "It is possible that Ning Po elevated her position by giving birth during his long absence."

Saina's stomach dropped.

The dyer gripped her daughter's arm, her gold bracelets slid down her wrists. "Could it be?"

"There have been whisperings of a pregnancy, and it is no secret that Kang Dahan has longed for an heir." She shrugged.

The dyer stood still, her face pinched in contemplation. Finally, her face softened, and she shook her head. "No. It cannot be. Word of an heir would have traveled through the city like a sandstorm."

"Something has occurred," her daughter said. "I heard that Ning Po's young servant went to the apothecary earlier this morning. The moment she walked through her door, Umida's demeanor changed. She immediately left several customers, including myself, to tend to the girl in the back of the store."

Saina's chest swelled painfully as she listened to the women speak, and realized she had forgotten to breathe. She exhaled a shaking breath and walked away.

Ning Po remained beside Kang Dahan, her smile forced, eyes wandering. Several times she glanced at the gates and frowned. Saina followed her gaze but saw only the guards and a few servants hauling items from the tents. Nothing of concern.

"I have longed to share with you a recounting of my journey," Kang Dahan said, his voice booming. "A journey that began with

221

the death of my lead puller who fell while securing goods on the back of a camel. It was an ominous warning, an augur of things to come." He paused, letting his head and shoulders droop heavily before continuing. "But a head caravanner, a *sartapao* such as I, has a terrible responsibility and must never give in to superstition. To do so would ensure that the far reaches of the world would never know the customs of the people of Samarkand or the workmanship of their hands. *Your* hands."

A loud roar erupted in the courtyard.

"Some of you have traversed the forest paths and parched desert lands of which I speak. As such, I will not waste my breath telling you of the dangers lurking on the Silk Road. But I know you expect a grand story, and in this way, I am obliged to tell you. First, fill your cups with fermented drink, for the story will go down easier that way." He tipped his head back and emptied his drink.

With cups in hand, guests pressed in around Saina and the servants beside her. She poured wine until the last cup was filled and all had returned to their places, their attention on Kang Dahan.

Gradually a hush fell over the courtyard as a servant approached him, and with great care placed a rectangular copper bell in his hands. Kang Dahan took hold of the bell's thick, scarlet cord and swung it gently, so its deep chime resonated in the stillness.

"How does one tell a story whose depths have yet to be mined, except to speak truthfully and hope the words reveal themselves?" He stopped to scan the crowd and smiled, no doubt pleased by their rapt attention. "I know what I tell you will be difficult to believe, but it was where we found ourselves as we cut through steep valleys and began our long ascent into the Pamirs.

"We had stopped to refresh our animals and fill our waterskins from the mountain stream when we were met by a single sojourner seeking to travel in the safety of our numbers. I denied him at first, having perceived that his tired donkey would slow us down. But he warned me of the robbers that had tormented several caravans in the days before our arrival. He assured me that he had traveled the mountain pass countless times and knew a different route.

"We set out, following this man of few words. When dense clouds descended on the mountains and we could not see beyond the noses of our animals, it was the resolve in his eyes and chime of his copper bell that gave my men confidence in their footing. Torrential rain followed, and for days it did not cease. We pressed on, silent in our suffering.

"The path became steeper, the ground saturated, unable to absorb another drop of rain. He led from the front while I moved to the back of my caravan to ensure every man and animal made it over the pass. But suddenly the earth began to shake beneath us, and the mountainside gave way. I watched in horror as a violent spray of boulders and mud thundered down the mountain, taking with it the sojourner and his donkey."

Kang Dahan paused as gasps of shock and concern spread through the crowd. When they quieted, he wiped the corners of his eyes with the hem of his robe.

"The responsibility of a *sartapao* is to press on, but how would I lead my men when the path before us was uncertain, and our only guide was gone? That night we pitched our tents, but I found no rest. For the first time in all my reckoning, I contemplated turning around."

Kang Dahan leaned forward. "Listen carefully, for you will not believe what I am about to tell you. In the morning, as we cinched the goods on our animals and prepared to turn back, I heard the distant chime of the copper bell and was struck still. Though I saw no one and no way forward, I followed its chime, trusting the source of the sound would guide me rightly.

"A full day had passed by the time we traversed the slide of earth and were safely on the other side and a shimmering object caught my eye. Tucked between a wedge of rocks was the copper bell." He held up the bell by its scarlet cord. "How did it come to rest so far from where the man was swept away?"

Kang Dahan straightened. "Many times, I have sought to placate my curiosity, but I have come to find solace in the unanswered questions and leave the mystery to remain as such." He rang the bell three times, its deep sound resonating in the courtyard.

When the chime stopped and silence settled over the courtyard, the mesmerized guests shifted.

Kang Dahan called out once more, "As you have all come to expect, Vandakk has prepared the finest meal to be found along the whole of the Silk Road. Please, partake of the banquet and enjoy the celebration." With a wave of his hand, he dismissed his audience and joined a group of merchants waiting nearby. Ning Po remained at his side as acrobats with painted faces and costumes resembling peacocks and snow leopards, black bears and lions tumbled into the courtyard.

Saina stood at the cast-iron *kazan*, serving pilaf to guests whose plates were soon filled with all manner of rich foods. By the time the long lines had become a slow trickle of people, the acrobats were well into their act, spinning plates and balancing on ropes strung high in the air.

The youngest of the acrobats climbed a tall pole set on the hewn stone ground, held by nothing but the black sky above. Saina stared in awe and cheers went up from the crowd.

Narisaf appeared beside her, his eyes wide with wonder. "I have never seen such a sight before." He leaned against the table and crossed his arms.

Comforted at his nearness, Saina laughed. For all the burdens that the caravanserai put on her, it was also filled with incredible beauty. This was a night of celebration, and she was delighted that Narisaf could partake of it.

"Bao Li has always insisted on hiring acrobats for Kang Dahan's feasts," Saina said. She leaned closer and lowered her voice. "They remind her of the acrobats her father took her to see as a young girl. She once told me that her greatest fear is losing the thread connecting her to the land of her youth."

"Such a display of her homeland is grand," Narisaf said. "I understand her longing for it."

"I wonder what it is like to be connected to something in such a way," Saina said, then paused. She looked into Narisaf's eyes. "When I watch you interact with your grandfather, I see how the threads of family bind you together, and I realize how strongly I want to be a part of it. A part of you."

Narisaf grinned. "You have been a part of me from the moment I first saw you in my grandfather's tent." He leaned closer. "Soon we will be free to announce it."

The ladle in Saina's hands grew heavy. How greatly she wanted to believe him. It was her only hope now, but it seemed impossible.

Narisaf picked up a small plate and tapped it in his hands. "When that day comes, I fear you will be disappointed. Life in this caravanserai is far more thrilling than the quiet home I share with my grandfather." He winked, and his low laughter sent Saina's heart beating.

Saina yearned to touch Narisaf, to assure him she felt the same, but she glanced at the crowd and drew back. "You are enjoying yourself, then?" she said.

"Of course."

She glanced at the weaver reclined at a warming fire near the sycamore tree. "And your grandfather?"

"He is tired," Narisaf said. He took a round of swirled onion flatbread and set it on the small plate, then topped it with roasted duck and sour cherry sauce. "But I promised to bring him a morsel of food and chai in hopes it would prolong his energy for the night."

Through the gathered crowd, Saina saw Kang Dahan approach the weaver and kneel beside him. She touched Narisaf's arm lightly and pointed. "It is well that you bring it to him soon. Your grandfather has a visitor."

Narisaf's eyes widened, then he frowned. "I should go," Narisaf said. But he hesitated.

"Take the food to him," Saina said. "I will prepare the chai and bring it to him shortly." She watched Narisaf leave and smiled. She would take any opportunity to be close to Narisaf, even if just for a moment.

By the time Saina filled a small kettle and brought the steaming drink to the weaver, Kang Dahan had acquainted himself with them and was reclining beside the weaver. Not wanting to interrupt, she stood back and waited for a lull in their conversation.

"I was told you are the man who has created these fine tapestries," Kang Dahan said, pointing to the banisters lined with the weaver's creations. "I have seen your work displayed in countless trade cities and have heard men speak of you with great reverence. But never did I expect to meet you in person, certainly not sitting in my caravanserai." He chuckled. "I could not be more pleased than I am at this moment."

The weaver bowed his head slightly and smiled. At his side was the small plate of uneaten food Narisaf had brought him.

Kang Dahan continued. "Did you come here directly from Merv? How was your crossing of the Kyzylkum Desert? Once, when I had not yet reached the height of a man, I crossed the loathsome desert with my father's caravan." He shook his head. "Never again. I dedicated my life to the mountain regions of the east. Nothing can compare."

Saina gripped the tea tray tighter, but the weaver smiled politely. "The land to the east certainly holds intrigue, as your tale of the copper bell suggests."

Kang Dahan raised his brow then paused. "Tell me, what compelled you to come to Samarkand?"

"I am acquiring the final thread for a design that was started many years ago."

"And this thread you speak of can only be found in Samarkand?"

The weaver looked up at Saina, his deep eyes penetrating hers. "Yes."

Saina's gaze darted to Narisaf. Flickering firelight cast a warm glow on his face and danced in his clove-colored eyes.

Kang Dahan pressed up on his elbow and jerked his head toward Saina. "Give my guest his tea," he said sharply. He looked back at the weaver and threw his hand in the air. "Forgive me of this servant. She has grown careless in my absence. I assure you, it will be dealt with."

Saina's face burned with shame as she knelt in front of the weaver and poured the steaming drink into his cup. Her hands trembled, but she was diligent not to spill and rouse Kang Dahan's anger even more.

Narisaf cleared his throat and shifted, but Saina gave a curt shake of her head, warning him not to speak.

"Your criticism of this servant is unwarranted," the weaver said. "She has tended to our needs with great attention. It is rare to find a person who holds both pride in her work and loyalty to her masters."

Kang Dahan's face reddened. He pulled the hem of his collar away from his neck and changed the subject. "If it is the finest threads and richest hues you seek, allow me to introduce you to the greatest dyers in all Samarkand. Indeed, along all of the Silk Road. You will not be disappointed in their work."

"Your offer is kind, but not necessary," the weaver said. "The thread has already been found. All that remains is for the design to be completed. As a master weaver, I have learned it takes great skill and careful diligence to draw it out."

Kang Dahan studied the weaver intently. "What has been said about you is true then," he said. "You hold the wisdom of a seer, the knowledge of things unseen?"

The weaver smiled and pointed to Kang Dahan's hand. "Like the copper bell you have in your possession, the answers to our greatest mysteries are often hidden in plain sight."

"You speak as though you know of this bell."

"No. But God of heaven stirs his purpose within all men, whether through a bell, a thread, or any other manner he chooses." The weaver held Kang Dahan in his steady gaze. "A wise man acts upon that calling, though it seems pure folly to do so. The opinion of the critic has no bearing on him."

Kang Dahan sat up.

"The ringing of that bell will stir a greater purpose in you as well," the weaver said. "Soon you will understand it."

Saina held her breath. What was the weaver saying? She looked at Narisaf, her eyes questioning.

"Grandfather?" Narisaf said, placing his strong hand on the weaver's shoulder.

Kang Dahan seemed troubled. He looked around the courtyard and stood slowly. "I regret that I must take my leave. There are many guests waiting to speak to me." He walked a few paces, then turned back, as though unable to resist the pull of the weaver's mystery. "I trust this final thread and design that you speak of will be something to behold. Show it to me when you are finished. If it is as rare as you say, I will make you an offer."

The weaver bowed his head and smiled. "An offer will be made, but not for the reason you expect."

Chapter Twenty-Three

Saina walked into the crowded storeroom and stopped. Cooks were arranging pistachio halva and stuffed apricots on platters, and bakers pulled fine flour and spices from shelves.

She pushed high on her toes, searching for Vandakk, and finally spotted him sitting alone in the far corner, away from the rush of sweaty bodies. His eyes were closed, his head resting against the wall.

Saina stopped to pour a cup of spiced tea, then grabbed two squares of halva, before weaving through the throng of people to reach Vandakk.

"Forgive my delay," she said, studying the plate of food that sat untouched on the low table before him. Whenever a feast was prepared, Saina and Vandakk had made a tradition of sharing a quick meal together. She knew to search him out in the lull between dinner and dessert, but on this night, Saina had been distracted.

Vandakk opened his eyes and smiled. "It is as I expected." He tapped the low table. "Sit."

Saina slid the tea and halva toward him. "If you eat only one morsel tonight, I recommend the halva. You will not be disappointed."

He chuckled. "You know me too well. I have never been able to deny myself dessert." He picked up the crumbling square, took a bite. "If my wife were here, she would scold me for eating this sweet before my meal."

"Is that not the way of all wives and mothers?" Saina said. She tried to smile, to lighten the unease that had her in its firm grip since Kang Dahan's arrival, but she felt no relief.

With his mouth full, Vandakk nodded, sliding the small plate of untouched food toward her.

She pinched jeweled rice between a piece of torn bread and put it to her mouth, studying the deep lines in Vandakk's face, which was framed by wisps of gray hair that stuck out in sharp points. How grateful she was to have been trained under his charge.

He smiled, his emerald eyes alight. "Do you remember when Miunai and Uta were here, and you asked me if I ever longed for children?"

The question surprised Saina, but she recalled how patient Vandakk had been with the curious, young boy. "You said it still saddens you."

"It was an honest answer," Vandakk said. "Children are like a strand of gold thread woven through a toilsome life. To not hold that honor is to be denied a heritage," he paused. "But I should have explained further."

Saina leaned in, straining to hear him through the clatter of dishes and the voices carrying across the room.

"My wife and I yearned for the honor of children, but when she died, I buried that dream. The notion was too insulting to consider without her by my side."

Saina's chest tightened at the depth of loss that still lingered on his face even after all these years.

"Life has a way of surprising us," Vandakk said. "It shines its warm light in the darkest moments and gives us hope in the bleakest of times. You must remember that, Saina."

She nodded but wondered at his deeper meaning that seemed to reside just beneath the surface.

He pointed to his head. "You understand it here, but you do not know it here," he said, as he moved his finger to his chest. "There comes a time when we all must learn this lesson." He paused, his eyes staring but unseeing, as though recalling a distant memory.

"I was returning from the canal the evening your father brought you to the caravanserai. From a distance, I heard the words exchanged between him and Bao Li and watched you curl into yourself standing between them. When he walked away, it was your desperate cries that struck me with such emotion I could not shake it from my mind." Vandakk's voice broke.

Saina stared straight ahead, trying to keep from falling into the abyss of that terrible memory.

"Time passed, but you did not emerge from your grief. Late one night, Bao Li came to my room. Worried, she expressed her concern that you would not survive much longer and wondered how we could help you. I offered the only thing I could, and the next day she brought you here."

Saina glanced around the storeroom, remembering how small and insecure she once felt standing within its unfamiliar walls and towering shelves.

"I remember," she said, grateful for the reprieve of thought. "You had just pulled a tray of samsa from the oven and offered one to me."

"The moment you took that first bite, I saw a spark of life in your eyes," Vandakk said, beaming. "From that day forward, you began to talk. It was just a word or two at first, but over time you laughed. And with your presence in my life, your youthful spirit in my kitchen, so did I." He reached across the table and touched her hand. "I should have told you long ago, that you are my strand of gold thread. A beautiful gift in a life of toil."

Saina was struck silent as she stared at Vandakk, his eyes glistening in the glow of cressets burning overhead. In all the years she had longed for a family of her own, one had been provided for her. How had she not recognized this before? She choked back tears. "I owe so much to you for your words of comfort, your gentle hand of guidance—given the way a loving father cares for his child. I see clearly now that I was wrong in my thinking. I was never alone but had the greatest example of a father in front of me all along."

She looked away for a brief moment, ashamed of the wasted years of longing. But before she could turn back to Vandakk, Zimat approached, his face and arms dusted with fine flour.

"The trays of halva, honeycomb, and fruit have been prepared, and the last of the sweet pastries are baked, ready to be taken to the courtyard," Zimat said.

Vandakk placed his hands on the table and shifted his weight to stand, but Saina stopped him. "I will go. Stay here and finish your meal or this time it will be you who withers away." She stood.

"But you have hardly eaten," Vandakk said. "And you need energy, for the night is long."

"I will be fine," Saina said, following Zimat to the table where the desserts were piled.

With a tray of sweet pastries resting on her shoulder, Saina walked into the music-filled courtyard where the *dayereh* beat a steady rhythm and dancers swirled in brightly colored silks.

She wove through the tangle of guests and set the tray on the table, then began arranging the desserts. When she straightened, Ning Po was walking toward her. Issik, the honey merchant, followed closely behind.

A strange mix of anger and dread gripped Saina's body. Her hands were suddenly sweaty, and she wiped them on her tunic. The honey merchant seemed larger, more vile, than she had remembered. She began to back away but stumbled into a servant behind her. By the time she straightened, Ning Po was standing in front of her.

"You look like you have seen a ghost, Saina," Ning Po said, a crooked smile forming on her lips.

Saina stood in silence, her knees shaking. She glanced through the courtyard, searching for Narisaf, but did not find him.

Ning Po took a plate from the table and gave it to the honey merchant. "Your arrival was too late for the evening meal, but you will be pleased with the offering of desserts nonetheless."

The honey merchant filled his plate with pistachio halva, fruit, and pastries, then stopped suddenly. His hand hovered over the stamped clay vessel of honey. He snapped his head up, his gaze falling on Saina.

She looked down, away from his icy stare.

Ning Po moved toward him. "I told you, Bao Li is not here, and her servant is powerless without her. Do not fear humiliation at her hands."

Saina's jaw tightened.

"I fear nothing," he barked. "But if your word proves false and the plan falls through—"

"I assure you, it will be worth your time." Ning Po turned to Saina, her chin high. "Show my guest to the finest room available."

Saina tilted her head and stared at Ning Po. What was she trying to accomplish with this grasp for power? Whatever it was, Saina would not cower before her. "All rooms were claimed early in the day. Even the courtyard is full," she said. She pointed to the servants standing near the caravanserai's entrance. "They will supply your guest with a lantern if he wishes to pitch a tent outside the gates."

Ning Po's eyes widened with surprise; her mouth grew hard. "Then I demand that you take him to the encampment and ensure his tent is raised."

Saina shook her head. "By direct order of Kang Dahan and

Bao Li, I am not permitted outside the gates when darkness has settled."

"Of course," Ning Po said, trying to gain the upper hand. "A servant like you cannot be trusted."

"It is for my protection," Saina said, looking from Ning Po to the honey merchant. "To be left outside of the gates at night is to be exposed to the beasts that lurk unseen." She let the words hang in the air.

Ning Po shifted uncomfortably, then reached across the table, her metal bracelets clanged as she pointed her sharp finger in Saina's face. "You will regret conducting yourself in this manner," she seethed.

Saina stepped back. "I am honest in my speech. If you take issue with the edict, speak to your husband. I have no say in the matter." Saina pointed to Kang Dahan who, having succumbed to drunkenness, was reaching toward a dancer dressed in layered silks in front of him.

Ning Po recoiled, the sight a blow to her pride. She growled low and spun around, facing Issik. "Pitch your tent outside the gates. I must attend to my husband."

He stepped in front of Ning Po as she turned, stopping her. He lowered his head, his hard eyes set firmly on her. "Assure me that I did not come in vain."

"The plan has already been set in motion. I will see it through," Ning Po snapped. She brushed past him, leaving Saina and Issik standing alone.

Saina looked at his pale eyes, the smirk upon his lips. Upach did well to leave him when she did. Who knows what would have happened to her. But where could Saina go? To whom could she escape? It was her duty to remain at the serving table, ensuring the guests were tended to.

Issik growled, then shoved a square of halva into his mouth, bits of the crumbled dessert falling into his beard. He walked away and disappeared into the crowd.

What had Ning Po planned?

Saina looked across the courtyard. It was filled with people talking and laughing, their high voices carrying throughout the caravanserai, but she had never felt more alone.

———

The feast continued with grand ceremony as the moon tracked slowly across the sky. The music grew louder, the tempo increased, and the dancers swirled with great skill to the frenetic beat. With pure delight, guests clapped and chanted, immersed in the performance before them.

When the refrain swelled to its height and seemed it could go no faster, both the music and dancers stopped suddenly. Stunned silence hung in the air as the dancers remained perfectly still, their chests heaving from the exertion.

Cheers erupted from the guests, the raucous applause filling the courtyard until the last of the dancers exited the caravanserai and returned to their tents outside the gates. Their departure made way for the final, most highly anticipated performance of the night.

Saina glanced across the courtyard, waiting.

At last, the bahkshi appeared from the hallway carrying a leather instrument case in one hand and a small rug in the other. A sudden hush fell over the crowd.

An unassuming man, he shuffled through the courtyard, the scrape of his leather sandals on the stone ground the only sound to be heard. Unrolling his rug, he sat down and pulled the *barbat* from its leather case. With great care he ran his fingers along its fretted neck, then set its pear-shaped base in his lap.

Saina recalled his song the last time he had come, how it brought to mind thoughts of her father and hints of a closure to the life he once lived. A gifted bahkshi had a way of telling stories that touched the heart of all its hearers, but only if they chose to listen.

"I have roamed the land in silence to glean many words," he

said, his voice as thin and wispy as his silver beard. "And when they grow heavy upon my lips, I pour them out, a revelation of that which is hidden." He began to pluck the strings of the instrument, sending a melody over the crowd.

To whom does this song belong?
Whose story will be pulled from the sands
And gathered in a tale before us?

Kang Dahan pushed up on his elbow and leaned in, his eyes glassy and red. It was customary that his wife remained at his side as the feast drew to an end, but Ning Po had not taken her place of honor beside him.

Saina drew her brow. What would keep Ning Po away from such an important matter of ceremony? And how would Kang Dahan react when the effects of his drunkenness wore off and he was made aware of his wife's insult?

She searched for Ning Po through the throng of people sated by a night of indulgences and found Narisaf, instead, leaning against the wall outside his room. The door was closed, no light flickered beneath it. The weaver had gone to bed.

She smiled, relieved at his presence, even as the roll of the bahkshi's tongue drew her into the cadence of his flowing song. Soothed by the words, Saina was unaware of how much time had passed. She leaned forward, straining to hear the song, which seemed to speak directly to her.

The sojourner's restlessness flows like a fountain
He slogs beneath pine and scales the mountain
Stirring within him he seeks to quell
The lonely beat of the camel bell

Beware the tongue split like a serpent
Her lies flow swift in a raging current
Take heed and listen leave it not to fate
A snare has been set created by hate

Look up incline the ear to hear
The time has come a testing draws near
If your stubborn heart holds sway
From Samarkand you will be carried away

The bahkshi's hands on the *barbat* slowed and the strings grew silent. His song was strung together, woven like a tapestry. Saina was struck by the depth and meaning behind each word, a glimpse into a grander design. But its whole she had yet to grasp.

The bahkshi stood with ease and rolled up his rug. Was he not weighed down by the immensity of his own words just as Saina was?

With a slight bow, he walked away, leaving all to ponder his song. His was the final act. No musicians, no acrobats rose to take his place, for who dared come after him?

Long after the silence had settled, the guests began to stir and slowly disperse to their rooms and tents. Others set out their bed mats in the courtyard and lay down beneath the canopy of stars.

Saina was stacking the food trays near the cauldrons when a swift movement above drew her eye.

Ning Po strode across the balcony and quickly descended the stairs. Her shoulders were hunched, and her arm was pressed tightly against a bulge beneath her thin, silk overcoat.

What was she up to? Caution pricked Saina's heart.

When Ning Po reached the landing, she rushed to Kang Dahan as he stumbled toward his khana. Together, she and his manservant struggled to usher him through the gilded doors.

The doors closed behind them, but Saina remained standing, unable to move.

———

Later, when Saina had finished helping clean the storeroom and the cooks and bakers had departed to bed down for the night, she walked into the courtyard. All was silent except for the sounds of men in deep sleep. A few dim torchlights burned in far corners, casting just enough light for her to see Narisaf sitting in front of his room, waiting for her. Just as he said he would.

Beneath the dark reach of the sky, Saina brushed a strand of hair from her face and quickened her step.

"Who am I that you would wait for me at this hour?" she whispered, kneeling in front of him. She looked over her shoulder at the still bodies sleeping in the courtyard but felt certain wakeful eyes were watching her. She would stay only a moment; she dared not get any closer to Narisaf.

"If this is what is required to be near you, then I will do it until my last breath," he said, studying her face. He tilted his head. "What troubles you?"

Saina desired to tell him about Ning Po and Issik, but the night of delight and glint of high wonder still lingered in Narisaf's heavy eyes. She would not trouble him with it now. There was time enough in the morning.

Narisaf drew his brow. "Saina?"

Her stomach tightened. To utter the words aloud would give voice to the danger, but to remain silent could prove deadly.

Someone stirred in the courtyard, and Saina froze. Narisaf peered past her.

She shook her head. "Go to bed, you are tired. But do not leave at morning's first light. I would like to see you before you go." She placed her hand on his arm, felt him soften beneath her touch.

He smiled. "I will stay. You have my word."

She left him standing by the door of his room and climbed the stairs, sensing his eyes were upon her. How safe and protected she felt in his gaze.

At the landing, she stopped to light a small wax candle from the burning torch, then walked to her room. The long-awaited feast was over, and her future was still uncertain. Bao Li had not returned, and Ning Po had clawed her way to the top. *With Bao Li gone, how can I defend myself against Ning Po?* Saina had no answers.

The candle shed its dim light on Saina's door and cast unfamiliar shadows along its frame. Something was out of place. She reached for the handle, but the door was already cracked open. A chill crept up her spine.

With the candle pulled close, Saina lowered her head and cautiously stepped inside. Clay cracked beneath her feet. Her hand trembled as she held out the candle, its light bouncing around the room.

Pieces of her shattered clay vessel lay strewn across the floor, along with her wooden elephant with the broken trunk, the colorful stones, and turquoise feather. Where was her bracelet?

Saina brushed aside shards of clay, but her hope of finding the bracelet faded quickly. She picked up her bed mat and shook it. Nothing. The bracelet was gone.

Pressing her back against the hard wall, Saina slid to the floor. She stared a straight silence, the room becoming a blur of dull color as a slow awareness took form.

Something else was missing.

Could it be...?

The thought was so wretched Saina could not utter the words, could barely force herself to search.

She pulled up the blankets and her bed mat once more, and her breath stilled. Nothing but the dusty floor.

The warhorse garment was gone.

Chapter Twenty-Four

Morning stretched across the sky, its pale light a reluctant herald of what had occurred in the night. With its rising, the events of last night could no longer remain hidden in darkness. Saina drew water from the cistern and stared long across the courtyard. Her body ached, and she was weary. Dread had wound its way through every muscle and sinew.

Many guests had risen early and were rolling up bed mats and gathering their items. Outside the caravanserai, servants pulled up pegs and took down tents, their backs already damp with sweat. It would not be long before the sun, fanned by the west winds, burned hot upon the sands. All manner of men who made their living trekking across the desert knew to heed its warning and seek respite in the midday shade.

But what kind of shelter would grant Saina reprieve from the anguish that had wrapped her body in its tight grip and darkened her thoughts?

She sighed and set her bucket on the ground, seeking a moment's relief from the swarming pressures. When she straightened, Narisaf had emerged from his room, tying his long knife to his belt. He smiled at her with that familiar boyish grin, but she looked away. His appearance brought her no relief.

How would she tell him that his father's warhorse garment was stolen? The thought had tormented her throughout the night, and she still had no answer except the painful, honest one.

The pervasive dread scratched at her throat. Saina could not hold back any longer, but the moment she stepped toward him, a man's voice called out from behind her.

"Saina."

She turned and saw Kang Dahan's servant, his tunic hanging loosely from his gaunt shoulders. His hands were clasped tightly in front of him.

He dropped his hands and took a step back. "Kang Dahan demands your presence." His eyes were troubled, his voice hesitant, as if he was not comfortable with the words.

"Me?" she said. "What reason does he seek me out at this early hour?" She understood the depths of Kang Dahan's impulsive nature, but even she had not anticipated this unusual demand while his guests were still in attendance.

The manservant shook his head, his gaze fastened to the ground. "You are ordered to come with me now."

Her heart raced. She looked at Narisaf and saw his brows drawn together in concern. She walked away, swallowing down the terrible sense that she would not return to him.

———

The gilded doors slammed closed behind Saina, engulfing the halls of the khana in ominous shadows.

The sound of sandals scraping against the smooth stone echoed off the narrow walls. Despite the heat of the morning, cold fear crept into her bones. She shivered. How alone she felt, shut away from Narisaf. He could not help her here. Did he even know the trouble she was in?

Saina had walked these halls countless times, had tended to

their upkeep and learned to serve Bao Li within them. With the care and attention of a deeply held friendship, she had come to anticipate her mistress's needs and provide for them without a word being uttered. What pride she had taken in it.

She walked past the bowl of rose water she had set out a few days earlier, its sweet fragrance dulled and stagnated in Bao Li's absence. Nothing felt familiar now.

The manservant led her to the entrance of the vaulted greeting room where the low murmur of voices stopped as they approached. He moved aside and fear seized Saina. Her body felt as rigid as fired clay, at risk of shattering with each forced step leading her into the room.

Kang Dahan sat in his carved chair. Gone was the merriment of last night's feast, the idiocy of drunkenness wiped clean from his face. He seemed to work out a thought in his mind, as though sobered by unpleasant news. At his side stood Ning Po, holding a bundle in the crook of her arm, her mouth twisting into a slow, cruel smile.

Saina shifted, fixed her gaze on the ground, and waited for Kang Dahan to speak. The terrible silence stretched out between them. She had seen his wrath poured out on other servants. What a cruel game he played. None could withstand it.

Finally, Kang Dahan cleared his throat, and Saina looked up.

"All servants in my caravanserai are governed by the precepts that were set in place by my forefathers long ago. Of course, obedience is demanded by all who live and work here, but the value of each servant is measured in their loyalty. For if a servant is not loyal, how can she be trusted?"

Saina looked at Kang Dahan's young wife and thought of the betrayal Bao Li must have felt when he brought her into Bao Li's home. For all his talk of loyalty and trust, Kang Dahan seemed unable to hold himself to his own standards.

"You have lived here long enough to know what happens to servants who have dealt in deceit," Kang Dahan said.

Saina's memory flashed back to the first time she had seen

Kang Dahan make an example of a young man accused of stealing saffron from a spice merchant. All servants were made to watch as he was dragged into the courtyard and pinned down. She had stared in horror, her body frozen, as his right hand was cut clean off and *thief* was branded on his forehead. The sight should have been deterrent enough, but since then, she had been forced to watch three other servants receive similar punishment. She had succeeded in honest work, but still, she found herself standing before Kang Dahan like a criminal.

He continued. "Now imagine the severe consequences of a servant who has taken an innocent life?" His eyes flashed with accusation.

Saina placed her hand on her churning stomach and shook her head, fearing she would become ill.

"Your high position does not exempt you from my decrees." He tapped his ringed fingers on the arms of his chair and leaned forward. "Do you find fault in my authority?"

"No, my lord," Saina said, her voice weak.

He raised his brow, his mouth a straight line.

He was forcing her to speak that which remained unspoken, to incriminate herself. But she could not do it, of this she was certain.

"What do I stand accused of?" Saina said, her voice measured and firm. "How have I found disfavor?"

"Coward," Ning Po lunged forward. "Admit what you did. Tell my husband that you killed my baby."

Saina stumbled back, her defense stolen from her mouth.

Kang Dahan stared straight, his eyes glassy and pained.

Ning Po had accused Saina before, but to hear it spoken in the presence of Kang Dahan, with his grief so evident, disturbed her in a new way.

"Tell him," Ning Po said, her face wet with tears. "Tell him that Bao Li was jealous of *my* child," she glanced over her shoulder at Kang Dahan. "Of *his* child that I carried within me."

"No. That is not true." Saina held out her hand, wishing Ning Po would stop.

"Tell him that you and Bao Li conspired to murder my baby. That the moment she was born you snuffed out her life."

"You speak lies," Saina cried. "Upach begged for my help in your distress, but your daughter was stillborn. There was no life within her." Saina turned to Kang Dahan, but he had collapsed back into his chair, his head in his hands. "There was nothing I could do. You must believe me," Saina pleaded, wishing he would look at her.

"Liar," Ning Po screamed. She wiped her eyes with the back of her hand.

"It is the truth," Saina said, regretting the compassion she had once felt for Ning Po, for the death of her newborn daughter and the reason they were here now. "I have always conducted myself with honesty and loyalty to my master Kang Dahan and mistress Bao Li—"

"Do not utter her name again," Ning Po said. "Bao Li has betrayed my husband, denying him the heir he has desired more than anything."

Saina turned to Kang Dahan. "Please, Bao Li is the wife of your youth. You know she is incapable of such a thing." Saina needed him to understand, to see through the veil of deception.

His eyes darted toward the entrance of the room, as though wanting to believe her, but his shoulders sagged, and he shook his head. "If what you say is true, then why has Bao Li not shown herself? Why has she left you to suffer the consequences alone?"

"No." Saina shook her head, but the moment the word left her lips, her thoughts darkened. Was that the reason Bao Li had not returned? Doubt clouded her mind, ate away at her confidence. "I am certain she has only been delayed. She will arrive soon. When she does, you will know the truth."

"Do not be fooled, husband," Ning Po said. "This slave is not the victim she claims to be." She shoved a bundle in Kang

Dahan's lap. "Ask her how she came to have these in her possession. Ask."

Kang Dahan's eyes darkened as he unfolded the bundle and held up the garment. The indigo bracelet tumbled to the ground at his feet. He slowly reached down to pick it up. "What is this?"

Ning Po sneered. Her cold eyes sent a shiver through Saina's body.

Saina clenched her jaw. It was true. Ning Po had been in her room. She had stolen them. Saina stared, unblinking. The garment and bracelet, which had been a beacon of hope, a reminder of the man she loved, would now be used to destroy her.

Her heart sank. Even with the risk of a harsher sentence, she would tell Kang Dahan the truth. She fixed her gaze on him, her voice shaking. "Those items were given to me by Narisaf, grandson of the weaver. Your wife stole them from my room last night."

Kang Dahan straightened, cast a confused glance at Ning Po.

Ning Po seemed startled by Saina's admission, as though she had not expected Saina to speak honestly. Her eyes darted around the room; her mouth worked nervously. She stepped forward and clenched her fists. "These were reported stolen by a guest at last night's feast. They were found in this servant's possession."

A snare has been set, created by hate, the bahkshi's words returned to Saina. If the truth was to be known, she must speak now. "No, these were created by the hands of the weaver and his grandson. Ask them."

"Do not mock us," Ning Po spat. "Dignified men would not gift such valued items to a filthy slave."

Kang Dahan held up his hand, silencing Ning Po. "Who reported these items missing?"

"A merchant who attended your feast last night," Ning Po said. "He is waiting in the courtyard."

"Not true," Saina said. "They are mine."

Kang Dahan pushed out of his chair and pointed a sharp finger at Saina. "If you will not answer honestly for this insult, then an answer will be given for you." He looked at his manservant. "Bring in the merchant who reported the items stolen."

Saina stared at Ning Po. "It was you," she said, her chin quivering. "I saw you on the balcony last night. You entered my room and stole them while I served the guests of my master's feast."

Ning Po's face hardened. "Who are you to accuse me of stealing? You stole the life of my baby, my only joy."

Saina closed her eyes, tried to still the panic in her chest. Ning Po had set her plan in motion. Nothing she said would change things now.

Down the hallway, the doors to the khana creaked open and the sound of heavy footsteps approached.

Kang Dahan's gaze fell on something behind Saina, and he grimaced.

The skin on Saina's neck prickled. She did not need to turn around to know that Issik stood behind her. Indeed, Kang Dahan's reaction was enough. If only she could speak the right words to illuminate the truth and shrink back the confidence of the darkness and the lies lurking in the shadows. But how?

Kang Dahan tilted his chin, motioning the merchant to step forward. "A serious accusation of theft has been brought before me. Tell me, do these belong to you?" He held up the warhorse garment and bracelet.

Issik bowed his head. "Yes." He cleared his throat. "I left them securely in my tent last night but grew suspicious when I saw this servant walking among the tents well after dark."

Kang Dahan's face reddened.

"That is not true," Saina said, tears springing to her eyes. "I have never left the gates after dark."

Issik stepped forward, speaking over Saina. "When I returned from enjoying the evening festivities, my garment and bracelet were gone. In my distress, I did not know who to speak to, so I brought it to the attention of your wife."

Saina's shoulders slumped. How wearisome their lies were.

Did she have the energy to continue fighting them when Kang Dahan seemed to have swallowed their deceit?

"Very well." Kang Dahan closed his eyes, beads of sweat built on his forehead. "I assure you that a swift punishment will be exacted for this great shame." He held out the garment and bracelet. "Take your items. A handsome payment will be prepared as compensation for your trouble."

The honey merchant glanced at Ning Po, his eyes questioning, before taking the items from Kang Dahan.

Saina swayed where she stood. No one could help her. Even if she cried out to Narisaf, he would not hear her through these walls.

"Husband," Ning Po said, her voice dripped like sweet honey as she knelt in front of him. Gone was the anguish of a grieving mother and the desire to destroy with words. "It would serve you well to inquire of the merchant's wishes regarding this servant. Perhaps he has an idea that you have not considered."

Kang Dahan raised his brow. He nodded slowly and bid him speak.

Issik gave a slight bow. "My request is simple. Release the servant from your charge. I will accept her as my slave. It will be payment enough for the distress she has caused me."

Saina spun around. "No! I will not go with you." Through her tears she saw his cold eyes. Indignation toward this man burned like fire through her body. She clenched her fists.

"It is a small matter for you," the merchant said to Kang Dahan. "In return for your cooperation, I will speak nothing of what happened here. There will be no blight upon your caravanserai."

Kang Dahan did not seem convinced. He shook his head slightly, but Issik leaned in, his voice lowered. "A man of your high status can acknowledge how this agreement would be of great benefit to *both* of us."

Ning Po stroked her husband's arm. "We can wash our hands of her," she said.

Kang Dahan bit his lip, as though working a thought over in his mind. "It is well," he said reluctantly, then turned to Saina. "You are fortunate that he is a forgiving man and has spared your life. I would not have been so kind." He dabbed sweat from his brow.

Saina's mouth fell open. Spared her life? She could barely form the words in her mind. She glanced around the room but found no focus. Richly hued tapestries, plates of honey cakes, and Bao Li's mural all blurred together.

The merchant wrapped his hand around Saina's arm and yanked her toward him.

Saina tried to pull away from him, but he tightened his grip. She winced in pain, and a smile of satisfaction crossed Ning Po's face.

"Please, be patient," Kang Dahan's voice cut in. "I understand your desire to be on your way, but this servant cannot be released to you until a contract has been drawn up and signed."

Issik growled with displeasure. "This slave has caused me more trouble than she is worth. Already the day is hot. I must leave."

Kang Dahan stood. "As a merchant yourself, you must know these things take time if we are to do them according to the law. I assure you, by late morning, you will have the contract in hand."

Issik cast a nervous glance at Ning Po, then shoved Saina toward them. "If your word proves false, the agreement is off," he barked.

"Please, you must hear me," Saina cried. Her legs collapsed beneath her. "This man, your wife, they are lying." She crawled forward and reached for Kang Dahan's foot. "I beg of you...speak to the weaver... He will tell you—"

"Do not touch my husband," Ning Po screamed. With a swift motion, her fists came down upon her.

Saina had no time to react. A sudden flash of light and searing pain tore down her face. Everything went black.

Chapter Twenty-Five

Ning Po had won.

This vague thought formed in Saina's mind as she emerged from the darkness that wrapped around her. She groaned, sensing the confines of a small room, the narrow walls rising up, and the cold ground beneath her.

Where am I? Pushing up on her elbows, she felt a stab of pain radiate down her face. She put her hand to her temple, felt the open wound and a sticky residue on her fingers. She quickly pulled her hand away. Her senses were awakened to the prick of hay against her skin, the faint hum of flies, and burning stench of the stables.

Following a dusty beam of light peeking through a narrow crack in the door, she looked out and saw Kang Dahan's lead rope and colorful bridle hung high on the rafters that spanned the width of the stable. The stalls across from where she was being held were empty, the grousing camels, donkeys, and yaks brought by last night's guests were gone. How long had she been here?

Saina straightened at the sound of two men conversing nearby. She pushed against the door but the metal latch on the outside was fastened. Panic swelled in her throat. "Please help!"

she called out, shaking the door. Her head throbbed, and the ground spun beneath her.

The men's conversation dropped off before Makh's resonant voice broke through. "Return to your previous task," he said, holding a measure of authority. "I will tend to her."

Makh's heavy footsteps drew near, and Saina pushed away from the door. Had Kang Dahan been told the truth and sent Makh to free her?

Metal scraped against metal as he slid the lock and opened the door. Bright light pulsated behind Saina's temples. She closed her eyes. When she looked again, she could just make out Makh's muscled silhouette standing in the doorway. His arms hung at his sides, and in one hand he held a leather strap.

Makh looked away. "I am sorry, Saina."

All hope was lost. A sob caught in her throat. "Ning Po has spun her lies. How will I bear this misfortune?" Her mind was strained, her heart even more so.

"I beg of you, do not harbor ill will against me for what I must do," Makh said. "I have no say in the matter."

Saina stared at him. Even he knew the truth about her. If only Kang Dahan saw it too. "You were there the night the honey merchant came seeking shelter from the storm. You saw how Bao Li dealt harshly with him. She would not stand for this."

Makh nodded. "The moment she returns I will tell her what has happened," he whispered under his breath.

"And if she does not return?" Saina said, her voice flat. She paused, studying the leather cord hanging loosely in his hand. Who was left to help her now? Had Narisaf already returned to the city?

She detested the doubt rising within her. If only he would show up and prove her wrong. But even if he did, what then?

Makh shifted his gaze, then rubbed his hand along the deep scar on his neck, as though reminding himself of his own distant battle wounds.

"Bring the slave girl," Issik called angrily from the courtyard.

Saina snapped her head up, and the sudden, rapid beat of her heart reverberated in her ears.

Makh looked over his shoulder, then sighed. "It is time."

Her hands shook as she lifted them toward Makh. She had seen him exercise the fierceness of his training when duty required it of him. Few could withstand his strength. But he bound her wrists loosely and led her into the courtyard. How grateful she was that he had treated her with a gentle hand, not as an accused criminal. This was the last kindness she would know.

The sun burned its oppressive heat overhead. It beat down upon every living thing. But Kang Dahan and Ning Po cooled themselves in the shade of the sycamore tree. Its leaves seemed to have withered as it lent itself to their comfort.

How fitting. All things gave of themselves where Kang Dahan was concerned.

Kang Dahan gazed long at Saina, then motioned to the merchant standing to her left, the warhorse garment draped over his shoulders. Saina bristled at the sight. How dare he robe himself with honor in this way.

Issik brushed past his donkey, which was readied and hitched to the cart. Inside, a few jars of honey remained, along with provisions of food, a single bed mat, and a blanket.

Fear seized her.

The merchant threw the garment into the cart and approached Saina, his mouth twisting into a sneer.

Saina stared into his eyes and shivered. What manner of unspoken cruelty had he inflicted upon others? She drew back, tried to still the tremble in her legs. If she must go with him, she would not give him the satisfaction of a slave cowed in fear.

"Get over here," Issik barked. "You have held me up long enough, and now I must walk in the heat of the day."

Strengthened by a deep resolve that had taken root in the marrow of her bones, Saina planted her feet. She would not move for him.

The merchant growled low and pulled her close. "You will pay for this," he said, his breath hot on her face and reeking of rot.

Saina turned away from the stench as he cinched the leather cord tightly around her wrists. Her skin burned and felt as though it was being ripped open, but she clenched her jaw to keep from crying out.

"What are you doing?" Vandakk called out. "Let go of her."

Looking over her shoulder, Saina saw Vandakk running across the courtyard. His brow was drawn, his finger pointed sharply at Issik.

The merchant studied Vandakk for a moment, then laughed.

Vandakk turned to Kang Dahan. "She is Bao Li's head servant. Will you condone this action?"

Kang Dahan wrung his hands and frowned, but he did not offer a response, nor did he step out from the shade of the tree.

Vandakk turned back to Saina, his hands shaking as he tried to loosen the cord.

"Leave us in peace, old man," Issik said, no longer amused. He shoved Vandakk aside. "This slave belongs to me."

Vandakk stumbled back and fell hard on the ground. He grunted as his head hit the stone ground.

"No!" Saina cried. With her hands still tied, she knelt at his side and helped him sit up.

Makh moved toward the merchant, but Kang Dahan held out his hand. "Wait," he said, his voice thundering.

Just then, a door swung open. Narisaf rushed from his room. The weaver appeared behind him.

Saina's breath caught in her chest. Could it be? Their presence stoked an ember of hope within her. She wanted to stand, to run to Narisaf, even if his protection lasted only a moment, but she could not will herself to move her legs.

"You were given rights to the slave woman, nothing more," Kang Dahan said, as he strode out from the shade and pointed to Saina. "Take the slave and leave, or I will have you held for assaulting a man in my charge."

Fire burned hot in Narisaf's eyes, his face flushed red. In an instant, he was barreling toward them.

Issik twisted Saina's arm and jerked her back, snapping her head. A sharp pain tore down her neck and arm. His grip tightened even more. "Leave the old cook be. Your duty is to me now."

"No," Saina said, sparked by a bold impulse. She would rather die having stood firm against this brutal man than be forced to live under his heavy hand. She twisted her wrists, trying to loosen herself from the leather chord, but the more she fought against it, the tighter it wound.

His lips curled back. "You will learn your place," he growled. Raising his arm, he opened the palm of his hand.

Saina shut her eyes and cowered. She braced for the blow, for the searing pain that was sure to tear through her body, but nothing came. Instead, a swift rush of air brushed past her. She heard shuffling of feet, low grunts, and the thud of a fist.

When Issik cried out, Saina slowly looked up.

Narisaf stood in front of her, his eyes wide, his nostrils flared. He was holding Issik's arm in his firm grip. His other hand was clenched around his throat.

Saina's shoulders slumped, her entire body felt weak. She fought to remain standing.

Narisaf shoved Issik so hard his feet came off the ground and he landed on his back, the stone shuddering.

Stunned, the merchant lay still, his arms splayed out. A groan escaped his lips.

"Calm yourselves!" Kang Dahan said stepping between them. Servants and sojourners began to gather along the perimeter of the courtyard, whispering.

The merchant sat up slowly and wiped blood from the corner of his mouth. He glowered at Makh. "Will you do nothing for this injustice? Deal harshly with this man."

Makh made no move to apprehend Narisaf.

"What is the meaning of this?" Kang Dahan said. Behind him, the weaver brushed off Vandakk's tunic and helped him stand.

Saina shot a glance at Ning Po who stood rigid in the shade of the sycamore tree, her eyes darting around the courtyard. Would she try to escape the web of lies she had spun?

"This thief is my rightful property," Issik said as he stood.

Saina drew close to Narisaf. His fists were clenched, and she saw how fiercely he struggled to compose himself.

"She is no thief," Narisaf said.

The honey merchant laughed. He pulled a small scroll from the pouch hanging from his belt and waved the contract in the air. "The evidence was brought before Kang Dahan. He issued the decree. Take up the matter with him if you must, but I am leaving with my slave." He reached for Saina, but Narisaf placed his hand firmly on his chest, his other hand resting on his long knife's hilt.

Issik threw up his hands, but his smirk remained.

"What did she steal?" Narisaf said, his face barely a hand width away from the merchant's.

"Please, husband, this man has been harassed enough," Ning Po said, her face pallid, even in the shade of the tree. "Let him be on his way."

"Am I a weak man that I require a woman's defense?" Issik said. "My word stands. I will speak it, so it is known to every ear." He reached into the cart and held up the garment and bracelet. "This slave stole these from my tent while I attended the master's feast. They were found in her possession early this morning."

Saina shook her head as a murmur went through the courtyard.

"It is true," Issik said, the hesitation in his voice belying his confidence.

Kang Dahan wiped the sweat from his brow and turned to Narisaf. "You see, then, the slave is receiving her due consequence."

"Consequence?" Narisaf gave a sharp bark of laughter, but there was no humor in his regard. He snatched the warhorse garment and bracelet from Issik and held them up. "You were played for a fool."

Kang Dahan's eyes flashed with anger. "What is the meaning of your reply? Have you come to insult me?"

Saina winced. She could not bear to see harm come to Narisaf.

The weaver left Vandakk's side and stepped forward, holding up his hand. "Forgive my grandson. At times, the impulsive nature of his youth gets in the way of his wisdom. He only seeks to point you in the direction of truth."

"Truth?" Kang Dahan threw up his hands. "What is the truth?"

"You have been deceived," the weaver said. "Saina is not a thief."

Issik stepped forward. "These men are liars."

"No." The Weaver shook his head. "I am the owner of this garment. I wove it for my son."

Kang Dahan's mouth twitched as he shifted uncomfortably. "If what you say is true, why were these items found in this slave's possession?"

The weaver motioned toward Saina. "We left them in the care of your honorable servant. Your caravanserai is held in high esteem, a place we knew they would be kept safe until we completed what we set out to accomplish."

Kang Dahan turned around. "You?"

Saina closed her eyes and nodded.

"How can it be? This merchant, my wife, they assured me..." Kang Dahan's voice trailed off, his confidence faltered. He spun around and looked at Ning Po. "What have you done? Why have you misled me?"

Ning Po took a step back.

Saina straightened. Kang Dahan had seen his error, but she dared not believe she was free from the merchant yet.

At the faint chiming of bells, a murmur of excited voices began to build and carry through the courtyard.

"Bao Li has returned," one of the servants called out, pointing toward the gates.

The recognition of the bells sent a thrill of relief through

Saina. Her mouth slackened, she watched as Bao Li entered the caravanserai, sitting high atop her camel, a dark silhouette in the shade of the howdah. A small train of camels and crewmen, dressed in the fine linens and robes of an accompanied dignitary, followed behind. Dust billowed at their feet.

Makh rushed toward Bao Li with Kang Dahan following close on his heels. But Saina stayed back. She sensed the withdrawal of danger but was still unsure to whom she now belonged.

Narisaf was silent as he took Saina's hands in his and untied the cord. His hands were gentle, but they held a strength she had not noticed before.

She studied his face. It had softened some, but his countenance still seemed troubled. "I...I thought you had returned to the city," Saina said.

He stroked his finger over the deep grooves and broken skin on her wrists. "I gave you my word that I would wait for you," he said.

She sighed. The scars of abandonment were deeply rooted within her, but it was unfair to hold him accountable for the actions of her father. "Still, what would have happened if you had not come out of your room when you did?"

He let out a sharp breath of air, a mix of anger and amusement. "I assure you, that man would not have taken you much farther beyond these walls before I caught up to him."

The courtyard was silent as Makh helped Bao Li down from the howdah. She straightened and smoothed out her silk dress. But the air in the caravanserai was still thick with tension, and Bao Li, whose sense of discernment was highly regarded by all who knew her, appeared to search for its source among the people gathered around her.

Her gaze settled on Saina, concern crossed her face. "What manner of trouble has occurred in my absence?"

Saina was overcome; there were no words. Every muscle in her body felt strained, until at once the tension released, flooding her eyes with tears.

Bao Li examined Saina's face, her mouth pressed in a thin line. "You are hurt. What happened?" Bao Li fixed her icy stare on Kang Dahan, and he staggered back.

Before Saina could speak, Issik hollered at his donkey, setting his cart in motion.

"Stop," Kang Dahan bellowed.

"You have kept me long enough," the merchant said. "I must go. Already my animal will suffer for this heat."

"Bind him," Kang Dahan said.

Bao Li spun around. "Who has let that man in this caravanserai? Who has done this thing?"

Kang Dahan's mouth hung open. He was unable to give a response.

"I am innocent," Issik barked. "It was Ning Po who deceived you. She conspired against this slave. I only sought payment for the humiliation I received at *that woman's* hands," he said, pointing to Bao Li. "She took my honey—"

Makh shoved him into the wall, silencing him.

Kang Dahan spun around and pointed at Ning Po, who stood unmoving beneath the sycamore tree. "What is your answer for this?"

"But...our baby," Ning Po cried out. "Will there be no justice?" She searched the courtyard, her gaze falling on the faint movement near the entrance to the hallway where Upach stood silently. "You, come here."

Upach slowly stepped forward, her hands clasped tightly against her body. The courtyard was silent, only the shuffle of her sandals was heard.

Saina's mouth felt as dry as the desert.

"Tell them what this slave did to my baby," Ning Po said.

Saina wanted to cover her ears and shut out the lies, but she held her hands firmly at her sides as Upach approached them.

Ning Po leaned toward Upach. "Do not hold back," she said through clenched teeth. "Tell them that she killed her."

Upach narrowed her eyes and stood firm. "No," she said, her

voice flat. "Your baby was dead at birth. I was there. I saw it. Saina acted honorably."

Saina exhaled, but Ning Po screamed and lunged for Upach, who quickly tried to back away.

"Seize her," Kang Dahan said.

Immediately, guards surrounded Ning Po, but she fought against them. "I gave you an heir, not that barren woman," she cried as they dragged her flailing body toward the stables.

Kang Dahan shrank back and covered his face with his hands. He seemed suddenly a shell of a man.

All was still. It seemed the whole of the people standing in the courtyard had taken a breath and held it in, unsure of what would come next.

When Kang Dahan finally pulled his hands from his face, his eyes were deeply troubled. He looked at Bao Li, then the weaver and Narisaf. "My ancestors have walked this land for so long that no event existed here without our knowledge of it. And now this great shame has been heaped upon me. Cursed be my name and that of my forefathers if you will not forgive me for the iniquity that occurred on my watch," he averted his gaze.

Forgiveness? Saina rubbed the tender marks on her wrist, and her head spun beneath the hot desert sun. She was safe now, but could a spoken word relieve Kang Dahan of the responsibility for his rash judgments? She could not differentiate her anger from her relief. Both overwhelmed her in equal measure.

The weaver spoke. "You seek a pardon for your offense, but we must not cheapen such injustice by a mere uttering of words."

Kang Dahan's eyes darkened. He scratched his beard, his ringed fingers glistening. "What are you asking of me?"

"A truly repentant heart. A sacrifice," the weaver said. "Therefore, I will present you with an offer, a way to wash your hands of this guilt. You would be wise to consider it."

Kang Dahan shook his head, but Bao Li stepped between them. "Come," she said. "We will speak to the weaver and his grandson in private." But as they turned to leave, they were stopped by the sound of a child's high laughter.

Saina shifted her attention to where a young boy was running through the gates. "Uta?" By the time his name had formed on Saina's lips, Miunai appeared, rushing after him.

"Uta, slow down," Miunai said, catching him by the arm. "Do not make the mistress regret her kindness."

Saina looked at Bao Li. "They have returned?"

Bao Li nodded. "It is the reason I was late." She took Saina's hand in hers. "Forgive me, Saina. I promised I would return, and I betrayed your confidence in me. Know it was not by choice. We arrived in Penjikent with the intent of leaving Miunai with her father's family, but after searching for several days, no surviving members were found. It was Miunai's decision to return with my caravan. She did not want to be left destitute in Penjikent." Her gaze followed Uta, a smile forming. "That boy has walked for hours and still has energy to spare."

Laughter escaped Saina's lips. She could not have anticipated how much would change in a short amount of time. She looked at Narisaf. Perhaps the God of heaven would provide a way for them after all.

Bao Li followed Saina's gaze and studied Narisaf with a slow, measured intensity. "I sense we have much to discuss. Let us not put it off any longer," she said, brushing past him.

Bao Li, Kang Dahan, and the weaver walked toward the khana. Narisaf turned back to Saina and flashed a boyish grin, an offering of unspoken certainty, before running to catch up with his grandfather.

Saina stared after him, pondering his confidence, which seemed to manifest in a thick form around him. Her love for him swelled. Could she truly hope to marry him? She was pulled from the thought when she felt a bony hand on her shoulder.

She looked at Vandakk next to her and Upach, who stood at his side.

"You are bleeding," Saina said, pointing to the trickle of blood behind his ear.

"It is a small matter," Vandakk said, brushing away her concern with a wave of his hand. He looked at Saina's temple, his green eyes glistening beneath pooled tears. "Your duty to me, to Bao Li, is admirable. How honored you are within these gates. You have sought the comfort of all others at your own expense. Now it is your turn to rest."

Uta approached them, and Vandakk turned toward him, his face beaming at the boy's presence.

"Come," Upach said, smiling at Saina. "I will tend to your wound."

Chapter Twenty-Six

S itting in a dark corner of the storeroom, Saina turned toward the sound of soft footsteps drawing near. Her head throbbed with the sudden movement, and she winced. Not even her relief at escaping the cruel fate of being a slave to the honey merchant helped dull the pain. How badly she wanted to be rid of it.

She opened her eyes and saw Upach setting a small basin of water on the ground at Saina's side, her lips pursed.

Upach's dark hair had been let loose, falling in untamed waves at her shoulders. The young woman draped a cloth over the basin's edge, then quietly left. She returned moments later with a cup of steaming tea and knelt down beside Saina, extending the drink toward her.

Saina inhaled the pungent scent and grimaced. "What is this?"

"A decoction made from nettle leaves and herbs," Upach said, managing a smile. "It will relieve your pain."

Saina choked down the bitter drink and leaned her head against the wall. "How long will it take?"

"Be patient," Upach said, her voice full of motherly tenderness far beyond her years. "Healing happens in due time." She dipped the cloth in the water and wrung it out.

Saina leaned against the wall and sat in silence as Upach placed the soothing compress against her temple. She studied Upach's amber eyes and the torchlight dancing in them. How weighty and troubled they seemed.

"Thank you for speaking the truth," Saina said, touching Upach's hand. "You...saved my life."

Upach looked away and dropped her hands in her lap. "It was my fault. All of it."

Saina leaned forward. "I do not blame you. It was a desperate situation."

"From the moment Ning Po went into labor, I sensed something was wrong," Upach said, sadly. "Unskilled as I was in matters of childbirth, I felt the weight of trouble in the air. I turned to you because I did not know what else to do." She shook her head. "But I never should have sought your help that night. I never should have involved you."

"It was my choice," Saina said. "We could not have known things would turn out this way."

"I knew what Ning Po was capable of," Upach said, exhaling a slow breath. How worn down and weary she seemed. "She made her choice and will receive due punishment, but what will happen to me? Kang Dahan and Bao Li know my loyalty was to her. Can I expect them to overlook that?"

Saina stared silently. It was a fair question, one for which she could offer no comforting answer. Even Saina could not be certain of the decisions that would be handed down to Upach. Indeed, she had no idea of her own fate.

"What if I am sent to the slave market?" Upach said, her hand trembling. "I have heard it is a cruel and terrible place."

The fear in Upach's eyes gnawed a tender ache in Saina's heart. What was to become of her? Of both of them? Her shoulders slumped as a helpless feeling washed over her. Saina would be unwise to offer words of hope that were contrary to the situation, but could she tell Upach that she must accept her fate? No. She resented the very thought.

"I will speak to Bao Li," Saina said. "I will try."

————

Adorned in her finest homespun tunic, Saina drew near the khana and stopped in the shade of the portico.

Moments earlier, Bao Li had sent a messenger requesting Saina's immediate presence, and she had not been able to calm her unsettled mind since. She studied the gilded doors she had walked through countless times, the carved dragons with bared teeth staring back at her.

As a young servant, Saina had viewed the dragons as a cautionary warning, too terrified to go near them for fear she would rouse the anger of those who lived behind the guarded doors. Standing before them now, her stomach twisted, thoughts swirling like a blinding sandstorm. If only the medicinal tea that had alleviated the throbbing in her head could do the same for her old fears.

She looked down, smoothed the creases in her tunic, then inhaled a shaking breath. Opening the door, she felt a rush of cool air envelope her as she walked inside.

The murmur of voices drew her down the hallway toward the greeting room where Makh was speaking at the arched entrance. His tone was serious, thick tension emanated from inside.

Saina stopped next to him and peered into the room. At the far end, Bao Li paced in front of the mural, her hands clasped behind her back. In the center, a low table had been set with wine and several small bowls of uneaten fruit and nuts. Narisaf, the weaver, and Kang Dahan reclined on brightly colored cushions around the table, their attention fixed on Makh.

Saina shifted and Narisaf's eyes met hers. He sat up. She smiled at him, her heart quickening for an instant before Makh's voice pulled her back to the weight of the conversation.

"Ning Po waged a fierce fight when my men brought her to the stables for holding," Makh said, his gravelly voice echoing through the room. "She was finally restrained, but not before causing great unrest among the animals."

"Have the animals settled?" Kang Dahan said.

"Yes, but a stableboy was trampled underfoot and sustained significant injuries. A messenger has been sent to retrieve Umida from the city."

Bao Li looked sharply at Kang Dahan. "Ning Po has caused immense damage. She must be dealt with harshly."

Kang Dahan held up his hand, his face wearied. "Her deception will not be tolerated. I will arrange to have her taken west by the Persian dye traders."

Why would he send her west? Saina thought as Kang Dahan rubbed his temples. Was he sending her to a slave market far away from here?

Bao Li nodded curtly. "Ning Po sought to ruin my maidservant but shackled her own life instead. As for her servant, Upach..."

"Please, my lady," Saina said, the words ringing loudly in her own ears. "Extend mercy to Upach." She shut her mouth, embarrassed by the sudden outburst, but Bao Li's posture seemed to relax. If she was bothered by Saina's words, she did not show it. She motioned for Saina to continue.

Sensing a hint of conciliation in Bao Li's regard, Saina continued cautiously. "Upach is but a young woman, a victim of Ning Po's deceit, just as others were. She is strong and caring and is gifted in the healing nature of plants and herbs. Even Umida has taken notice. I assure you, she is skilled enough to tend to the stableboy if you allow it."

Bao Li studied Saina intently, her lips pressed together. She broke her gaze and turned to Makh. "My maidservant's word is trustworthy. We will find a suitable position for the girl. For now, show her to the injured stableboy. Ensure that she has whatever supplies she needs until Umida arrives."

Makh bowed and left the khana.

A rush of relief flooded Saina, but she had no time to consider it as Bao Li drew near her and glanced at the wound on her temple. "You are too good for this place, for my husband...for me. Your loyalty has never ceased. And I am filled with shame knowing that in your time of greatest need, you were denied that same loyalty from us. You did not deserve what happened."

Standing in the middle of the room, Saina felt naked before their silent stares. She wanted to nod in agreement, to acknowledge their failure, but to concede Bao Li's regret would admit their guilt. Dare she speak so freely?

The weaver cleared his throat, and everyone turned to him. Frail as he was, his presence filled the room. His wisdom, coupled with Narisaf's strength, brought Saina a measure of peace. Whatever she faced, she would do so with them at her side, at least for the moment.

Bao Li motioned to the Weaver. "You said you would not proceed with our meeting until my servant was present. She is here now. Tell us how we can correct this injustice. Let us hear it. Let us make it right."

Saina glanced from the weaver to Bao Li. Why had the weaver requested her? Who was she to give ear to words exchanged between such people?

The weaver took the folded garment from his side and set it on the table before him. "Many have asked why I traveled all this way from Merv with the brittle body of an aged man. Indeed, when I first spoke of making the trek, my grandson refused me, fearing my mind had gone the way of my body." He chuckled and clapped Narisaf on his shoulder, the tension in the room easing.

"What I told you earlier is true. I wove this garment for my son. But when he was killed in battle, I thought it was lost to me forever. After a time, a man traveled to my home, said he had acquired it from my son and wanted to return it to its rightful owner." The weaver paused and ran his fingers over the pale threads of the warhorses. "He trained these animals. He trained my son's horse."

The air in the room felt still and hot. Saina's mouth was

suddenly dry. She glanced at the wine on the table and swallowed. If only she could wet her parched lips.

"This man," the weaver continued. "He told me that his job took him away from home, sometimes for days. And when his wife and unborn child died in labor, he saw no way forward in caring for his only living child. Grief had stolen his judgment. In desperation, he sold his daughter into the home of the only woman he knew who would treat her well."

Bao Li's eyes flickered.

The weaver continued. "Time brought him to his right mind, and he realized his mistake. It was his greatest regret." He placed the garment on the table and looked once again at Kang Dahan and Bao Li. "In return for reuniting me with a part of my son, I made a promise to the man. I held these things close to my heart until recently, when I felt the stirring to make good on my word to seek out the daughter he left in your care."

"In our care?" Kang Dahan said, his confusion cutting through the silence. "Who was this man?"

"Turghar," Bao Li said, quietly, her eyes holding the weaver's.

Saina felt the dampness of sweat on her forehead and pulled the collar of her tunic, trying to cool herself.

The weaver offered a knowing smile. "The threads of each of our lives have been bound by one man. Though disparate and stretched across vast lands, they have drawn us together." He paused. "We stand at the culmination of a grand design. Only now have each of our hearts been prepared for what comes next."

What was he saying? Saina looked at Narisaf, but his gaze was set firmly on Kang Dahan, as though reading his every move.

"Next?" Kang Dahan looked at Bao Li, then back at the weaver. "I do not understand."

"We have come to procure Saina's freedom and return her to the heritage of her father."

Bao Li's mouth fell open, her face ashen.

"Of course, she will not be left to start a new life alone," the weaver continued. "My grandson seeks to be joined with her in a marriage covenant."

Bao Li stared at Saina, her pained eyes demanding answers.

Saina stepped back, searching for an explanation she had not known to have prepared.

The weaver cut in. "If you seek answers, you will find no suitable response in Saina. She did not know that such a request would be made. But this proposal of marriage is our offer. To accept it is to wash your hands clean of your offense."

Saina felt as though her heart had been pulled taut. Her masters would never agree to such a notion.

"There can be no marriage," Kang Dahan said, slamming his fists on the table.

A muscle twitched in Narisaf's jaw, but the weaver remained calm, his cerulean eyes holding Kang Dahan's. Unblinking, he leaned forward. "Consider the debt that you owe."

"You are asking me to release my wife's personal slave," Kang Dahan said, shifting uncomfortably. "Why must Bao Li pay the penalty for *my* offense?" his voice rose.

"Because you demanded the same of Saina. She deserved none of it," the weaver said.

Kang Dahan opened his mouth to protest, but Bao Li placed her hand on his shoulder, silencing him. She fixed her watery gaze on the corner of the wedding mural, at the boy holding the basket of fish, then to Saina.

"Do you love Narisaf?" Bao Li asked, her voice flat.

The question stunned Saina, left her searching for words. She looked at Narisaf. Suddenly, the hurried need to explain herself released. His eyes held gentle strength, and his character was unmatched. Everything faded away except for her certainty of her feelings for Narisaf. "Yes, I love him," Saina said, the words sweet upon her lips.

"And you would choose to marry him over this life that I have given you...the garden and the high standing you possess over any other servant?" Bao Li said.

Saina inhaled a slow breath. How would she speak of her heart's greatest desire knowing it would hurt Bao Li immensely? But even as the question formed, a shift occurred, bringing clarity, a pressing need to speak honestly.

"Yes," Saina said, trying to still the quiver in her voice. "When my father left, I believed that I was worthless, unwanted. But your kindness gave me dignity. A sense of belonging. You showed me that I am worthy of these things."

Bao Li straightened, her lips pressed together in a thin line.

"Be assured, I hold these things close to my heart, but you asked the question and deserve an honest answer." Saina's body felt light, as though an oppressive burden had been lifted from her shoulders. Was this what freedom felt like, to speak honestly?

Bao Li's face fell as silence opened a chasm between them. Saina wanted her to say something, anything. But instead, Bao Li turned on her heel and walked out of the room.

When the shuffle of her footsteps had faded away, Kang Dahan leaned forward and whispered, "My wife, she has just returned, and this...this thing you ask of her...it is all too much." He leaned back, flicking his wrist in frustration.

Saina closed her eyes and hung her head. Had Bao Li regarded Saina's honesty as another betrayal? Could she bear to lose her high standing and the man she loved all at once? She glanced at Narisaf. He was shaking his head, his jaw tensed.

How terrible it was to love a man and be denied a life with him. She had taken a great risk in speaking the truth. No matter what happened, they would both carry that with them the rest of their lives.

"It is our only offer to remove the guilt from your name," the weaver said, his voice firm. "You would be wise to consider it fully."

Kang Dahan rubbed his face, his eyes weary. "Please, I beg of you, ask anything else of me. Just do not heap such pain upon my wife. You see how much Saina means to her. It was my offense alone, she did nothing to deserve this."

He stopped talking at the sound of approaching footsteps. Bao Li appeared once again at the entrance of the room clutching a yellowed scroll.

In silence she drew close to Saina, the soft skin around her eyes red and swollen. "I do not harbor resentment for your honest speech. Indeed, I have known the sweetness of the love in which you speak," she said. A thin smile, a distant remembrance, softened her face. "I was young once. I had dreams too..."

Kang Dahan snapped his head up, looked at Bao Li, but she kept her eyes firmly fixed on Saina.

Saina's breath grew shallow, her legs weak. She waited to hear Bao Li speak the words that would bind her to the same suffering, to deny her the love Bao Li was denied many years ago.

Bao Li broke the seal of the scroll and unrolled it. "This contract was a binding agreement between me and your father. I gave him my word that as a slave, you would be provided shelter and food. In return, he vowed never to interfere with your life from that day forward."

Saina stepped back. The stabbing pain of her father's memory, of watching him walk into the desert, had dulled. He had not blamed her. Her mother's death was not her fault.

Bao Li ran her finger along the signatures scrawled at the bottom of the scroll. "Your father did not keep his word."

Saina nodded. She understood why.

"Such a contract is not easily undone," Bao Li said. "Not because the words on the contract hold more power than I,"—she closed her eyes, inhaling a slow, steady breath—"but because you have become the joy of my barren womb, and I do not know how to release you."

Saina's throat ached as she absorbed Bao Li's admission. She had not considered what her leaving would do to Bao Li—indeed, had never thought it a possibility. Did she dare ask Bao Li to accept that heartache, to drink a double portion of its bitterness?

Bao Li continued, her words building one upon another. "But if I claim to love you as my daughter, then I must be honest with myself when confronted with this question. Can I bear the responsibility for your suffering by denying you the man you love?"

Saina straightened. From the corner of her eye, she saw that Narisaf did the same.

"Bao Li?" Kang Dahan said, but she shoved her hand toward him, silencing him. Tears pooled in her eyes, spilled down her face.

Bao Li held Saina's gaze and searched deeply, as though trying to hold on to an unspooling thread that was slipping away from her grasp. She shook her head slowly.

"Saina, I grant you freedom from the bonds of this contract, from servitude in this caravanserai. I release you to marry Narisaf and live as you desire," she said, her voice faltering. She tore the scroll in half and dropped her hands at her sides.

Saina stared, her mouth open. She had heard Bao Li's words, seen the scroll torn, but she could not form their meaning in her mind. Nor had she anticipated the tears that stung her eyes, flowing without warning. She buried her face in her hands, ashamed of such an expression of emotion in front of Kang Dahan and Bao Li.

"Bao Li, are you certain of this?" Kang Dahan said, rising from the cushions. But Bao Li did not respond as she stared straight ahead.

The weaver and Narisaf stood up, but Saina kept her focus on Bao Li. What could she say that would express her gratitude? No utterance of words would ever be enough. In an instant, and without thought, Saina found herself kneeling on the floor, her arms wrapped around Bao Li's waist. Bao Li stiffened, but Saina pressed harder against her and wept. "Who am I to deserve such kindness?"

"Sweet child," Bao Li said, softening. She stroked Saina's cheek. "You deserve to live as a free woman and be loved by a good man." The certainty in her voice faded, and she pulled away. "I only ask that you do not forget me when you go."

"Where could I go that you would not be with me in my heart?" Saina said, standing.

Bao Li closed her eyes, a reluctant smile creasing the corners of her mouth. "Narisaf is waiting for you."

Saina turned around and saw the man she loved reaching out to her. Beside him stood the weaver, the warhorse garment tucked in the crook of his arm.

Placing her hand in Narisaf's, Saina went to him, each step drawing her farther away from her life of slavery, from her early mornings with Vandakk and her quiet loyalty as a possessor of Bao Li's deepest secrets. There was a measure of lament at the loss of this familiar life, the parental love she had known within these mud-brick walls. But love beckoned her away from these things, toward a new life with Narisaf, the man with the clove-colored eyes and warrior heart.

Taking her place beside Narisaf, feeling his calloused hand wrapped around hers, Saina looked across the low table, where Kang Dahan had joined Bao Li, his hand resting on her back.

The weaver unfolded the warhorse garment. "The thread that began its work in your parents long ago has woven its way through time and distance and found its end in the love shared between you," the weaver said.

He draped the garment over their shoulders and stepped back. "It is my honor to witness the betrothal of Narisaf, son of Arash, and Saina, daughter of Turghar."

The betrothal was announced in the caravanserai, and the news spread quickly.

When Narisaf and Saina left the khana, allowing Kang Dahan, Bao Li, and the weaver to continue discussions about the wedding that would soon take place, Vandakk was the first to greet them outside the gilded doors. He was beaming.

"I hoped this day would come," Vandakk said. He tipped his head back and laughed, then pulled Saina into an embrace.

She could hardly bear her emotions. The fatigue of weariness, the buzz of exhilaration, both overwhelmed her in equal measure. "If only I could have expected the events leading up to it," Saina said. "Then I could have been prepared."

"Ah, but the unexpected is a gift," Vandakk said, his green eyes alight. "To come about things in a manner that is out of our control is where gratitude is birthed."

Saina nodded. Vandakk spoke the truth, but it would take a lifetime to gain his wisdom in these matters.

"I have prepared a table of roasted meat and accompaniments for you and Narisaf in the garden. Go there now. Rest together in the cool of the evening." He led them through the courtyard swarming with a newly arrived caravan of merchants and their noisome camels. Colorful saddlebags and leather cinch ropes were strewn along the ground. The scents of cinnamon bark, black cardamom, and alfalfa hay filled the air.

Miunai called out to them. She quickly set a tray of fresh cut watermelon on the serving platform and embraced Saina. Behind her, Uta grabbed a slice of melon from the tray and held it proudly in his small hands.

Vandakk shook his head and laughed, ruffling Uta's dark hair. "We must be careful, or Uta will eat all our food," he said.

Saina was delighted at the way Vandakk's face lit up in Uta's presence. The young boy had captured his fatherly heart, and she was glad for it.

They left Vandakk and Miunai and entered the garden. When Saina stopped to close the door, Narisaf continued down the shaded path. From behind, she studied the shape of him, his muscled shoulders and confident stride as he walked past orchard trees and plump figs growing on tender limbs. By the time he neared the low table, set with lamb kebabs, fresh melon, and wine, Saina caught up to him.

He brushed a strand of hair from her face. "Do you remember

doubting me when I told you that one day soon you would become my wife?"

Heat spread into Saina's cheeks, but she could not pull her eyes away from Narisaf. "I wanted to believe you but saw no way forward. To me, you were worthy of so much more than I could offer. How foolish my doubt seems now."

A bird flitted freely in the branches of the fig tree beside them, its high song filling the evening air. She recalled the turquoise bird that was once freed in the sudden crushing of its cage, how it flew to the top of the caravanserai before spreading its wings and disappearing over the wall.

She was that bird. Only God of heaven could have broken her cage and set her free.

Narisaf untied the long knife from his belt and set it on the table. "When I left my home in Merv, I did not know that my heart was being drawn by something far greater."

Saina studied the gleam of the blade, its carved-bone handle. As a man with the blood of a warrior running through him, he kept it always at his side. She drew closer to him. He had let down his guard, and she was learning to do the same.

"Without knowledge of it, I crossed the desert sands in pursuit of you, Saina. You are the thread that binds my heart from my past to my future." He gently pulled her into him, wrapped his arms around her waist, and kissed her.

There, in the cool evening shade, with the heady scent of night-blooming jasmine thick in the air, she felt the thrum of his chest against hers. Overhead, the setting sun cast the desert sky aflame in a vibrant tapestry, and Saina's heart, now free, burned with it.

Chapter Twenty-Seven

Saina walked through Bao Li's room one last time, taking in the beauty of the carved furniture and fine rugs awash in golden sunlight streaming through the window. She set the satchel holding Bao Li's gift on the windowsill and straightened vials of perfume on the small desk. Inhaling the familiar scent of rose water, she pulled her hands away. This job belonged to Miunai now, she must leave the task for her.

Saina sighed. How bittersweet it was to fall into old habits of servitude but no longer be forced to claim them as her own.

"Are you ready?" Bao Li said as she walked into the room holding the bridal headdress. It was a beautiful piece made of dyed silk and wool, with glass beads and silver roundels dangling from its rim.

"Yes," Saina said, exhaling a shaky breath. Her stomach felt like a hollow cavern. "But I am nervous too." She bent low as Bao Li placed it on her head. "If only Upach was still here...I would drink some of her calming tea."

Bao Li lifted the embroidered mantle off her bed and, turning back to Saina, paused. "I saw her when I visited Umida at the apothecary yesterday."

"Oh?" Saina said, surprised. It had been almost two full moon

274

cycles since Upach became Umida's apprentice and moved to the city. Saina had not seen her since. "How was she?"

"Busy preparing tinctures," Bao Li said. "But she held a measure of peace I had not seen in her before. With her gift of healing, her work in the apothecary is suitable. She will do well in time."

The news soothed a restless, aching spot in Saina's mind. She sighed. "Umida will be good to her. I trust she is where she needs to be."

"As you will be soon," Bao Li said, draping the mantle over Saina's shoulders, its vibrant hues standing out from her ivory, silk gown beneath it. She drew back, scanned the length of Saina's body. "Narisaf will not be able to take his eyes off you."

Saina laughed, her face warming at the compliment, but the sudden blow of a ram's horn shocked her into silence and sent her heart beating. She reached a shaking hand out to Bao Li. "My time with you has drawn to an end. Soon I will join Narisaf and the weaver and sojourn to a land I do not know."

Bao Li's eyes flickered, a smile played on her lips. "Trust Narisaf," she said. "He will not lead you astray."

Saina pondered Bao Li's reaction, sensing she held a secret. Something remained unspoken, but what? There was no time to press her further. She took the satchel from the windowsill. "Before I go, I wanted to give you this."

Bao Li pulled the porcelain vessel from the satchel and ran her fingers along the delicately painted fish and summer grasses. Her eyes pooled with tears.

"For your tea," Saina said. "To replace the old vessel that was shattered."

Bao Li nodded, pulling it to her breast. "I will cherish it."

"You will visit me in Merv?" Saina said, seeking assurance that when the ceremony was over and the distance spread out between them, she would see Bao Li again.

Bao Li pursed her lips together and smiled.

The silk traders who had just come from Merv told Saina it

took them eighteen days of travel to reach Samarkand. A portion of that time was spent crossing the Kyzylkum Desert. It would be no easy feat, but she trusted Narisaf to guide her there safely.

The ram's horn blew once again.

Cheers were sent up in the courtyard, flowing through Bao Li's window as Miunai burst into the room. "Your groom has arrived!" she said, breathless, her voice light with mirth.

Saina stepped back, the silver roundels of her headdress danced and chimed, an outward manifestation of her heart, which thrummed like a thousand running horses.

"He stands at the gates waiting for you!" Miunai said.

Saina adjusted her mantle and straightened. "I am ready."

With Bao Li and Miunai following close behind, she walked out of the khana and into the shade of the portico where Makh greeted her, the hard lines of his warrior face softening into a smile.

The drumming of the *dayereh* set the beat as musicians filled the air with the celebratory sounds of the stringed tanbur, ney flute, and tambourines.

Saina searched for Narisaf through the press of the crowd but saw only a tangle of merchants and livestock handlers, sober men with the similar sand-worn faces she had looked upon time and again. Who better to join her in the day's festivities?

Vandakk stood at the front of the crowd, smiling proudly. Uta, who now spent his days shadowing the aged cook, stood at his hip. Beside them the weaver leaned on his walking stick. He nodded in satisfaction, as though acknowledging that what he set out to accomplish had finally come to pass.

Kang Dahan approached Saina, bowed his head, then faced the courtyard. When he raised his arms, the crowd parted, giving full view of Narisaf standing beside his horse at the gates, adorned in a woven wedding mantle, silver cuffs wrapped around his wrists.

Saina met his dark eyes, her breath catching in her chest.

Narisaf thrust the reins of his horse into the hands of the

stableboy, then approached Saina, his smile widening, his deep laughter calling out to her.

Her heart beat strong and steady. Her ties to the caravanserai and the people living within loosened when he took her hands in his and led her onto the richly hued rug rolled out in the center of the courtyard. As cheers erupted, they stepped beneath the covering of the silk wedding tapestry raised overhead by the outstretched arms of people who gathered around, witnesses to the ceremony that would join them in marriage.

———

Light shifted, casting long shadows along the ground as the wedding feast continued into late afternoon. Serving platforms were piled with the traditional foods of roasted meats, spiced vegetables, and hot bread, as well as wine. As the main course began to dwindle, trays of varied sweet pastries and fresh fruits were brought out.

When Narisaf stepped away to speak to the weaver, Saina sought out Vandakk, stopping him as he passed by with a tray of honeycomb. "You have not forgotten a single detail," she said.

"Of course," Vandakk said, his voice thick with pride. "Only the finest foods will do on your day of celebration."

"Thank you for all you have done for me," Saina said. She tried to swallow down the knot of emotion rising to the surface, but it was no use. How difficult it was to cut all ties to Samarkand, the land of her youth.

"Do not cry," Vandakk said, drying her cheek. "There is always something beautiful to fix your eyes upon, even when you step into the unknown." He embraced Saina, then walked away, but not before she saw him dry his own tears.

Saina took the quiet moment to scan the courtyard, hoping to keep the memories of this day alive in her mind. She closed her eyes, felt the cool air on her skin beneath her silk gown, and inhaled the strong scent of cinnamon and aromatic cedar.

When she opened them again, Narisaf approached, holding out his hand toward her. "Come," he said, then winked. He led her toward the gates where a stableboy held the reins of his warhorse.

Narisaf helped Saina mount the sturdy horse, then climbed on behind her.

She turned to him. "Your grandfather...we cannot leave him here."

"All is well," Narisaf chuckled. "I have arranged to have him join us in seven days' time."

They set out from the caravanserai, the music and laughter of the wedding feast fading in the distance. Lulled by the sway of the horse beneath and the strength of Narisaf's body behind her, Saina was silent, pondering the swelling of her love for her husband, the anticipation of a life freely lived with him.

"We must hurry if we are to reach our destination before nightfall," Narisaf said. But instead of taking the Silk Road west, toward Merv, he led them north, crossing a stone bridge that spanned the Zarafshan River. It was the same bridge Saina had crossed often as a child with her father.

"Where are we going?" Saina said, as they began their trek toward the hills, crowned in the distance with the golden light of the setting sun.

Narisaf stretched out his arm and pointed toward the familiar fields where Saina had roamed as a young girl. Ahead was the stone well where she had fetched water for her mother whenever she helped her with chores and cooking. A new bucket had been set on the ground beside it.

Narisaf guided the horse along the worn path leading toward the towering karagach and sycamore trees, where her old home once sat in a clearing of land. Saina gazed in surprise at the newly built, mud-brick structure in the old home's place. Leaning forward, she went still as she studied its colorful awning and carved wooden door.

"Is...this..." Saina stuttered, her heart quickening.

"I have brought you home," Narisaf whispered in her ear, his deep voice spreading waves of warmth throughout her body. "To the place I have prepared for you."

He helped her dismount the horse. Once steady, she looked into his eyes and wrapped her fingers around his. She was finally home, where her heart had always longed to be.

Afterword

A Note on the Silk Road

The term Silk Road was first used in 1877 by German geographer Baron Ferdinand von Richthofen to describe the series of ancient trade routes stretching across the Asian and European continents.

From China in the east, to the Mediterranean Sea in the west, the trek was arduous. With geographical barriers such as the 600 mile-long Taklamakan Desert, as well as towering mountain ranges, unpredictable weather, and robbers seeking to pilfer goods, few people endured the entire 4,000-mile journey. Rather, goods were trekked from outpost to outpost by traders well versed in short sections of the road.

For this reason, the trade route was not given a single name in the way we think about the Silk Road today. Instead, it was broken up into small stretches and would take on the name of the next outpost or city a traveler would come to along the route.

In writing this novel, it proved difficult to follow a consistent name where one did not exist. I went back and forth on whether to use the modern term Silk Road, or instead, the various city names that merchants would travel to when they set out from Samarkand. While the former is not historically accurate, the latter was downright messy.

Ultimately, I settled on using the Silk Road, both for reasons of familiarity to today's readers, and to create a sense of the flow of goods with as little interruption in the narrative as possible. This decision was mine alone.

Caravanserais were important outposts for merchants and sojourners along the Silk Road. Not only did they provide protection at night, but some even had bath houses, prepared meals, and stables for livestock. Many caravanserai's can still be viewed today along these ancient trade routes, but Samarkand's Grand Caravanserai, along with the characters who lived and worked within its stone walls, were formed in the sands of my imagination.

The Sogdian people were well known traders and played a key role in ensuring the continuous flow of goods. Kang Dahan's character represents such movement. As a young man, he conducted trade in China, earning him the Chinese surname 'Kang'—a name which corresponded to his hometown of Samarkand. Some of what we know about the Sogdians today, including matters of business and craftsmanship, their dealings in slavery, and even their given names, have been found in various letters and locales along the Silk Road. I have taken great care to give my characters traditional Sogdian names, at times having to choose between different transliterations.

Lastly, in my research for this book, I benefitted greatly from the countless resources made available by historians, authors, academic articles, and travel writers. But there were three invaluable books I kept within arm's reach whenever I sat down to write. *The Silk Road: Two Thousand Years in the Heart of Asia*, by Frances Wood; *The Silk Road: A New History* by Valerie Hansen; and *The Silk Roads: A New History of the World* by Peter Frankopan.

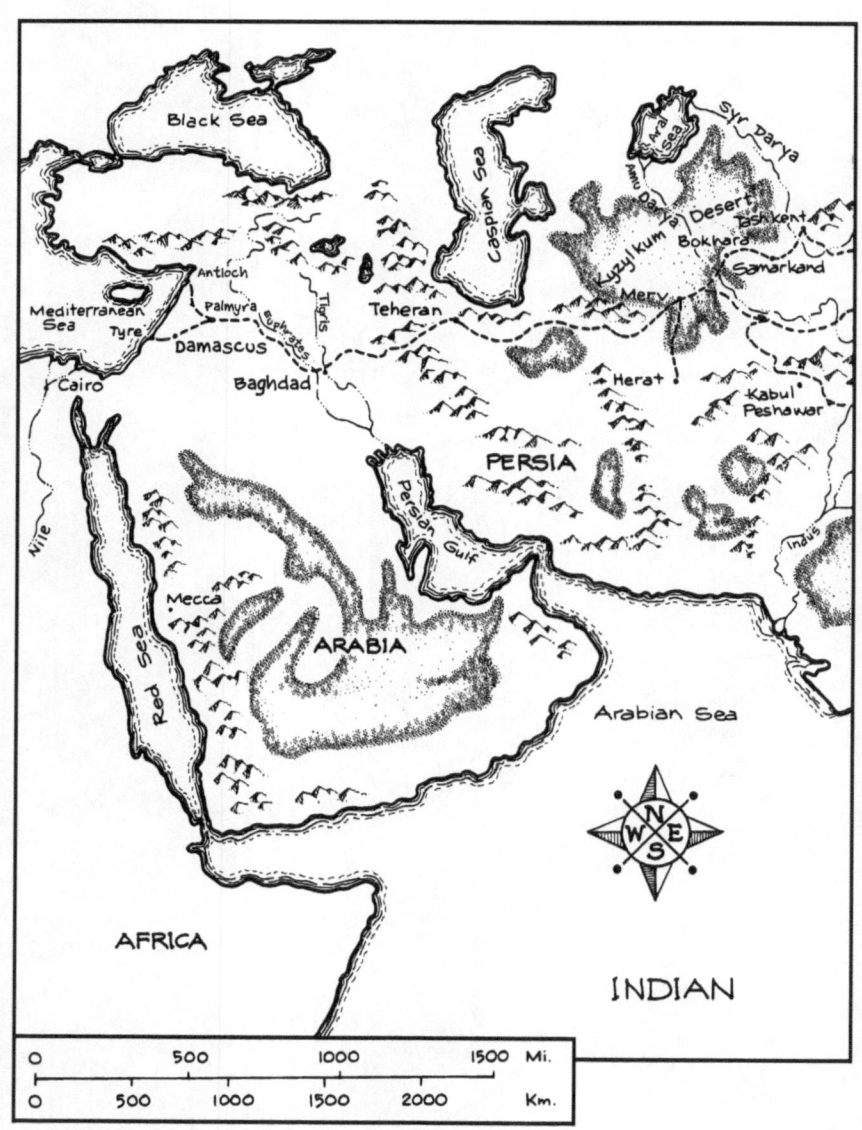

Acknowledgments

First, I want to thank you, dear reader, for being here. Your time is valuable, and I don't take it for granted that you've spent a portion of it reading this book.

There's a saying: 'The journey of a thousand miles begins with a single step.' I suppose the journey to writing *The Weaver's Tapestry* was the same. It began when my husband and I set out to adopt our daughter, not knowing what lay ahead. She was the inspiration for this book as I researched her lineage which traces back to Central Asia. That first step led to a series of steps—a long obedience, of sorts—that showed God's goodness in putting the right people in my path at exactly the right time.

With that, I must extend my sincere gratitude to Jon Carlisle, whose phone call one afternoon urging us to journal our adoption was the catalyst to all the writing that has followed since.

To my friend, Jessica Jones, who encouraged me to write this book in the earliest years of its inception while we pushed our youngest children in strollers up the butte near our houses. She continued to encourage me when we'd meet for long runs, or while attending our eldest sons' hockey games, or when we'd spot each other at the grocery store.

I'm infinitely grateful to the gifted writers in my critique group who both challenged me to be a better writer and encouraged me to keep going: Rosanne Croft, Lindy Jacobs, Julie S. Johnson, and Yvonne Kays. Without your careful guidance and sharp eyes, I would still be trying to put down the entire story in my first chapter, and believing it was good.

To my faithful writing friends, with whom I've enjoyed many

hours of laughter and fellowship over a shared meal: Jan Sheerin, Joanne Bowles, Mylissa Salvatore and Lorraine Stuart.

To my editor, Alison Imbriaco. What can I say, except that you're incredible. Your keen eye for detail is exactly what I needed to ensure that even the most minor details in both grammar and historical accuracy were not overlooked.

To my parents, Gary (the artist for my Silk Road map) and Carolyn Bartlett, who have encouraged and prayed for me along the way. Also, to Randy Hutton, and to the memory of my beautiful mom, Sandra Hutton, who lost her fight with cancer, but won the ultimate battle and is now at home with Jesus.

Lastly, to my husband, Adam, who encouraged and supported me through the gauntlet of emotions that came with writing this book, and whose quiet patience sustained me on the days when I questioned whether I should get a 'real' job, or at the very least an easier one.

About the Author

Anna C. Snyder grew up in the beautiful Rogue Valley in Southern Oregon, far away from the Central Asian lands which she writes about. As a lover of history, she considered pursuing a degree in archaeology, but beginner's algebra at the college level proved incredibly difficult, so she married her high-school sweetheart instead.

She's the mother of two sons and a special needs daughter whom Anna and her husband adopted from Russia. Her daughter was the catalyst for her writing. Through studying her Central Asian lineage, Anna's passion was reignited. On the page, she sought to weave a thread connecting her daughter to the beauty of the land and her rich ancestral history.

Through countless hours of research and rewrites the task felt herculean, but God placed within her a burning desire to tell a story. She agreed, of course, but only with the promise that algebra would not be involved.

You can visit her website at annacsnyder.com

Also by Anna C. Snyder

Beneath the Ginkgo Tree
A Silk Road Short Story

CHANG'AN CHINA, AD 605 Bao Li, daughter of a Chinese dignitary, has fallen in love with a peasant boy named Chen Tien. When Bao Li reaches the age of marriage, she and Chen Tien make plans to run away before her father finds a suitable husband for her. But first, she is required to attend tea with her father and the Sogdian merchant from Samarkand—a wealthy man with plans of his own.

The Silk Road Series
Tales of Mystery and Wonder from the Silk Road

I'm currently working on book two in the series. For updates, including release dates and opportunities for pre-orders, as well as bookish giveaways, sign up for my newsletter at annacsnyder.com. As a special bonus, you'll receive an email with my short story, *Beneath the Ginkgo Tree*.

Has this area of the world piqued your interest? Would you like to know more about its incredible history, but aren't interested in yet another newsletter filling up your inbox? If so, I think we'd be good friends in real life. I've put together a list of articles and recipes just for you on my website. No commitment required.

www.ingramcontent.com/pod-product-compliance
Lightning Source LLC
Chambersburg PA
CBHW050027120726
47903CB00006B/1943